"That our audience?"

Brant pointed to the porch, indicating the people collecting there.

Marley nodded.

"Break a leg," he said and pulled her into his arms. "Relax," he whispered against her ear. "You want to convince your family we're engaged, you'll have to loosen up. I may be good, but you'll need to cooperate a little. I can't carry the whole show by myself."

"You arrogant..." She stopped when his lips brushed hers. The kiss, if that's what it was, turned out to be very short. A disappointment, actually. "You call that a kiss?" she asked breathlessly.

He turned, dragging her toward the porch. As he smiled and waved, he said under his breath, "That's what I give mannequins. You want something better, you'd better put some life into those bones."

Dear Reader,

Thank you for choosing *An Act of Love*. I started this story a long time ago with Marley going back to her hometown in Pennsylvania for a wedding and reconnecting with Richard, her love in college. Well, by about chapter seven, I was in love with Brant and couldn't figure out how I could continue with my first premise. I put the story aside. But the idea kept coming back to me, and I decided to try again. Eventually, Marley came around and fell for Brant as well, but you can see through the story it was a difficult challenge to get her on board. With Brant's help, we showed her he was the one for her even though Richard wasn't such a bad guy.

In the first go-around, I didn't include Brant's viewpoint. Can you imagine not letting an "actor" with an ego keep his opinions to himself? The reasoning behind not having a male viewpoint was simple: if I included one then the reader would know immediately who the hero was. I wanted everyone, including Marley, to think Richard had possibilities. Brant got a little pushy so I gave in and let him have his say.

Do I sound as though my characters rule what goes on in my books? The best possible scenario is yes. I love it when their voices take over in my mind. I can see them, hear them and empathize with any problems they may be experiencing. However, they never let me strong-arm them into something they know is wrong and often won't allow me to sleep.

Marley plays my favorite music on her guitar, and I share her delight that Brant is able to sing and play music with her, as well.

I hope you've had a few laughs as well as poignant moments and maybe shared some similar experiences. Reach me through marionekholm.com or heartwarmingauthors.blogspot.com. I'd love to hear from you.

Marion

HEARTWARMING

Marion Ekholm
An Act of Love

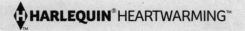

H HARLEQUIN®HEARTWARMING™

Recycling programs
for this product may
not exist in your area.

ISBN-13: 978-0-373-36689-7

An Act of Love

Printed in U.S.A.

MARION EKHOLM

was writing stories and reading them to her friends back in fifth grade, in Plainville, Connecticut. She always wanted to be either a writer or an artist. Neither one seemed like a possibility in her day, when most women became either teachers or secretaries. But she had determination on her side and a mother willing to help with her dreams. She earned her BFA at Rhode Island School of Design and became a lace designer in New York City, met her husband and moved to New Jersey. Years later, she took stock of her life. She had a career, two children, a beautiful home and opportunities to travel extensively—but she'd never written anything other than letters. She began writing for real and eventually became an editor of a newspaper and sold numerous short stories and magazine articles. Thanks to Harlequin Heartwarming, she's now a novelist. Her second novel, *An Act of Love*, follows her first, *Just Like Em*. She's found signing her books and talking to people who've read them an absolute delight.

Books by Marion Ekholm

HARLEQUIN HEARTWARMING

JUST LIKE EM

This book is dedicated to Jane Toombs who died this March, 2014. Jane introduced me to Romance Writers of America when RWA was in its infancy by sponsoring a romance writers conference with Ruby Frankel in New York state. Thanks to their efforts, Hudson Valley Romance Writers came into being. Jane asked me to be the newsletter editor for the group. There I learned about deadlines, writing articles, interviewing and a host of other skills necessary to becoming a writer. Over the years, she not only critiqued my writing but also offered friendship that led to many delightful trips as roommates to RWA national conferences. Thank you, Jane, for your dedication in helping people learn their craft.

Acknowledgments

I have wonderful opportunities to take classes at Glendale Community College where I work. David Thibodeaux, my instructor at GCC for *The History of Jazz* and *Rock Music and Culture,* instilled in me a passion for all types of music.

Chuck Hulihan taught my acoustic guitar class at GCC. Even though I should have started a hundred years earlier, I learned about the dedication and enthusiasm required to play well. So much of Marley's love for playing the guitar comes from those lessons.

Hank Glogosh, who helped with his knowledge of Pennsylvania.

Sheryl Zajechowski, the acquisition editor for Brilliance Audio, answered all my questions about narrating books, Brant's profession.

To Shelley Mosley and Sandra Lagesse—my best friends, mentors and critique partners—a heartfelt thank-you.

Additional thanks to Harlequin and its editors whom I've been fortunate to meet or work with over the internet, especially Paula Eykelhof, Victoria Curran, Kathryn Lye and Beverley Sotolov. I really appreciate all your help and encouragement.

Love to my daughter and granddaughters for their support. And special thanks to my son, David, who answered so many of the questions I had about acting. His experiences in the theater in college and after were very helpful.

CHAPTER ONE

AFTER WORK ON Friday night, Marley Roman and her friend Dede Sanchez met for drinks at a downtown bar in Phoenix to escape the July heat before heading home. Marley pushed her long hair away from her neck to let the cool air-conditioning sweep around her.

"Here's to you, Lindy." Marley lifted her oversize margarita to her lips and licked at the salt before taking a sip. "Thanks for beating me to the altar." Saturday morning she'd be flying to her youngest sister's wedding. Memories of the last sister's ceremony still haunted her. How could she handle the next week and keep her sanity?

"I've never seen you so glum." Dede placed her glass of wine on the bar. "Why not avoid this ritual? Tell your family you've come down with the plague or something."

Marley leaned toward her friend. "Right. Like anyone would believe me." She hastily readjusted herself on the bar stool to catch her balance. The drink hadn't helped Marley's funky mood one bit. Maybe skipping supper hadn't been such a great idea.

"I'm the first of six girls, five of whom... who...whom..." After pausing, she took a deep breath to clear her thinking. "Why do I have to be the last one?"

"Since when has marriage become one of your priorities?" Dede dusted a speck off her black dress, which was the same shade as her long hair. "I thought you liked being single."

"I do, but everyone in my family questions it. And they keep asking me when will it be my turn." Marley tried to focus. "Well, maybe someday I'll meet someone—and then...then I'll think about it."

"It won't happen. Not when you refuse to accept the drink that cute guy at the end of the bar is offering." Dede smiled at him and waved a finger; Marley ignored him. He didn't appeal to her. For that matter few men had since she'd finished college more than a decade ago.

Dede continued where she'd left off. "You won't date anyone in your office, and you completely blew it when I tried fixing you up with the guys I work with."

Marley propped her cheek against her hand and leaned her elbow on the bar to support her head. "Jerrod was ten years younger than me—"

"Nothing wrong with being a cougar."

"And Lincoln looked like the original Lincoln, minus the beard."

Marley finished her drink and motioned to the bartender.

"Want the same margarita, Red?" He reached for her glass.

Red. She hated that reference to her hair color. Did he call other customers Black, Brown or Blonde when he addressed them? Her father was always called Red. Anyone calling her that brought back memories of him. She didn't need reminders of all the pain associated with her father's abandonment.

"The name's Marley, and, yes, I'd like the same."

"You sure?" Dede attempted to shoo the bartender away. "You rarely ever finish one, let alone two."

"I'm not driving, so it's okay."

The bartender hadn't moved. He jerked his thumb toward the end of the bar. "He'd still like to buy you one."

Marley glanced at the man, gave him a half-hearted smile, placed a bill on the bar and shook her head. The motion momentarily destroyed her vision, making her realize she'd already had enough. "No, thanks. Don't fix another. Your margaritas are way too potent."

"You know, you're avoiding the real problem." Dede stood and went through her purse in search of money.

"Which is?"

"Guilt."

Marley furrowed her brow. "What guilt?"

"You moved away from your family, and every time they bring you back, you try to make it up to them." Dede dropped a bill on the bar. "Like this wedding. You've practically paid for most of it yourself."

Marley shrugged. "Maybe so, but this is the last wedding so…No more guilt."

"Yeah, right. Until the next baby is born."

Hesitantly, Marley placed her foot on the floor, got off the stool and held on to the bar for support. "See, no hands." Marley lifted both palms, only to lose her balance and grab the back of the stool.

"At some point, you'll have to say no." They started for the door. "Practice. It could make your life so much simpler."

Now that the sun had gone down and the night air felt tolerable, they walked the few short blocks to the light-rail station. Marley slung her jacket over her arm and hiked her purse's strap onto her shoulder. Her feet ached in her open-toed heels. Getting home, then into a bath, was her only priority.

"What you need is a fiancé, not a marriage." Dede slipped her arm through hers.

Just a fiancé. That's all I need, Marley mused.

"A fiancé you can talk about and get rid of the moment you return to Phoenix."

When they reached the red light and stopped, a city bus with a giant poster on it also stopped. The poster had recently popped up all over the city—an advertisement for a special business symposium to be held at the Civic Center. Here it was again, Brant Westfield smiling at them.

"You see that guy?" Marley said, pulling back and pointing at the bus.

"Yeah. Cute."

"He's my neighbor."

"Really?" They both turned to face yet another announcement of "The Convention No One Should Miss," this one posted at the bus stop. And this one with another smiling Brant Westfield.

When Brant had first introduced himself, she'd been welcoming but had kept him at arm's length. For several reasons. First, she avoided relationships where she worked or lived because problems arose when the people became too involved or they broke up.

Second, and more important, she'd seen Brant with a parade of women. Obviously a player, he brought a lot of gorgeous females home with him. Better to avoid potential problems. Problems likely to occur with a man whose smile left her breathless.

Now that smile was plastered everywhere.

"Give me your phone." Dede held out her hand and snapped her fingers.

"Why?"

"I'm taking a picture of you with your new fiancé. Stand over there."

Laughing, Marley did as Dede ordered. After several unsuccessful shots, Dede handed the phone back. "I don't know if there's too much or too little light. Sorry it didn't work, because he sure makes a decent fiancé."

After reaching the Metro station, the women took seats to wait for the next light-rail that regularly made trips up and down Central Avenue. A breeze had picked up. Instead of offering relief, it felt more like a hair dryer blasting them. At least Marley wouldn't have to deal with the Phoenix summer once she reached Pennsylvania.

"To create a make-believe fiancé, it's better if you focus on someone specific, so you'll be able to remember the details."

A make-believe fiancé. Was she really going to invent a guy? Marley nodded slowly. *Who?* She went through all her acquaintances, including the few men she'd dated. No one stood out. Certainly no one she'd like to be engaged to.

Another poster of Brant flashed by.

Maybe...

Brant could be her fake fiancé, especially since he'd never know about it.

WHEN BRANT SAW the woman approaching his condo building, he backed under a tree out of sight. Since his picture had started appearing in all the ads for the convention campaign, everyone who recognized him accosted him. Particularly women he didn't know. Better to be safe and not broadcast his address by walking in. His three-day beard and grubby clothes provided some disguise, but the celebrity status the poster afforded made anonymity nearly impossible.

When he could finally see her clearly under

the streetlight, he recognized his neighbor—Marley. And she was obviously feeling no pain.

Beautiful she might be, but beauty was a common sight in his profession, and often the women had little more than their looks going for them. But he'd heard Marley play the guitar. He'd wanted to talk to her about possibly jamming together. Unfortunately, she shot him down before he could even suggest it.

He stayed put as water from the yard's sprinklers hit his calves, refreshing after the day's heat. He watched, waiting for her to go inside. Instead of entering the building, though, she took out her cell phone and paused in front of his picture on a bus stop billboard. It was an older likeness, from when his hair was shorter—

Great. His flip-flops were getting soaked. He stepped onto the sidewalk.

In the British accent he'd been practicing for his next gig, he asked, "You're taking a picture of my picture?"

She screamed and tossed her phone in the air.

He managed to catch it before it hit the cement. "Sorry. Didn't mean to alarm you, love." Reverting to his natural voice, he asked, "Why are you taking my picture's picture?" If it was to become rich on Facebook or Twitter, it was a wasted effort, since his image was already all over the internet. He held out the cell phone and waited. Finally, he took her arm and placed the phone in her hand.

MARLEY'S HEARTBEAT CONTINUED to race. How on earth could she explain this? She might as well be truthful, since she couldn't think of any plausible reason. "I needed your picture to show my family."

"Why?"

"I…I needed a fiancé and decided you'd do."

"What?" After a moment's pause, possibly to focus on what she'd said, Brant held his sides and roared with laughter. "Lady, you've absolutely made my day."

That annoying accent again. What was it, anyway? British? Australian? She knew he'd spent several months in Australia doing a movie and had returned only a few weeks ago. And she knew he was an actor. But that's all she really knew about him—well, that and his propensity for cowboy outfits. Usually he wore boots and a cowboy hat; today, though, he looked more like a hobo. His chambray shirt no longer had any sleeves and his shorts were cutoff jeans with white threads hanging around his knees. Instead of boots he wore grungy flip-flops.

"So we're engaged?" Brant said as he continued to gaze at her. The accent was gone but not the smile in his voice. "When's our wedding?"

"I'm leaving tomorrow to attend my sister's and…" She stopped and took a deep breath.

"And?"

"And I have five sisters, all younger and married or about to be. You have no idea what it's like when everyone gangs up on you and asks when you're getting married."

"Oh, but I do. I'm asked the same question by my family. Okay if I tell them I've finally found the woman of my dreams and plan to tie the knot?" He took out his cell phone. "Here, let me take your picture so I can show them."

"No!" Marley held her hand in front of her face.

"All these weeks you've barely given me the time of day, and now we're engaged." He grasped her hand.

Marley pulled free and pushed past him.

"We're not having a spat now, are we, love?" he said, returning to that accent. "Our engagement is only minutes old, and you're already breaking it off. What will your family think? That you prefer to remain a singleton?"

Marley halted. Every nerve in her body fired. Feeling queasy, she faced him. "I'm not in the mood, Brant, and one more word in that phony accent and I'll—"

"It doesn't sound genuine?" He raised his eyebrows and stared in disbelief.

"I haven't the slightest idea if it is or not. I just know it's not you, the Willie Nelson cowboy I see every day." She walked past him and continued to their condo building.

"Oh, so you *have* noticed me." Slipping back into his usual voice, he pushed the door open for her. "But Willie Nelson? I look that old? I always considered myself more of a young Tim McGraw."

Once in the elevator, Marley removed her shoes and leaned against the metal wall. The coolness seeped into her skin, a delight after the warmth outside. She closed her eyes. When she heard Brant drop his backpack to the floor, she opened them. He had one hand on the wall above her head and was bending over, getting way too close.

"Hmm. Brown. Aren't redheads supposed to have green eyes?"

She placed her palms against his chest and pushed him away.

He grinned—that smile that thoroughly unnerved her. "Why pick me? We've never even been on a date."

"I didn't pick you. My girlfriend Dede did when your picture passed by on a bus."

"Not that I haven't tried. I asked you out for coffee and a walk in the rain. Both times you refused. Really did a number on my self-confidence."

Marley stared down at her feet and wiggled her toes. She remembered. Only someone who lived in Phoenix would consider a walk in the rain a fun thing to do. "You've obviously recovered."

"What is it? You've got a thing against actors?"

"No." She looked up into very dark eyes only inches from her own. "I don't like dime-store cowboys."

"What's that supposed to mean? You think I'm not for real?"

Oh, he was for real, all right. And promised nothing but trouble on a grand scale.

He backed off but still kept eye contact. "I'll have you know that unlike most of the residents in this fair state, I'm a native Arizonan. I own my own ranch and raise horses."

They got off the elevator on the seventh floor, and Marley put her key in her door. "Sure you do." Before opening the door and walking into her living room, she faced him. "I can smell the horse manure emanating from your condo every time the wind shifts."

Laughing, he stood in her doorway, his hand braced against the doorjamb.

"This engagement will be over by the time I get back."

He pulled his hand away before she could close the door on his fingers.

Brant stayed in her thoughts for some time while she packed for her trip. As long as the engagement was in her imagination, why not stick with him as her fiancé? He did have some qualities she found attractive. That smile, for instance. Yes, she could definitely wrap a fake engagement around that.

Marley glanced at her watch and decided Dede should be home by now. When she answered, Marley said, "You'll never guess what. I met Brant coming into our building." She choked back laughter. "I can't believe he caught me taking his picture and..." She paused to gain control of her voice. "I told him I needed a fiancé, and he's it."

Marley would need a ring, she suddenly realized, something concrete to show her family so they'd believe she'd finally found her man.

"Meet me tomorrow, Dede, before I catch my plane, and help me pick out an engagement ring."

CHAPTER TWO

BRANT HARDLY SLEPT. When he did Marley Roman appeared in his dreams with the guitar he'd heard her play on occasion. In fact, he was quite sure he'd heard her playing the previous evening. Maybe it was his imagination. The condo was pretty soundproof, and he'd only heard her the few times she'd gone out onto the balcony they shared. And she had been good, progressing through chords he'd struggled with for years. Not to mention her riffs. She could certainly teach him how to improve his technique.

His sister Elaina, oddly still dressed in the fancy outfit she'd worn the previous night, had coffee ready when he came into the kitchen. She used one of his guest rooms whenever she came into Phoenix. "Morning," he said as he took a seat on the stool in front of the bar, deciding not to ask her why she hadn't changed clothes. "How was the concert?"

"Perfect. It was a duo with a cello and guitar. Got to meet both the man and woman after and thought I might take up the cello again." She pushed a full cup of black coffee over to him.

"I remember you playing back when I was in grammar school. You sure you want to put my poor nieces and nephews through that torture?" He moved away from her attempt to swat him. "Usually you're out of here before the rush hour. Who's minding the ranch while you're away?" Elaina managed their father's ranch a good 50 miles northwest of Phoenix. His two other sisters were also involved in the family's large holdings. Something he'd managed to avoid.

"I delegate." Elaina took the stool next to him and watched over the brim of her mug. "Dad wants to talk to you."

Brant swiveled around so that he faced a window. "You know what about?"

"No, but I think you do. He expected to see you when you finished that last picture. You're on hiatus now, aren't you?"

Brant got up and walked over to the sink. "Yeah. I have a few things to take care of and then I'll come up." Brant had dreaded the day when he'd have to give in to his father's wishes and take over the responsibilities at the ranch.

If only he could delay the inevitable. He excused himself and headed to the vestibule.

Brant had every intention of meeting Marley again this morning, and this time it wouldn't be by accident. After opening his door, he picked up his tablet and a book, the former to read and the latter to keep the door ajar so he wouldn't miss her. Then he sat in his foyer, facing the door.

"What are you doing?"

"Waiting to see my neighbor."

Elaina laughed. "Why not ring her doorbell?"

"It's awkward. We got engaged last night and—"

"You what?"

Brant held up his hand when he heard Marley's door open and placed his finger against his lips. He stood, tossed the tablet onto the chair, pulled open his door, and kicked the chair with the tablet aside before entering the hall.

"Well, what have we got here?" In a Texas twang, another accent he'd perfected for the detective book he had to read for his next gig, Brant added, "My lovely fiancée. Aren't you just the morning sunshine."

That elicited a dirty look from Marley.

Maybe he was being too obnoxious. "Sleep well?" She didn't answer as he walked her to the elevator.

Reverting to his normal voice, he asked, "Care to join me for that cup of coffee?"

"No, thank you." Finally a response. "I'm meeting someone."

"It better not be a male acquaintance. I can be ferocious if another man shows my fiancée any attention."

"I'm meeting my friend Dede to pick out a ring for my false engagement."

"Well, then I have to come, too. How else would you know what I'd choose for you?"

As they got off the elevator, he put on his straw cowboy hat, hoping it would offer some concealment. He still hadn't shaved, and his beard was starting to itch, but it did help hide his face.

For what felt like the hundredth time, he wished his face wasn't plastered all over Phoenix.

SHE'D SPOTTED HER before the door closed. A woman in Brant's condo. Brant the player, with beautiful women at his beck and call. No matter how much Marley tried to focus on something else, she couldn't. An attractive woman had closed Brant's door, and it wasn't the maid. Marley had glimpsed chiffon and glitter, dressy for a Saturday morning.

What did she care? As a bachelor, Brant could have a dozen girlfriends. Since his return from Australia, Marley had noticed him with at least two.

Brant stayed right next to her every step of the way to meet Dede. Still unshaven, he wore another chambray shirt, this one with long sleeves rolled up to the elbow. The shirt had its breast pocket ripped off, the stitching visible around the square of unfaded blue. The jeans must have been new, though, since they didn't have any observable holes. Marley herself was dressed in black pants and a white shirt for comfort on the plane.

Any thought of losing Brant disappeared when they reached the restaurant where she and Dede planned to meet.

"Hi, there," Dede said to Brant. "I'm Dede Sanchez and you must be Marley's fiancé."

Brant stuck out his hand. "That I am. Glad to meet you, Dede. Shall we get some coffee before buying the ring?" He put his hand on Marley's shoulder, aiming her toward the entrance of the restaurant.

She stopped. "We don't have the time. Need to get that ring before I catch my plane."

Brant pointed down the street. "There's a great pawnshop a block from here with a large selection. I know the owner, and I'm sure he'll give us a deal."

Why did he include himself in everything as though they really had a relationship? Annoyed, Marley said, "I'm buying the ring, Brant. This engagement is fake, remember?"

"Precisely, love." Again with that British accent. "I wouldn't have it any other way."

Once inside the store, Brant shook hands with a man who was clearly the owner. "Gee," the guy said, "I haven't seen you since two seconds ago when you sailed down the street on that bus." Amused at his own joke, he turned to Marley and Dede. "Going to introduce us?"

Brant placed an arm around each of them. "Gus, this is Dede and my fiancée, Marley."

Marley shuddered. *How can he do that, tell someone he obviously knows well that we're engaged?*

"We're looking for rings. Have you got anything suitable?"

"Inexpensive," Marley interjected.

"Isn't she wonderful?" Brant removed his

arm from Dede but continued to hold Marley.
"Won't let me spend a dime on her."

"Over here."

Marley managed to slip from Brant's grasp
as they followed Gus to a display case with
jewelry. Brant leaned over and pointed to an
elaborate ring. "What about that one?"

"Excellent taste." Gus reached under the
glass, took out the ring and placed it in Brant's
hand.

Brant eyed the tiny tag that dangled from
the ring and his eyebrows went up before he
reached for Marley's hand. "Try it on for size,
love."

Marley grabbed the ring and put it on herself. It fit. And it was gorgeous. Something any
potential bride would want. White gold, with a
large diamond surrounded by several smaller
ones. And a price of over five thousand dollars! Marley managed to pull it off and place
it on the counter before it scalded her finger.
"I want a ring as fake as our engagement."

With a sigh, Brant turned to Dede. "You talk
to her. I can't deal with this constant change
of heart. The engagement's on—the engagement's off." He motioned to Gus. "I'll let her
decide what she wants. You have any new instruments to show me?"

Gus directed another salesclerk over to help Marley while he and Brant headed to where various musical instruments hung on the wall.

In a rush, Marley settled for a similar ring costing less than fifty dollars and was out of the store before Brant had a chance to involve himself again. Left with barely enough time to catch her plane, she shouted a thank-you to Dede and raced home.

Quickly, Marley slipped into sandals that would be easy to take off at airport security. Thank goodness she'd had the foresight to pack the night before.

How was she going to manage transporting everything? She left the guitar and pushed the two pieces of luggage into the hall, planning to return for it once she parked her gear at the front entrance. She was locking her door when Brant stepped off the elevator.

"Let me help you."

"I can handle it," she said as he reached for one of her suitcases.

"Darlin'." He took off his battered cowboy hat and placed it against his chest. "I know you can, but my ancestors would rise from their graves if I permitted my fiancée to do any manual labor."

While putting his hat back on, he placed his

hand over hers, trapping her fingers around the handle. "I'm catching a plane, Brant. Let go of my hand."

"Just protecting that gorgeous ring I gave you. So, may I help you with your luggage?"

Again Brant interfered with her thought process, jumbling her concentration. She drew a deep breath and let it out slowly. Realizing he wasn't about to let her alone, she yanked her hand free and said, "Take it."

He grabbed her two bags and rolled them to the elevator, leaving her with a small carry-on and an extra-large purse. Afraid he might run off with her belongings, she decided to stay glued to him every step of the way.

"Why so much luggage? Dede said you were going for a week. I didn't have this much when I spent three months in Australia." Probably because he wore the same rags Marley saw him in every day.

The doors opened and he greeted a man leaving the elevator and finagled the luggage inside. "You got a dead body in here? This weighs a ton. Want me to come to the airport? I could fly out with you to…Where we going?"

Totally frustrated, Marley pressed her hand against her aching forehead. At some point, all the tension had turned into a headache. She said authoritatively, "I am flying—alone—to Pennsylvania."

Brant leaned against the wall, studying her. "I see pain in those beautiful brown eyes. Headache?"

She nodded but didn't go into detail.

When the elevator stopped on the fifth floor, he moved to give the woman entering some space. "You're breaking my heart. You know that, right? How can I exist a whole week by myself?" He smiled at the newcomer and waved offhandedly at Marley. "We're newly engaged, and she's taking off without me. After I gave her that gorgeous ring."

Marley compressed her lips and tried her best to ignore Brant. She would not talk to him. She would not acknowledge his remarks. The elevator stopped at the fourth floor and the woman got out. The doors were closing when he raised his voice and said, "She'll probably hock it as soon as she gets to Transylvania."

Marley finally shook her head and turned to stare at him directly. "You're a real nutcase," she said before the door opened on the first floor.

"So when are we going on a date? Engaged for twelve hours, and we haven't even shared chopsticks." The door started to close, and

Brant pushed one of the suitcases forward to stop it. He rolled the other bag into the lobby, pushed both out the front door and down the ramp into the parking area.

"Where are you going with those?" Was he about to make off with her luggage? Marley gripped her purse and carry-on even tighter as she started after him. "I have a taxi coming."

"I'll drive you. I've got my truck parked right here."

"Stop." She grabbed one of his arms, accidentally whacking his chest with her purse. "I mean it, Brant." She backed away to put some distance between them. "Sorry. I didn't mean to hit you."

He leaned against the white truck, hooked one scuffed boot over the other and folded his arms across his chest. "May I have a serious word with you?"

"Are you capable of being serious?"

He stared her down. If she missed her plane…

"What do you want to say?"

"I'm between gigs right now." He paused. "No work for maybe a couple of weeks."

Defeated, she let out a sigh. Given the panhandler outfits he wore, he had to be broke. Probably hadn't had work since they'd first met and wouldn't get more till that convention, which was still weeks away. She wasn't about to start lending him money. But...if he was desperate. "How much do you need? I don't have a lot with me but..."

Brant frowned, lines puckering his forehead. "I don't need money. Let me finish what I have to say, okay? I have work coming up later this month, and I'd like to get away from my picture posted on every free space in Phoenix while I wait for the assignment." He looked away. "And I have personal reasons to disappear for a while."

He put his index finger to his lips when she tried to interject a comment.

After another pause he said, "You need a fiancé, and it could be fun to act the part. My upcoming job is in New York, so if I stop off in Pennsylvania, I'll be more than halfway there."

Marley's heart raced. No way could she ever have him show up in front of all her relatives and embarrass her. She held her breath and hoped the panic she felt wasn't visible. "My turn?"

He tossed a hand in the air.

"I don't want to hurt your feelings, Brant." He straightened slightly. "But you're not the type of person I want to present to my family as my fiancé."

He edged away from the truck, and she backed off so he couldn't get too close. Since last night when they'd become "engaged," he had begun to take up too much of her space. And that casual touching of his when he got near her played havoc with her sense of well-being.

"As an actor, I can make myself into anything you want. A Texas billionaire?" he twanged. "How about an English count related to the royal family?" he asked, switching to a British inflection.

The accents rankled. Unable to think rationally, she attacked an obvious fact to distract him from the truth: that his very presence had begun to mess with her comfort level.

"You don't have the wardrobe to carry it off. I doubt either the billionaire or the member of the royal family shops for clothes at the local Goodwill." When he looked as though he might continue to argue, she said, "My taxi's here," and motioned to the yellow cab pulling to the curb nearby.

Brant shook his head, rolled the luggage to the cab and put the bags in the trunk once the cabbie had flipped the lid. When Brant opened the cab door for her, he said, "It'd be fun, and you'd be saving me from a week of boredom."

"No way, mister." She got into the cab, grabbed the door handle and shut the door. The last thing she wanted to do was provide him with entertainment.

"I have other clothes," he shouted as the cab took off.

It was only when Marley was on board her plane for Pittsburgh that she realized she'd forgotten her guitar.

The one thing she could rely on to get her through this pending wedding.

CHAPTER THREE

MARLEY SAT BACK AND WATCHED the young women, relatives and friends, gathered for Lindy's shower on Sunday. She had intended to remain nonchalant and not mention her engagement. And she managed it, right up until Chloe, the sister closest to Marley in age, noticed her ring.

"You're engaged!" Chloe grabbed Marley's hand and nearly pulled her arm out of the socket.

Questions flew at her from her other sisters. "What does he look like?" from Jen. "How long have you known him?" asked Morgan. "When do you plan to get married?" squealed Franny. "How come you never said anything before?" The last from Lindy, who looked very upset. Marley managed to answer questions by showing Brant's picture on her cell phone. Her well-rehearsed lies seemed to satisfy everyone and eventually, when the spotlight returned to Lindy, Marley thought she could finally relax.

No such luck. Lindy took her hand and examined it. "Your nails are so...so stubby." She looked up. "People will notice it, Marley, when they look at the ring."

Marley glanced down at her left hand. Had Brant noticed her fingers when he'd held her hand a few nights ago? "I play the guitar, remember? I can't have nails touching the strings." Her hands never matched, the right one having longer nails because she used them as picks.

"Well, you'll need to do something about them for my wedding. Maybe some fake nails."

Once Lindy finished with the examination, her focus turned to the ring. "He must be very rich."

The large cubic zirconia that served as Marley's engagement ring overshadowed the half karat wrapped in a Tiffany setting on Lindy's hand. Marley cringed from the comparison and slowly pulled her hand out of her sister's grasp. If only she could soothe Lindy's pride and tell her the obnoxious stone had no value compared with her genuine diamond.

Why had she created this bogus engagement? Why? She never meant to hurt Lindy. Marley tried to remain inconspicuous and concentrated on crafting a bouquet of all the ribbons from the gifts for the wedding rehearsal.

With Chloe's help Marley took the many presents from the bridal shower and placed them in her rental car. Keeping the gifts dry had turned into a nightmare, thanks to the unending rain. It would have been welcomed back in Arizona, but since she had arrived in Pennsylvania the previous day, it had become nonstop depressing.

"Why have you been so secretive?" Chloe asked. She added another group of packages to the collection. "When did he ask you to marry him?" Chloe's short blond hair had lost its stylishness and now hung limply because of all the rain, whereas Marley's hair had begun to curl, a problem she always had in high humidity. Marley pulled her sister under the protection of her umbrella.

"It just happened." Marley really wanted to avoid the subject, fearful she might not be able to keep her false story straight.

"Well, I expect a great deal more explanation." Chloe dragged Marley into the open garage. "We talk, email, text nearly every day, and Brant's name never came up."

Marley crossed her fingers. "I don't have secrets, honest." She hoped this would end the discussion.

"Well, I do." A warm glow brightened Chloe's features. "I'm pregnant." She clutched Marley's arm. "Now, don't go saying anything. We want to be sure before..." Chloe paused and a shadow crossed her face. Two years ago, into her second month, Chloe had lost her baby. Marley empathized, remembering the struggle her sister had gone through.

"A baby! That's so exciting." Marley drew her into a hug. "Does Al know?" A small part of Marley wished she was the one having a child. No chance of that when she'd had to create a fiancé and her biological clock was running out.

"Of course. I don't show, yet, and Lindy will absolutely kill me if I can't fit into that form fitting bridesmaid dress." She paused. "But we haven't mentioned it to Michelle. She's been dying for a sister, so once I start to show, we'll tell her."

"When's the baby due?"

"In seven months." Chloe pressed her lips together. "And I have a favor to ask."

"Sure, what?"

"Could you watch Michelle?" When Marley hesitated, Chloe added, "Not all the time. Just on those days I have morning sickness. Which has been a freaky misnomer this pregnancy. I spend more time with nausea at night. We end up exhausted, and Michelle tires us out even more during the day."

"Of course. I'd love to."

"Wonderful." Chloe gave Marley a quick kiss on her cheek. "Michelle adores you. I'll bring her over tomorrow and tell everyone… tell them you want a chance to…I don't know, see what it's like to have kids. Since you're getting married and you want the practice."

Great. Another lie. Only this one had some truth. She really would love to have children.

AFTER SEVERAL TRIPS carrying the shower presents through the living room of her family's house, Marley met her grandfather. "You haven't even given a decent hello to your poppy. When you plan on doing that?"

Marley smiled. "Soon as I get these gifts upstairs. Want to join me?"

"Can I help?" he asked, following her.

"Thanks, but this is the last of it and this one's lightweight."

Once she deposited the package on the stacks collected in the large playroom, she turned to her grandfather and threw open her arms. She welcomed his strong squeeze.

Although his thin white hair gave away his age, he still had the trim shape and posture of a much younger man. She grasped Poppy's arm. "Come with me to my room."

When they reached her old bedroom, Poppy glanced around. "Looks like this has turned into a storage area." He pointed toward a collection of dressers piled on top of each other. Several other pieces of furniture, including her old desk and chair, stood stuffed in a corner. "And I don't see your grandmother's favorite rocker."

"It's my favorite now. I took that and the antique treasure chest to my place in Phoenix." She paused. "And you know that because you helped me get them into my car."

Poppy chuckled. "Sure wish you'd had room for some of this other stuff. But at least you left me some place to sit." Poppy lowered himself into a wooden rocker, and Marley sat on the patchwork quilt that covered the double bed. He started rocking slowly.

"Honestly, when you and your sisters get together, it turns into a regular hen party, and us old roosters never get to see you."

"What do you mean? I've been here for every wedding, baptism and special birthday."

"It's not enough. I'd rather have you close by so you could play the guitar for me." He lifted a gnarled hand. "Since Mr. Arthur Ritus took over my hands, and you moved away, I gave the guitar to one of the great-grandkids. Don't know as I'll ever hear it again."

"I'm sorry I didn't bring mine. Too much luggage this time. I'd love to play a few songs for you." She felt really down, not being able to give him that tiny pleasure. *Darn Brant.*

Poppy rocked several times, staring past her. "You're not upset with me, are you?"

Leaning toward him, she asked, "Why would you say that?"

"You wanted to major in music, and I...I should have kept my mouth shut." He looked away and pressed his lips together.

"Poppy. You didn't steer me wrong. I asked for your opinion because I knew you'd give me good advice. I love mathematics, and it's led to several excellent jobs."

"You still teach math?"

"No longer in the high school. But I work as an adjunct, a part-time teacher, at a local community college in the evening."

"Pay well?"

Marley chuckled. "No. I make my real money as an accountant. See, another reason math was a good choice. And I never gave up on my music. Play every day and often with some bright young men who live in my building. They're forming a band." Marley fluttered her fingers in front of him. "Lindy says I need to do something about my nails. Can you imagine me strumming away with false nails?"

Poppy shook his head and grew thoughtful. "So I hear you're next in line..." *Good, the rumor mill was already working.* "...if your mother doesn't beat you to it." He chortled. "You going to show me that ring?"

Marley hesitated. *If her mother didn't beat her to it? Was her mother seeing someone? Maybe so. Marley hadn't seen much of her since she arrived.*

Marley kneeled in front of him, lifting her hand so that he could grasp it.

He nodded several times before releasing her hand. As she stood, he said, "Sure hope you found someone stable."

Marley was momentarily unable to speak. She hated deceiving her grandfather. He had always been forthcoming and honest with her. Finally, she said, "I certainly hope so."

"What's he do? Heard he had a horse ranch. Those things cost a pretty penny. Sounds like you've found yourself someone with money." Visions of Brant in his threadbare clothing momentarily clouded her thoughts. But then he did have a unit in her high-rise condo building, and those didn't come cheap. Hers had cost every last penny of the inheritance from her grandmother.

"He manages."

"Well, you bring him around here so I can check him out. I can tell if he's a prowling alley cat."

MICHELLE ARRIVED MONDAY before lunch, and after a busy day Marley and Michelle went to bed early. Sleep was a sometime thing with a four-year-old kicking and squirming through the night in Marley's double bed. A crack-of-dawn riser, Michelle was already up, poking and pulling Marley's hair to get her attention.

Marley dragged herself to a seated position, barely able to open her eyes. Since Chloe had dropped Michelle off the day before, Marley had spent every hour with the girl, playing games, puzzles, hopscotch and anything else she could think of. Again she cursed herself for forgetting her guitar. If Brant hadn't distracted her...Marley playing the guitar had always worked at occupying her sisters' attention.

"Let's play hide-n-seek," Michelle said and bounded for the bedroom door.

Didn't Michelle ever tire? Marley wondered. "Wait. Wait till I'm up," she told her niece. "Go down and see Granny and get breakfast. We'll play when you come back."

When Michelle took off, clunking down the stairs to the kitchen, Marley flopped back on the bed. At least she'd have a few minutes of undisturbed sleep...

She awoke to someone screaming in the hallway.

"I could kill you!" Lindy yelled.

When Marley made it to the hall, she found Lindy staring at Michelle, who was sitting crying on the floor in the spare bedroom. The room Lindy had her wedding dress in. A room that was usually locked.

Lindy turned on her in fury. "Aren't you supposed to be watching her? She just ruined my wedding dress!" A bright red blotch ran down the back of the gown where the plastic covering had been ripped away. An empty pink child's cup decorated with princesses lay on the floor.

Marley rushed in and picked up the child.

"I tripped," the little girl said, burying her tear-streaked face in Marley's neck. "I'm sorry." Lindy came into the room, and Michelle tensed in Marley's arms.

"Sorry doesn't cut it." Lindy turned to Marley. "Why is she here, anyway?"

"I'm…" *What was the reason?* "I wanted to see what it would be like taking care of children…now that I'm getting married."

"Well, my solution is don't have any!"

CHAPTER FOUR

THE NEXT TWO DAYS didn't improve as tempers ran hot, especially the bride's. At least the woman at the cleaners promised to do her best and return the dress by Saturday morning in time for the wedding.

Marley's babysitting assignment turned into several days of dealing with Michelle while Chloe suffered through bouts of nausea. And her mother, who usually could be found in the kitchen when she wasn't serving meals to clients in her catering business, had disappeared. Maybe she was dating someone.

Lindy avoided her and Michelle, and everyone else managed to disappear into their own activities. On Wednesday morning, Michelle again woke Marley by pulling her hair.

"We have to get ready."

Marley opened one eye. "Why?"

"We're going to Kenny."

Instantly, Marley felt revived. Kennywood Park. Her sisters and their children had planned a day trip to the park, including Chloe, provided she was up to it. As much as Marley adored her niece and enjoyed the park, she wouldn't have to go. And that meant she'd be free! After several days of watching the munchkin, she'd have some time to herself, even if it only meant catching up on her sleep.

Marley pawed through the girl's clothes that she'd washed the night before. "Shorts?" Marley held up the red ones and saw a frown settle immediately on her niece's face. "Great! I'll put on my red shorts, and we'll be twins." Magically, Michelle's expression brightened. Marley packed all the girl's cleaned clothes into her Dora suitcase.

Was it only Wednesday? Four more days, not counting today, to go before she could take off for home. *Home.* She missed Phoenix and its low humidity. Marley forced a comb through her hair, endless curls that had assumed a life of their own. Her constant companion started to laugh and pointed at the uncontrollable bush on top of her aunt's head.

"You look funny." After some tickles, the giddy girl dropped the subject.

The rain had subsided for the present, and the dreaded daytime heat hadn't started yet. Marley dressed in red shorts, a sleeveless

T-shirt and her sandals, grabbed Michelle's hand and headed for the kitchen staircase. They passed the assortment of gifts stacked in the playroom on the second floor while Michelle pulled her pink suitcase with Dora emblazoned on the side.

Buster, the family's old mixed-breed dog, bounded over, and Marley leaned down to pet him, roughing his neck and ears the way he liked. Michelle went to her knees and wrapped her arms around his neck. "He's glad to see me." After the watchdog wagged his tail and pulled out of the embrace, he rambled toward the stairs that led to the living room, where he usually stayed.

Michelle started after the dog, and Marley had to rush to reach her. "Come with me. We'll get some breakfast." She pulled the girl in the opposite direction and headed toward the stairs that led to the kitchen. Having two staircases had provided easy access and escape for her and her sisters but had often proved a bane to their parents and grandparents.

Michelle pulled back. "I don't want to. I want to go to Kenny."

"Your mother will take you later." Marley sighed. This experience with her niece had been a wonderful revelation. Children were tolerable in small doses.

As they passed Lindy's room, Marley had another idea. Should she risk waking her? Had Lindy finally forgiven her for the stained dress? Hesitantly, Marley knocked on the door. "Lindy, you decent?" They'd had little time to talk since her arrival thanks to the spilled juice.

"Marley? Sure, come in."

Lindy sat in the middle of the bed, dressed in summer pajamas, rubbing sleep out of her eyes as Marley entered the room. Lavender violets covered the white walls as well as the curtains, bedspread and canopy bed. A menagerie of stuffed animals lay strewn around the purple rug and topped every available surface. Marley pushed several aside to sit on the edge of her sister's bed, while Michelle warily glanced at her aunt. When Lindy didn't appear ready to scold her, Michelle dived into a group of bears on the floor and began to play.

Although twenty-one, Lindy still looked like a child hardly old enough to take on married life. Her long blond hair was swept over her shoulder in loose abandon. Marley had always considered Lindy—the baby of the family—a little spoiled. But then hadn't she contributed, always giving in to any demands made by her sister or the family.

After making a face at Michelle, Lindy leaned across the bed to greet her niece. "Hi, Shelley."

"My name's Michelle."

"Oh." Lindy straightened, suppressing her amusement. At least she wasn't scolding any more. She turned to Marley. "You're sure an early riser, all dressed and everything. Did the past few days make you decide to have kids?"

"This one has been way more active than any of you were."

"As I recall, you always calmed us down with your guitar. Why didn't you bring it this time?"

My fake fiancé made me forget it! "Too much luggage." As the firstborn, Marley had received lessons in guitar and dance, an opportunity that dried up as more and more daughters joined the family. Lindy patted the mattress close to her. Marley moved over and was immediately entrapped in Lindy's arms.

"Oh, I'm so excited for you," Lindy said as she squeezed.

"Me? Why me?" Marley asked, returning the hug. She avoided entangling herself in the long blond hair. Memories flooded back of trying to brush out her sister's snarls and listening to her scream. During their early years, they had been devoted to each other.

"Your engagement, silly." Lindy pushed away, flipped her hair behind one ear and focused those blue eyes on her. "If only we could have made it a double wedding. When am I going to meet this Brant? He's coming to my wedding, isn't he? The best man can't get leave from the army. I know it's last-minute, and we're devastated, but I was hoping maybe Brant could fill in."

Marley choked on her own saliva and started to cough so hard, Lindy gave her a couple of whacks on the back until she was able to catch her breath again.

Michelle walked over carrying a large gray rabbit and attempted to climb onto the bed between her aunts. Marley quickly picked her up and placed her on her lap, relieved by the distraction. Lindy pulled the little girl away and handed her another stuffed toy before setting her back on the floor. "Your aunt Marley and I want to talk." She turned to Marley. "So tell all. I want every detail. Can you get him here for the wedding?"

Marley smiled in an effort to match her sister's gush of joy over Marley's engagement, which every member of their family had duplicated. The struggle at false effervescence strained her cheeks, and she fought to remember what she'd spent hours rehearsing on the five-hour plane trip. The double wedding bit was something she hadn't anticipated.

Marley cleared her throat. "Unfortunately, Brant has to work." She tried to swallow without choking this time. "He really felt bad about not being able to attend." Another lie. She'd nearly had to hog-tie him to keep him from joining her.

She had fabricated him to suit her family: a businessman and mechanic for Marley's pragmatic grandfather; a traditionalist and financier for her conservative mother; an outdoorsman and athlete for her active brothers-in-law; and a cowboy for her romantic sisters. Only the cowboy part bore any semblance to the truth. That acting career? She'd never speak of it. Not to mention that Brant's scruffy beard and worn-out cowboy attire would have sent her mother into a fit.

Lindy reached for Marley's hand. "Where's your ring?" Marley had placed it in her pocket, not feeling it necessary to always wear it, especially when she washed her hands or worked in the kitchen making meals.

Lindy watched as Marley slipped her ring back on. "Where did you meet him? At his ranch?"

"He…" Marley hesitated, not willing to continue the deception. Clearing her throat, she replied, "Enough of that. I'm here for your wedding, not mine. Give me the rundown on the future Mrs. Dennis Kellner." Marley had met Dennis when she'd first arrived. She'd helped all her brothers-in-law before their weddings and, at Lindy's insistence, taught Dennis some fundamentals in dance. Marley liked him, a nice man who obviously loved her sister.

Marley forced herself to relax as Lindy accepted the spotlight and elaborated on the details of the big event only a few days away. Most of the rest of the conversation blurred as Lindy made glowing statements about Dennis, the love of her life.

"Oh, and you'll get to meet Denny's older brother." Lindy's shoulders dropped, and she looked a forlorn heap in the middle of the bed. "I had planned to pair you off with him, but now that you're engaged…"

In an attempt to avoid discussing her engagement again, Marley asked, "So what's Denny's brother like?"

Lindy leaned closer. "Looks to die for," she said in a conspiratorial whisper. "He told Den he'd steal me away from him if I wasn't a blonde."

"Sounds like you've got a crush."

"On him? No way. He's too old. Besides he likes redheads. When Denny mentioned that you were a redhead, Rick sounded interested. Maybe you know him. He went to your college."

"PITT?" Marley asked, referring to the University of Pittsburgh. "Sorry. It's a pretty large campus, and I don't remember any Rick Kellner."

"His name's not Kellner. His mother remarried after divorcing Rick's father. His last name is Brewster and most people call him Richard, but I know him as Rick."

"Richard Brewster," Marley said, drawing the name out. It couldn't be. Not her Richard.

Marley held her breath, waiting to hear more about Richard. Maybe getting engaged to Brant hadn't been such a good idea after all. It would create a few obstacles if flames from her earlier romance with Richard fanned to life. Then again…their romance had been brief. Both had drifted away, and she hadn't seen or heard from him since his college graduation.

Marley drew her fingers through her hair, only to get the ring caught in the curls, something her hairdresser back in Phoenix had managed to control. Walking over to the mirror, she concentrated on freeing her finger, wanting with all her might to find out more about Richard.

A knock on the door startled her.

"Time to get up, sleepyhead. Lots to do before the big day," a man shouted through the closed door.

Michelle bolted for Marley and hid her face in her aunt's lap.

Marley stiffened, then turned to face the door, enclosing her niece in a tight hug. Was that their father's voice? Why was he here?

"Yeah, Daddy. See you later," Lindy called.

Slowly turning around, Marley stared openmouthed at Lindy.

"Don't be mad. He's giving me away." Lindy knelt in the middle of her bed, clutching a large panda bear. She added in a whisper, "Please don't make a scene, Marley."

"He's back?"

Lindy nodded. "He moved his things in with

Poppy last night, and I really want him to give me away instead of Poppy."

Michelle glanced up at her aunt. Had the little girl picked up on Marley's tension? Her niece's face began to twitch.

Marley picked her up and cradled her in her arms. "It's okay, honey." She brushed kisses along the girl's forehead to calm her down. A few moments later, Marley placed her on the floor and said, "See if you can find the baby kangaroo for me." Distracted, Michelle went searching through the menagerie.

"Is he just here for your wedding?" Marley kept her voice cool for Michelle's benefit and hoped the disapproval boiling inside her wouldn't erupt.

Lindy jumped off the bed and deposited her bear on the crowded dresser. "I hope not. He and Mom have been talking, and who knows? Wouldn't it be wonderful if after all these years Mom and Dad discover they're still in love?"

Marley swallowed the bile rising in her throat. *Was that what Poppy had meant when he said her mother might beat her to the altar? Were her parents getting back together?*

She'd seen her father only occasionally since her parents' divorce. When he'd returned the first time, she'd been in college. To her relief, he had left without getting involved in her life. As the eldest, she'd witnessed all the torment during her parents' breakup. And she couldn't conceive how they could ever get back together.

Marley picked up Michelle and her suitcase and backed out of the room. "I've got to get this one off to Kennywood Park. I'll talk to you later."

How could Mom put up with the man? Marley thought as she headed toward the front staircase. The trauma from his return and departure a dozen years ago had left her mother inconsolable, yet she continued to love Red and want him back? Marley hadn't been able to stay and watch back then any more than she wanted to be around now.

Upon graduation from PITT, she had moved to Phoenix and accepted a position teaching math in a high school, even though the same opportunities were available in Pennsylvania. And then she began building her fences.

She would never love a man to the extent her mother loved her father.

No man would ever be allowed to hurt her that way.

CHAPTER FIVE

BRANT ARRIVED HOME after several days at the ranch visiting with his sisters and their families. His father, who had asked to speak with him, had taken off with Brant's mother, so Brant never did have the opportunity. Now he was back in the Phoenix heat, dodging people who recognized him. Several actually asked for his autograph. He didn't look forward to hiding in his condo until his gig in New York.

His answering machine had several messages, and, for a moment, Brant hoped one might be from Marley. Wishful thinking. She wouldn't know his number. Plus their last meeting pretty much put the kibosh on anything neighborly between them. Tough, because she intrigued him, and he'd really like to know her better.

Three messages were from Gus, and he sounded stressed. Maybe he'd found another musical instrument Brant could add to his collection. Brant picked up his home phone and dialed Gus's store.

"What is it, Gus? Another instrument? I liked that mandolin you showed me the last time, but I still feel it's a little pricey."

"No. This is something different. Could you come down to my shop?"

Brant checked his watch. It was nearly nine, and Gus rarely kept his store open this late. "Can't it wait until tomorrow?"

"No. It's important you see this tonight."

"Okay. It'll take me a few minutes." *Might as well see what he wants,* Brant thought as he locked his door and headed for the elevator. In the few years he'd known Gus, the man had sold him several beautiful instruments, including a banjo and guitar. Gus opened the door when Brant arrived and led him to the back. A policeman stood at the counter where Marley had purchased her ring.

"There's a problem," Gus said, not making eye contact with Brant. "When your fiancée paid for that ring?"

Brant chuckled. "She's not my real fiancée."

"Let him finish," the officer interjected.

Brant turned to him, aware that the usual relaxed atmosphere in the shop had disappeared.

He looked back at Gus. "What about my fiancée's ring?"

"She paid for this one." Gus held out one that looked exactly like the ring Brant had pointed out to Marley. "It costs less than fifty dollars. She walked out with the one for five thousand."

"How…?"

"I don't know." Gus held up a hand and glanced at the officer. "I'm not saying she stole it." He swallowed. "But if you could pay for the ring, there won't be any…problems." He cleared his throat.

"And if I return it?"

"I'll take it back. No questions asked."

Brant stood there for several moments, his hands braced on the glass counter. *Wow. Five thousand dollars. An okay price to pay for a real fiancée, but not for a possible thief.* What did he know about Marley? For that matter, what did he know about Gus?

Swiftly coming to a decision, Brant pushed away from the counter, reached for his wallet and handed Gus his credit card. "Put it on this." Gus had never cheated him in the past, and Marley owing Brant wouldn't hurt one bit. She played a guitar better than most professional musicians he knew. If she wouldn't return the ring, she could teach him a few things about playing the guitar—a good five thousand dollars' worth of lessons.

But he had no intention of waiting until his "fiancée" returned to Phoenix to acquire that ring.

By the time he reached his condo, Brant had a plan. He'd follow Marley and trade the expensive ring for the one she actually bought. Besides, he wanted to get out of the city, and, as he'd told her, Pennsylvania was a lot closer to his New York gig. Well, it might be a plan if he knew where she had gone. Pennsylvania was a large state, and there had to be hundreds of people with the last name Roman. Still, there couldn't be that many Romans marrying in Pennsylvania this coming weekend. He turned on his computer and began searching social media.

MICHELLE WAS NEARLY finished with her pancakes when her mother came into the local restaurant and gave her a quick kiss. "How was it?" Chloe joined them in the booth next to her daughter. Dressed in shorts and a T-shirt, she in no way looked pregnant. "You ready to have a dozen kids?"

"Only if I can drop them off on someone else occasionally."

Chloe reached over and gripped Marley's hands. "Thank you, a thousand times over." She leaned back and sighed. "I feel good today, and, hopefully, I'll make it through to the wedding."

"He's at the house."

Chloe turned, her forehead puckered. "Who?" Then in delight she blurted, "Brant!"

Startled, Marley immediately shook her head. "No. Red. Our father."

After a moment's hesitation, Chloe glanced at her daughter. "Oh?" She leaned over and wiped some syrup off her daughter's chin.

"He's giving Lindy away. Did you know about this?"

Chloe studied her hands and swallowed. "Yes." She looked up. "We all did."

"I don't believe this." Marley shifted in her seat and glanced at her niece. Instead of having the screaming fit she felt entitled to, she controlled herself so as not to disturb the little girl with her outburst.

"When was anyone going to tell me?" Marley stood, choking back tears. She bent over and kissed her niece on top of her head. "You have fun, sweetheart. I'll see you…" She turned to Chloe. "When will I see her? You dropping her off when you get back?"

"No. She'll stay with us."

Marley went for the door, ignoring all the pleading calls behind her.

MARLEY FUMED. How could she avoid her father during her stay? Why hadn't anyone told her he'd be there? That question she could answer herself. *Because you'd never have come.* Well, the family was right on that score. She drove to the house and parked in the driveway. Easy access in case she wanted a quick escape.

Poppy sat in the living room with a newspaper when she entered. "Hi, Poppy. May I speak to you a moment? In my room?" She headed for the stairs after he nodded.

Marley took a seat on the bed and waited for him to take the rocking chair. "You heard?" he asked as he took the seat.

"Are you okay with this?"

Poppy sighed. "If there's one thing my old age has taught me—you can't force people to do what you think is right for them. You're parents are grown and maybe they might even have developed a little maturity over the years."

He looked past Marley and his expression

neutralized. Poppy got out of the chair and started for the door, acknowledging the man standing there. "Hello, Red. I guess you and Marley may have some catching up to do. Well, see you around," he said over his shoulder as he stepped through the doorway.

Basil Roman hesitated in the door frame. "Heard you had returned from Phoenix."

For a split second, Marley could only stare. "Dad?"

"Have I changed that much?" he asked, moving into the room.

The puffy quality in his jowls and his additional girth hardly resembled the athletic man she remembered. "Red," as family and friends called him, had provided the genes that gave her hair its distinctive color and curl. What little he had left no longer resembled its former brilliance. She wouldn't have recognized him if she'd met him on the street.

When she didn't answer, he said, "Lindy asked me to give her away."

Marley cleared her throat. She moved over to the rocker and stood behind it, not only distancing herself but also providing a barrier between her father and herself. "She mentioned you were coming to the wedding."

"I'm staying here with your grandfather

until the wedding." When Marley didn't respond, he added, "He invited me."

Marley couldn't handle it. Not when painful memories impaired her ability to see straight. She gripped the back of the rocking chair so hard her knuckles turned white. *Why Lindy?* Marley's thoughts screamed. Why had he chosen to give Lindy away, when he'd never bothered to even attend any of his other daughters' weddings? Lindy was the youngest, the one he'd abandoned soon after her birth along with the rest of his family.

He must have honed in on her thoughts because he said, "I was hoping to give you away, as well. Sort of make up for lost time."

Coldness slithered down her spine. No way would she ever allow that to happen. "Thanks for offering, but I don't plan on marrying for quite a while."

"No? I thought your mother said you'd just gotten engaged."

*Of all the stupid...*Marley twirled the ring around her finger with her thumb. How had she forgotten that minor detail? "Right. I...I..." She looked down at her hand. The fake diamonds caught the sunlight and tossed rainbows around the room. Placing her hand in her pocket, she tried to think of something to say that wouldn't jeopardize her engagement and still keep her father out of any future wedding. "We haven't set a date."

"I look forward to meeting your young man." He nodded and walked toward the hall, only to retrace his steps. "I know you took all the problems between your mother and me hard. We pushed a lot of responsibility on you because you were the oldest, and I'm sorry for that. I hope you can forgive me and let me make it up to you."

Like that's ever going to happen. She remained silent until he left. Marley tried shaking off the unwanted thoughts. More than half her life had been spent despising her father for destroying their family and hurting her mother.

She paced her room, feeling drained emotionally by having to participate in yet another wedding. Just once she'd like to see a wedding from the front pew and not have to deal with all the backstage drama. Then to top everything, her father had to show up asking for her forgiveness? She couldn't face it. Not now. Maybe never.

She took out her cell phone. A little after nine o'clock. The three hour difference from Arizona switching to Pacific Time when everyone else went on Daylight Saving Time meant Dede might still be at home before heading for work. *"¡Hola!"* Marley said. "I really need to talk."

"You sound horrible. Didn't the engagement thing go okay?"

"Yes and no." Marley paused, hoping to control her voice. "Everyone's happy about that, but my father's here!" She ended on a high note, unable to contain her frustration.

"What?"

"He's staying with Poppy and giving Lindy away." Dede knew all the details of Marley's past; she'd understand her friend's dilemma.

After a short pause, Dede chuckled. "So the soap opera goes on."

"It's not funny."

"Right. But there's nothing you can do about it, so chill out." After another pause, she continued, her voice lilting. "I saw your betrothed." When Marley didn't offer any remark, Dede added, "He asked about you. Sounded very concerned. Wanted to get in touch."

Marley collapsed onto the rocker and began to rock. "Right. The guy's an actor, remember? Did he give you his 'I adore you—let's make love' smile?"

"No." Dede giggled. "He must save that one for you, although it comes close on that poster you see everywhere. He's having a hard time dodging all the people who recognize him." After another short hesitation, she said, "He hopes to connect with you, maybe go out on a date. He wasn't specific, but he asked for your cell phone number."

Marley stopped rocking. "You didn't give it to him, did you?"

Dede sighed. "No. I don't do that without people's permission."

"Thank you."

"What do you plan to do? Move to avoid him?"

Marley loved her condo, but... "If I have to."

"Forget your ditsy rules. This guy could be the one. Give him a chance."

Remembering how much Brant's nearness had upset her, Marley shuddered and said, "No way." Totally flustered, she stood up, headed for her bed and flopped onto it. "Getting engaged was a mistake. The groom's brother is in the wedding, and he's Richard Brewster, my old flame from college. If I wasn't in this fake engagement, I might be able to start something with him."

"Oh, so there *is* some man around who intrigues you? I was beginning to worry."

Even though she hadn't heard from or seen Richard in years, he still brought back fond memories. "You got me into this mess with Brant. Now how do I get out of it?"

After a long pause, Dede said, "I have the solution."

"I'm listening."

"Tell everyone you broke off your engagement with Brant. That frees you to start something with this new guy. Then you move back to Pennsylvania so you'll never have to deal with Brant again. Problem solved. And I've got to run."

Agape, Marley just lay there. The call hadn't helped one bit. She had to come up with a solution, but telling everyone she'd just broken her engagement? No. That would require fabricating a whole new set of lies.

CHAPTER SIX

FOUR MORE DAYS, not counting today, and she'd be back in Phoenix. How would she avoid Brant once she returned? Did she want to avoid him? What should she do once she met with Richard? Annoyed, Marley tossed her phone into her purse and glanced out the window. Her father was getting into a car, heading out. *Good.* She wanted to talk with her mother and see how she felt about Red's return.

Marley found her mother standing at the kitchen counter, wearing a skirt and blouse covered by the ubiquitous flowered apron.

"Morning, Mom." Marley considered mentioning her father's presence and decided to wait until her mother brought up the subject.

Nora Roman turned with a warm smile. "You're here? I thought you'd take off with your sisters and their families to Kennywood Park. The weatherman promised a few sunrays."

"No. Michelle's back with Chloe and they

plan to go. I'm way too tired. The tyke exhausted me." How had her mother managed to take care of five girls, for the most part all by herself once Marley left for college?

"Aunt Effie will be arriving soon. Do something with your hair, dear. You know how she always hated that kinky look." Aunt Effie was ten years older than Nora's fifty-five years and the matriarch of Nora's side of the family. Aunt Effie rarely had a problem with anything, yet whenever her mother didn't approve of something, Aunt Effie suddenly became very opinionated.

Kinky? Marley automatically touched the springy curls. It had taken a long time to get her stubborn tresses to grow, and she liked how her hairdresser had managed to control the curl.

"Your hair looks like you put your finger in a light socket."

For the hundredth time since she arrived, Marley felt trapped in a time warp. The years of living alone as an adult in Phoenix, plus those spent in college, were whisked away the moment she returned home. "I'll tame it into a tight French twist by the time Aunt Effie gets here." But it wasn't kinky, never had been. It was merely curlier than usual, thanks to the high humidity. And a real pain in the neck to control.

"You know how critical Aunt Effie can be. I want everything perfect for...for everyone."

Marley picked up a box of cereal, took out a handful of small cubes and began eating them dry. "Where's she staying?"

"Here, of course. Use a bowl."

"Here where?" Marley reached into the box again and took out another handful. The three bedrooms upstairs were full. So was her grandfather's with Red staying there.

"I thought she could use your room, and you can stay with me."

"Why not have her stay with you?" Marley really needed her sleep after dealing with the squirming Michelle. If her mother planned to discuss her present situation with Red, Marley knew sleep would be impossible. Her mother would want to talk all night.

"She snores, and I'd never get any sleep." Nora looked pointedly at the box of cereal and pushed a clean bowl in Marley's direction. "Can't you use this? I thought I raised you to have some manners."

"The cereal's all gone." Marley placed the last handful in her mouth. "Empty." She turned the box upside down over the trash to show only a few crumbs remained before depositing it.

"Can I help with anything?"

"Thanks for asking, but everything's under control. Actually, there's little to do since your sisters refused to let me handle the wedding." Nora eyed her daughter accusingly, knowing full well that Marley had instigated the rebellion.

Convincing her mother to relax and enjoy the festivities this time around, instead of wearing herself out with the catering, had been a fight. But Nora not doing the work also meant her sisters, who helped Nora in her catering business, would be able to enjoy the wedding, as well. Marley had been so concerned about her sisters. Why had they backstabbed her and not told her…? *Oh, stop this. Just get through it.*

"You work too hard. You need to enjoy a wedding, for a change."

"Since it won't be the last, I hope you'll let me cater yours." Nora gave her daughter a hopeful smile, and Marley inwardly cringed. *No way,* she thought. *No way.*

"There is something you can do."

Marley wavered. If it had anything to do with her father…

"You're the organized one in the family. Could you help Lindy with the thank-you cards? She'll never get to them without help." When Marley nodded, Nora continued, "She sure got a lot of presents.... You can expect the same."

Not wanting to discuss her own wedding plans again, Marley left. She'd have to pack her things and take them to her mother's section of the house. As children they had referred to the two additions as "mouse ears." The additions stood on either side of the main building, one for Poppy and Nana when she was alive, the other for Nora and Red until the divorce.

When Marley went upstairs, she found Lindy on the floor of the playroom, sitting among all her gifts. "Mom said you haven't written any of your thank-you cards."

"I thought I'd do it after my honeymoon."

"Why not get it over with now? I'll help."

Lindy rose and shook her head. "Nah. It can wait. Come on back to my room so we can talk."

"Okay, but I need to get my things out of my room before Aunt Effie arrives. She'll be using it."

"Where are you staying?"

"Mom asked me to stay with her." Marley followed her sister into her room.

"That's no fun. Why don't you sleep with me?"

Marley took in the bed surrounded by a few hundred beady glass eyes and shook her head. "Mom probably wants to talk." She grimaced. Her mother would probably want to talk about Red. Maybe she should reconsider Lindy's offer.

"I'm so glad you're getting married," Lindy said while climbing onto her bed. She turned around. "I didn't want you to end up alone like Aunt Effie."

Marley picked up a giant teddy bear off the only chair in the room, intending to toss it at Lindy. Instead, she plopped down on the seat, holding the bear to her chest in a death grip. For several seconds she hid her face against the back of the bear's soft neck. Well, what had she expected? Hadn't the family breathed an audible sigh of relief when she'd told them about the engagement?

Once she felt composed enough to show her face again, Marley peeked out from behind the bear's head. "I better get going before Aunt Effie gets here."

"No, no. Wait! Silly me!" Lindy shouted,

bounding off the bed and reaching for her purse. "I got them right here. Ta-da." She lifted a bunch of keys and jingled them in front of the bear. "They belong to Rick. You can use his place. He won't be home till Friday, another two days."

Marley hesitated. A night at Richard's place sounded too intimate. "Why on earth do you have his keys?"

"I feed his cat when he's away. You can do it so I won't have to." She handed the keys to Marley. "At least you'll get one good night's sleep while you're here."

"Are you sure he won't mind?"

"Who will tell him?" Lindy grabbed Marley's shoulder and pushed her toward the door. "Use his guest room. That's the one I always use when I want to get away from the family. It's on the right when you enter the townhouse." Marley hesitated. "Just change the sheets and leave the room like you found it."

Still undecided, Marley asked, "What's the cat's name?"

"The Baroness. But she answers to 'Kitty, Kitty.' Now go. I'll explain to Mom."

WITH RICHARD'S ADDRESS punched into her cell phone's GPS, Marley drove to his townhouse in her rented Toyota. Rain had started, again. Normally, Marley loved the sound of rain in Phoenix because it was infrequent and so welcome. But the intermittent downpours since her arrival in Pennsylvania had become annoying. She hoped the rain would end before the wedding.

What would it be like to see Richard again? Had he changed much? Did he still have that golden hair, those eyes that melted any resistance? Did every woman he came in contact with still swoon and long to be in his arms?

Their short romance had occurred while he was a senior at PITT and she a junior. Because he'd been popular with the women, Marley had felt special when he singled her out. Just as things between them had begun to heat up, her father had reappeared unexpectedly in her mother's life. Nora accepted the situation, but Marley refused to.

No way would she be like her mother, chattel, used by a man who tossed her aside when something better arrived. That promise to herself ruled Marley's life. All her relationships had turned into slow fizzles the moment she detected any resemblance between the man and her father. At the time, she'd seen all the signs in Richard.

She parked across from Richard's townhouse in a guest parking space and dragged her one suitcase up the front steps. The Baroness, a solid gray short hair with a white bib, greeted her at the door and rubbed against Marley's ankles. After cleaning the cat's box and providing fresh water and food, Marley ran a bath for herself. The Baroness followed every step, demanding constant attention, which Marley gladly provided.

Marley picked up a crocheted ball, one of the many cat toys scattered on the floor, and tossed it. "Here, chase this." The Baroness ran after it, and Marley could close the door and slip into the tub. However, the cat scratched at the door, determined to get back in the room.

When bubbles trapped around the cubic zirconia made a radiant rainbow of color, she thought of Brant. What made that man tick? He liked being engaged to her way too much. She hoped it wouldn't create more problems for her when she returned to Phoenix.

Marley slipped off the ring, wiped it dry and dropped it into her shoe. Once back in her T-shirt that served as a nightgown, she bustled about with a need to straighten the bathroom and destroy any evidence of her presence.

Spotting underwear in the corner, Marley retrieved them, only to realize they weren't hers.

She dropped them into a hamper. The discovery of something so personal made her feel uncomfortable. What did she really know about Richard or his lifestyle? He could be having a steady relationship with someone. What a depressing thought. How could she resolve her muddled feelings for him if he already had commitments?

Determined to get some rest, Marley closed the guest room door on the Baroness. She had no intention of sleeping with the cat, especially one whose purr had to equal Aunt Effie's snoring.

Oh, what quiet, what solitude. Climbing between the sheets, she relished the cool, smooth texture. Finally, a peaceful sleep.

THE BED UNDULATED, bringing Marley from a dreamless rest to semi-consciousness. When something hit her head, she woke completely. Ominous epithets from a masculine voice brought her back to her surroundings.

I'm going to be murdered! Marley thought as the overhead light turned on. She pulled the sheet over her face and prepared for death.

"What are you doing here?" a man shouted. "Sheba, get out!"

Marley dropped the sheet to her nose. As her eyes adjusted to the light, she took in more and more of broad shoulders and flat waist. She gulped. Richard Brewster. His long pajama bottoms were covered with Pittsburgh Steelers logos.

"Richard! What are *you* doing here?" She sat up, keeping the sheet protectively under her chin. His expression turned from questioning to incredulous.

"Marley?" he asked. "Marley Roman?"

"Yes," she said, wishing she was facing a serial killer instead. Anything was preferable to having Richard discover her in his home. She gulped again and stared back as he breathed deeply, dropped his arm and relaxed his shoulders. "Who..." She faltered. "Who did you think I was?"

Oh, the years had added more muscular weight, and his hair had a trimmer cut. Laughing, teasing, virile. The same old Richard, she thought as she clamped her teeth into her lower lip.

"Sheba." The single word came out in a whisper. Obviously not one of his favorite playmates. The Baroness jumped on the bed and came over to be petted. A welcome distraction.

He still appeared stunned, so she asked, "Who's she? Some exotic belly dancer?"

"No." He stared right into her eyes. "My mother's poodle."

Marley's stomach knotted at his easy admission. He didn't even have the grace to look disconcerted. She bristled. "A dog? You thought I was a dog?"

"Yeah. It's your hair." He flipped his fingertips through his own blond waves. Another reference to her hair. One more time and she'd shave it all off. "I thought my mother left her dog here." His voice got softer as he continued to stare at her. "She sometimes brings her when she takes care of my cat."

"Really?" Adrenaline poured into her from her aborted fear. "Lindy said she was taking care of the Baroness."

Richard collapsed against the wall, rubbed his head and closed his eyes. "Right, I forgot. When the Baroness was scratching at the closed door, I came over to see why."

"The dog and cat get along?"

He nodded, straightening, his eyes still on her. "So why are you here? I hoped we'd have a chance to get together. I just never figured you'd take the initiative."

"Hey, wait a minute." Marley jolted upright. If he thought she'd planned this... "You've got the wrong idea here. I didn't expect you home." She paused. "I needed a place to stay, and Lindy gave me the key." Had Lindy planned this so that Richard would discover her this way?

Richard rubbed his head again. "I should have told her I changed my plans." He faced Marley. "I'm in charge of Denny's bachelor party tomorrow night...tonight, actually...I think. Tonight's Thursday, isn't it?"

Marley reached for the clothes she'd placed at the end of the bed. "I should go."

"No. Stay. The room's available. Not exactly how I planned our first meeting but..."

"You had something planned?"

Richard chuckled. "Not really. Just figured us meeting again would be a surprise. Figured you probably weren't aware of your sister marrying my brother. I know it certainly shocked me."

The humor in Richard's voice helped ease her tension. "Say, I'm wide-awake now. Want to talk?" He started out, but at the door he turned. "I'll meet you in the living room."

After dressing in her shorts and another blouse, Marley settled on the brown leather couch, her legs curled under her. Richard had added a white T-shirt. After flopping onto a leather recliner, he sent the bottom out to support his legs.

"Not much has changed with you, has it?" Marley said.

"What's that supposed to mean?"

"That woman's stuff in the bathroom, the discarded lace underwear. I remember you were quite the ladies' man in college."

"What should I have done after you brushed me off?" He pushed the handle on the side of his chair and his legs came down. He leaned toward her. "Why did you? I thought we had something good going."

Marley sighed. "I don't know. Immaturity, I guess."

"I was immature?" He looked about ready to jump out of his chair.

With another sigh, Marley fluttered her hands to indicate he should stay seated. "Don't get your hackles up. I was the immature one. You were this real popular guy, and I didn't know how to handle you."

Richard leaned back in his chair. "That's

great. I had to be handled in some special way."

Marley bit her lower lip. "I'm not saying any of this right. Back then, I was having issues with my father returning."

"I remember."

"And I thought you might be like him."

His voice nearly exploded. "You thought I was like that womanizing cheat you complained about all the time?" He gripped the chair arm, getting control of himself before adding, "I wouldn't do that to you. It wasn't until you ended it that I even looked at another woman."

"I was young and naive." Marley averted her gaze. "It wasn't my grandest hour." Oh, if only she could relive those days with some maturity. "The issues I faced got in the way, and I confused them with you. I didn't want to go through what my mother did. What she's going through now," she added in an aside.

Richard glanced at her, then looked away. "He's back?"

"Yes. Lindy wanted him to give her away. This is the first time he's been at any of the weddings, and he's staying in the house."

After a long pause, Richard asked, "You have any extra room in your luggage?"

Perplexed, Marley nodded.

"Then you might want to pack the other things you mentioned. They belong to Lindy. She stayed here a few times when I was gone while taking care of the Baroness." As if prompted by the sound of her name, the cat jumped onto Richard's lap.

"Did your brother stay here with Lindy?"

"I wouldn't know. I haven't been invited to watch the videos."

"Oh, you!" Marley tossed one of the cat's toys at Richard, but he managed to catch it in midair and gave it to the Baroness.

After a long pause, Marley asked, "So how many times have you made it to the altar?"

"Once. No kids, and it ended several years ago. What about you?"

About to say never, Marley sat up with a start. With nervous energy, she tucked her hands between the cushions and found an earring and some change but not the ring. Where had she put it? After a quick search around the couch, Marley headed for the bedroom.

Brant sat forward. "What are you doing?"

When she didn't answer, he followed her.

"I lost it."

"Lost what?"

"My ring. I took it off and put it in my shoe

while I was taking a bath." She paused before sputtering, "My open-toed, you-can't-put-a-ring-in-it shoe!" On her hands and knees, Marley crawled across the plush rug, sweeping her hand around.

"This it?"

Marley turned to find Richard standing above her with the ring. She accepted his offered hand and got to her feet. "Yes. Where was it?"

"By the tub." He dropped it into her hand and returned to the living room.

She slipped it on the proper finger before following him. "You're engaged?" Without waiting for an answer, he continued in an emotionless voice, "I'm going to bed. See you in the morning."

CHAPTER SEVEN

MARLEY COULDN'T SLEEP, not after seeing Richard's disappointment. More than a decade ago, she had loved this man, and at one point had expected to marry him. Now...now she was "engaged" to Brant. Marley turned over and pounded her pillow. Why was she stuck with Brant when Richard was available—and interested?

Marley tossed again. An engagement bound two people. She had to respect that...mainly because the truth would make a liar out of her. Still... She flipped again, unable to dislodge her thoughts. And why did Brant have to continually invade them?

Brant, needling, flashing that smile. She hated this engagement. She hated him for his utter enjoyment in being engaged to her. She hated him....Finally, exhaustion set in, and she fell asleep.

Marley awoke to a light tap on the door and the smell of bacon and coffee. Richard peeked in. "Breakfast's ready. I have to make a quick trip to the office."

She joined him a few minutes later. "Nice," she said, taking a tall chair at the bar. An array of jams in jars plus wheat toast sat on the counter along with two plates filled with scrambled eggs and bacon. The Baroness came over and rubbed against Marley's ankles.

"If the cat's bothering you, I can put her in my room."

"No, she's fine." Marley reached down and petted the cat's soft fur until she purred.

"You like anything in your coffee?" Richard poured, then pushed containers of sugar and cream toward her. "Can't remember if you even like coffee."

"I do." She added cream. "You cook like this on a regular basis? I usually grab a breakfast bar and pick up coffee at a local coffee stand when I'm off to work."

"I like breakfasts. My specialty is omelets. Not enough time this morning." He took a sip of coffee, put his cup down, then placed his hands on the bar, leaning slightly toward her. "As I recall, you made a few breakfasts for me back when—"

"Let's not go there, Richard."

"Sure." He smacked the bar and turned back

to his plate. "So when are you getting married? Is this the first time?"

Marley slowly chewed the bacon before speaking. "First time. Haven't decided when, exactly."

"Someone you met in Phoenix?"

Marley nodded.

"Not your usual womanizing guy?"

"No."

Richard chuckled, then returned to his food. "He coming to the wedding?" he asked, picking up his plate and bringing it to the sink. The Baroness jumped on the bar, and he shooed her down.

"No."

"What? You're not letting your family put him through the inquisition?" When she shook her head, he added, "Aha. You don't want him exposed to all your beautiful sisters. It might weaken his resolve, and he'd show just how unfaithful he can be."

Marley stacked her dirty dishes and brought them over to the sink. "I'm safe. He doesn't go for blondes." At least not from what she'd observed. All the women she'd seen him with had hair as dark as his. She found the dish soap and began running water into the sink.

Richard placed several items in the refrigerator before joining her. He slipped his hand under her hair and ran it through his fingers. "A man after my own heart. I always loved your hair."

The touch felt nice, comforting. She faced him with a smile. "Yeah, sure. Because it reminds you of your mother's dog."

"Don't put Sheba down. She's a true champion, and except for a telltale doggy odor, she could make any man happy. Maybe I'll introduce her to your fiancé and see if there's any attraction."

Marley said, "You won't get the chance. I told you—he's not coming."

"We'll see about that." He gave her a kiss on the cheek. "Got to go. Let me know if you need the place again tonight."

Marley dallied at the sink, enjoying the moment. Reuniting with Richard felt comfortable. Maybe…Then she noticed her ring, surrounded by a rainbow of soapsuds. No maybes or anything else until she had this ring off her finger for good.

ON THE WAY to her mother's, Marley passed the local motel and pulled into the parking area. She sat in the car, mulling her choices. She had no desire to stay with her mother and learn more about her mother's present feelings for Red. Nor did she consider Richard's offer a possibility. A motel room would probably max out her credit card, but it did offer a solution. After running through the drizzle to book a room, she gathered all her belongings from the car and placed them in the motel room. At least she was set for the night.

Her aunt Effie, who had arrived at her mother's earlier, wanted some time alone with Marley, so the two took off for lunch. Over the years, she and her aunt had developed a close relationship. Since Marley's discussion with Dede hadn't provided any solutions, she decided to be forthcoming with her aunt.

"Tell me everything—spare no details," Effie said, patting Marley's hand and fingering the ring. "You never even mentioned Brant in your last letter." Her aunt hadn't advanced into the technological age, so all their correspondence went through snail mail. Effie had gained a little weight since the last time Marley had seen her, and her short coiffed curls now had a hint of blue in the gray.

"It's a lie. All of it." Marley sat back against the padded booth in the restaurant and watched as her aunt slowly put her glass of water back on the table.

"What's a lie?"

"My engagement. I just couldn't come back here and face everyone old and alone."

Effie flipped the menu open and stared at it. "We better order. I think I'll need something that sticks to the ribs." She smiled at the waitress and said, "Give me the highest cholesterol thing you've got. I'm looking forward to my heart attack."

After the waitress took their order of burgers and fries with gravy, a delicacy in western Pennsylvania, Effie turned to Marley and said, "There's nothing wrong in being alone. I've certainly enjoyed it. Saved me from a lot of heartache and a great deal of crap."

"Oh, Auntie, I didn't mean—"

"You've heard the saying—I never realized the last man who asked me to marry him would be the last man to ask me?"

Marley nodded.

"Well, that wasn't me. I never wanted to spend my life waiting on a man, and I never needed one to wait on me. And I sure never wanted the type of relationship your mother settled on. She's, pardon the expression, turned into a yo-yo." With a wave of her hand, Effie added, "Forget all that. Let's get down to what's bothering you. Who's this Brant and how long have you known him?"

"He's my neighbor, and he's lived in the condo next door to mine since before I moved in. Not that you'd notice. I didn't know he existed until about two months ago, when he showed up."

Effie picked up a roll and began buttering it. "Good-looking?"

Marley flipped on her phone and showed her aunt Brant's picture.

"So in two months you fell in love with this good-looking—"

"No. I'm not in love with him. In fact, I feel ill at ease when I'm around him. Besides that, we've never even dated."

"Then how did you get engaged?" She looked at Marley over the top of her glasses.

"It's made up. Not real, not even this ring." She fluttered her fingers, which sent a rainbow of lights around the room. "He's hardly real," Marley added in frustration.

"That part's a lie. He's real." Effie wiped a spot of butter from the corner of her mouth. "Your mother was talking to him this morning."

Marley's jaw dropped. "She what?"

"Yes, he called, trying to contact you. Said

he needed to talk to you about something very important."

Leaning across the table, Marley gripped her aunt's hands. "The guy's loony. There's nothing that could be important between us."

"From what I gathered, your mom invited him to the wedding."

Marley half stood. "No!"

"Sit, sit." Effie gestured with a fluttering hand. "I don't think he's coming."

Patting her heart, Marley said, "Maybe I should call him." While her aunt busied herself with the roll, Marley picked up her phone. How could she reach him? How had he been able to call her mother?

Effie pointed at the phone. "You have one of those newfangled things that can do everything but drive a car?"

Marley nodded, still concerned about Brant's call. Maybe she could phone the condo management and get his number. But why bother? Brant merely wanted to annoy her, and she couldn't imagine him spending money on a plane ticket to do that.

Sidetracked by her thoughts, Marley was surprised when Effie asked, "Is there another problem besides this Brant?"

"Well, yes. Richard's in the wedding."

"Richard?"

"Denny's brother, Richard. I told you about him. I met him in college and—"

"Wait a minute." Effie picked another roll. "Denny's brother, Richard, is your Richard? Didn't that end a few centuries ago?"

Aunt Effie had been the only one in her family to know about Richard, the only one Marley could trust to keep her secret. "Yes, but I saw him again last night and he's…" She paused and thought about how pleasant the morning had been. "He's really nice, and he thinks I'm engaged. But I'm not, and I wish I weren't. Oh, Effie, it's such a rotten mess. How can I get out of this?"

"Let me get this straight. You got engaged, so no one would consider you an old maid. Now you want to go back to being an old maid so you can get engaged to Richard?"

"Well, no, not exactly. I just want to be free of this fake engagement so I'm available. I can't have anything start with Richard if I'm tied down to Brant."

Effie moved her hands so that the waitress could place her food in front of her. "You realize this wouldn't even be a problem if you were anything like your parents. Either one would ignore the engagement, fake or not, and do what suits them at the time."

Marley shuddered. "I broke it off with Richard because I thought he was like my father." She gave the waitress a smile and moved her water, indicating she and Effie both needed a refill. "I'd like to give him another chance."

"Then it's obvious, Brant has to go. And since the whole thing is fake to begin with, problem solved." Effie dipped a French fry in the gravy and waved it to emphasize her point.

CHAPTER EIGHT

WOULD SHE EVEN recognize the Emersons, Marley wondered as she scoured the people coming from the gate at the Pittsburgh airport. After Marley had returned her aunt to the house, Nora had sent her to pick up some distant relatives Marley hadn't seen since the last wedding. She held up the sign she'd made with their name on it in bold black letters.

"Here we are! Here we are," a woman shouted as she approached. She wore a brown fur wrap and a tiny pillbox hat—something from the Kennedy era, Marley guessed. "No need for a sign, dear. I'd recognize you anywhere. The hair." Marley moved out of her way before the woman could touch it.

"Your bags?"

"Harold has them. Come, come now." She beckoned to an elderly man dragging two carry-ons. "We don't want to keep her waiting."

"Marley?"

Marley turned to see who had called her name. A tall, handsome man approached, wearing a long-sleeved dress shirt and black pants and holding a jacket over his arm. For a moment she stared, unable to place the short dark hair, the face...the beardless face. "Brant?" She gulped. "What happened to your beard, your hair?"

"What happened to yours?" He grinned. "Looks like you went wild with a curling iron."

"What are you doing here?" She took a panicked breath and hoped she wasn't delusional. His being here was impossible, wasn't it? However, he'd been in her thoughts so often, Marley was sure her subconscious had created him.

"Do you mind?" Mrs. Emerson said. Marley didn't move, frozen in place by the surreal image in front of her. It was as though the poster had come to life. "I'd really like to get going." Mrs. Emerson pushed between them and pulled on Marley's arm. Beads of sweat had already formed on the older woman's forehead as she directed everyone to the outer doors. Her fur piece was whipped off the moment they reached the humid air. A drizzling rain fell. Mrs. Emerson turned to Brant, who had followed the three of them as they left the terminal. "He coming with us?"

Brant nodded. "We're engaged."

Mrs. Emerson seemed startled but made no comment. And Marley was beyond words. What on earth would she do with him? She felt her chest constrict and momentarily thought she might be having a heart attack...hoped she was having one. At least that might eliminate the need to deal with Brant.

Brant turned to Mr. Emerson. "Can I help you with that?" Surprise crossed his face, and he brought his carry-ons over. Brant placed one of them on his own rolling luggage and carried the second as the four trooped over to Marley's car.

Thank goodness Mrs. Emerson sat in front with Marley and did all the talking. There was no way Marley could have contributed to the conversation. Her brain was focused on the man in the backseat, and she kept glancing at Brant through the rearview mirror. Each time, he caught her eye and either smiled or winked, destroying her concentration. If only she hadn't had to pick up the Emersons. She had a million questions for him. Why was he here? Who paid for his plane fare? Where was he staying?

Then again, maybe it was a good thing he had come. They could have an argument, break off the engagement and she'd be able to spend the rest of the time with Richard.

Marley snapped back to the present when Mrs. Emerson said, "Where are you taking us, dear?"

"Mom said to come for supper. Would you rather go to the motel?"

"If you wouldn't mind, I'd like to freshen up first."

Marley drove into the motel parking lot and got the room key for the Emersons. Once they were settled, she turned to Brant, who had been shadowing her with his own luggage. "I have a room here. We can wait for them there. You may as well leave your bag there instead of in the car."

"Your father said I have a room here, too, or will I be staying with you?"

All the annoyance she had managed to control suddenly erupted. "My father! Did he buy your plane ticket?"

"Whoa. Why so hostile?"

She glared at him. "Take a wild guess, Brant. I told you not to follow me here. How is my father involved?"

"He made the arrangements. I paid for everything."

"Well, I'm not paying you back."

"Oh, yes you are, and for way more than the plane fare." When she started to protest, he cut her off. "Wait. I've got a lot to tell you."

The room was cool and dark with the shades drawn. Marley turned on a lamp and took the only chair. Brant deposited his bag near her luggage, then sprawled on the bed, feet crossed on top of the covers. This time he wore well-polished black lizard-skin cowboy boots. She wondered if he had one of his cowboy hats stuffed in his suitcase. At least his present outfit wouldn't embarrass her, now that he looked more like his poster.

Restless and agitated, Marley swatted his boots. He sat up and threw his legs over the side. Leaning toward her, he held out his hand. "Mind if I see our engagement ring again?"

"My engagement ring." Warily she placed her hand in his. "I paid for it, remember?"

He reached into his pants' pocket and pulled out an identical one attached to a pink ribbon. "No," he said. "You paid $42.98 for this one." He dangled it in front of her. "The genuine diamond you're wearing cost $5,347.84."

Marley's jaw dropped.

He squeezed her hand so she couldn't pull away. "And there's no way I'm letting that little treasure out of my sight."

"What are you talking about?"

"When you bought this," he said, continuing to dangle the ring in front of her, "you paid with a credit card, one that couldn't cover the five thousand."

Right. She had only a small amount of credit left, barely enough to cover the motel room and her car rental.

Brant continued, "Gus phoned the police."

"The police!" She pulled back, but he still gripped her hand.

"Yes. He called me into his shop with the police there and explained how you took off with the wrong ring."

"I...I...I did?" She placed her right hand over her mouth and continued to stare at the ring he dangled before her, as though hypnotized.

"Gus agreed to take the ring back, providing we return it after the wedding."

"Of course, of course. Here," she said, finally freeing her hand and pulling on the ring. She paused and looked up at him. "Wait a minute. How do I know you're telling the truth? The police? Really? This all sounds suspicious." She pointed at the other ring. "That's just another fake diamond."

In one continuous motion, Brant grasped her wrist, whisked her out of her chair and dragged her over to the mirror in the bathroom. He ran the ring on her finger over the glass. The mirror now had a scratch. "Here," he said, pushing the ring with the pink ribbon into her other hand. "Your turn."

Shaken, Marley ran that ring over the glass. Nothing. Making a fist with her left hand, she tried again with the ring she wore. Another scratch.

"You want more proof? I've got the receipts in my bag."

"And I suppose you've got a video, too. You plan to put it on the internet?"

"Boy, have you got some attitude." He followed her back into the bedroom. "I save you, and you act like I turned you in."

"Well, what do you expect?" Marley collapsed onto the chair, struggling desperately to control her tears. "You call me a thief, and tell me I could be facing a jail sentence, and I'm out five thousand dollars."

Brant sat across from her on the bed. "Gus isn't pressing charges. Besides, I paid for the ring."

"You what?" Marley leaned forward, gripping the wooden chair arms for support. "Where did you get five thousand dollars?" For most of the time she'd known him, he'd looked more like a homeless bum than someone with any money.

"I put it on my credit card. The charge comes off when we return the ring."

Calming down somewhat, Marley asked, "What shall we do with it? I've already lost it once."

"You wear it. I'll keep this," he said, putting the fake back in his pocket. "Until we decide on a safe place for the real one." He stood and glanced at his watch. "Should we go get the Emersons? I'm starving. Haven't eaten anything since breakfast."

"Wait." Marley raised a hand, and Brant sat back down on the bed. "My family isn't expecting you."

"Yes they are. Your mother and father invited me."

She stopped his protest by shaking her head and indicating he should stay. "They're not expecting *you*. They're expecting a very rich guy who owns a horse ranch and is a successful businessman in finances."

"Am I the Texan or the British count?"

"Neither!" Marley stood, her eyes wide, and shook a finger at him. "And don't you dare try one of those accents."

Brant fell back on the bed, his arms over his head.

She sat back in the chair. Marley needed to concentrate, and she held her head in her hands while she tried to decide what to do next. When she looked at him about to fall asleep on the bed, she ordered, "Pay attention, Brant."

"I am. Tell me more so I can get into character."

How could he be so relaxed while she felt as if her brain were exploding with the ramifications of his arrival? How could she tell him to act like a normal person? "Please don't... don't make waves. I mean, act like...a person who just got engaged." She had almost said act normal, but she didn't know what normal was with Brant.

He sat up. In that same British accent he'd used previously, he said, "And I'm obviously totally enamored and think you're the love of my life."

"Stop talking like that." She stood and pounded her fists against her hips.

His eyebrows went up. "I'm not to act enamored?"

"Stop using that accent."

"But I could really use the practice for my next gig."

"Your acting thing is never to come up." Marley looked away and placed her hands on either side of her head to contain the explosion in her brain. Taking in a deep breath, she turned to him, determined to control the situation. "You do anything to embarrass me, Brant Westfield, including that phony accent, and you'll never see this ring again." Flashing her left hand at him, Marley walked over to the door. Brant trailed her closely.

No NEED TO practice for his part. Just play himself. *Rich successful businessman. Had she looked him up on the Internet?* Brant followed her out the door and worked hard at containing his amusement. This could be a whole lot of fun if Marley wasn't so uptight. Why had she gone berserk when he'd mentioned her father? Brant sobered, remembering his own father. If only he'd been at the ranch when Brant had been there so they could have had that serious discussion. It still nagged at him. What had his father wanted to discuss?

Brant climbed into the backseat next to the older gentleman, while the man's wife continued to carry the conversation. Lush green scenery passed by, so different from the land in Arizona. No need to irrigate with this constant drizzle. He leaned back against the seat and closed his eyes.

The drama was about to start. He'd find out more about Marley and what she was like around her family once he met her parents. He'd steer the conversation to how she learned to play the guitar. Maybe go through family photos. What had she looked like as a child? When the car pulled to a stop, Brant sat up and regarded the house stretched across the property.

A wraparound porch covered the first floor and an addition peeked out on the left side. A rambling ranch his father would call it. Homey.

Brant felt excitement build, a tension he experienced whenever he was about to play a part. *Let the show begin.*

LINDY AND THEIR mother were on the porch as Marley pulled into the driveway. Panic gripped her. What if this whole pretense fell apart? She'd never be able to hold her head up again.

The Emersons took off for the house, calling out greetings, arms raised. About to follow them in, Marley stopped when Brant grasped her arm. "That our audience?" Brant pointed to the porch, indicating the additional people collecting there.

Marley nodded.

"Break a leg," he said and drew her into his arms. "Relax," he whispered against her ear. "You want to convince your family we're in love, you'll have to loosen up. I may be good, but you'll need to cooperate a little. I can't carry the whole show by myself."

"You arrogant—" She stopped when his lips brushed hers. The kiss, if that's what it was, turned out to be very short. A disappointment, actually. "You call that a kiss?"

He turned, dragging her toward the porch. As he smiled and waved, he said under his breath, "That's what I give mannequins. You want something better, you'd better put some life into those bones."

Marley controlled any retort, not wanting to sound like a surly malcontent in front of their audience. However, his remark galled her. This guy who had gone out of his way to be with her, and acted as though he really liked her, now found her lacking? No one had ever complained about her kisses before.

As they approached the house, Lindy and Denny made a quick exit toward one of the parked cars in the circular driveway. Instead of coming over to Marley and Brant, they got into their car and drove away.

Marley grasped Brant's arm and stopped, staring at the couple who left rubber on the road in their speedy getaway.

"What's wrong?"

"I don't know. Lindy wanted to meet you so badly, and here she is driving off without even saying hello."

"Trouble in paradise?"

"I certainly hope not."

Marley made quick introductions to her mother, grandfather and Aunt Effie, thankful that her father wasn't in sight. The three delighted in welcoming him into the family, and, miracle of all miracles, Brant didn't embarrass her.

None of her sisters or their husbands and offspring were around. "Where are they off to?" Marley asked, pointing toward the departing car.

"Lindy just notified Denny he has a bachelor party he needs to attend." She turned to Brant. "You'll be expected to go, too. Marley can drive you." Nora glanced at the car pulling into the drive. "Or you can go with Denny's brother." With a wave and no further explanation, Nora turned and entered the house as a convertible with the top up pulled close to the porch.

Marley went over to the driver's side.

Richard rolled down the window and leaned an arm on the door frame. "I'm creating the best send-off a guy ever had. I have a private room with food and drinks and a surprise or two you don't want to know about." He did a drumbeat on the outside of the door.

"You're not putting Denny on some plane to Chicago or something harebrained like that?"

"No, but that's not a bad idea."

"Just don't do anything to delay or spoil the wedding."

Brant came up behind her and wrapped an arm around her waist possessively. Richard eyed him, his jaw tightening. "Who's this?"

Brant maneuvered her to the side and stuck out his hand. "Brant Westfield, the newest fiancé. I'm supposed to help give your brother a spectacular send-off?"

Without acknowledging the outstretched hand, Richard said, "Sure, hop in."

Brant didn't move. "Mind dropping me off

at the motel first, if it's not out of your way? I'd like to get a clean shirt."

"Wait." Marley grasped Brant's arm and moved him away so she could speak directly to Richard. "I have to go to the motel for my clothes, too. Why don't you let me drive everyone in my car? You'll probably all get wasted, and I can be your designated driver."

As they headed to her car, Brant said, "Bossy, aren't you?" and got into the passenger seat of her Toyota. "I don't drink, so I can be the designated driver."

Richard climbed into the backseat and sat behind her. Marley glanced into the rearview mirror and caught Richard's attention. "I'm the only one allowed to drive the rental." She smiled. "I'll be at the motel, so give me a call when you're ready to go home."

Brant moved closer. "Think you can stay away from the hard stuff in the room's refrigerator?"

With a perfunctory nod, she said, "No worry. I don't drink."

"Really? You gave it up after taking the picture of my picture?"

Marley glared at Brant.

Richard spread his arms across the back

of the rear seat and glanced out the window. "Wow. They're only just engaged and they bicker as much as an old married couple."

CHAPTER NINE

"WANT TO COME IN?" Marley asked Richard when they arrived at the motel.

"Sure he does," Brant said, exiting the car. "Nothing he'd like better than watching an engaged couple change clothes."

While Richard stayed behind, Marley seethed. "What's your problem?" she asked Brant once they were inside the motel.

Brant shrugged. "No problem. I'm just trying to get my head into this part I'm playing, and I haven't figured out what's going on with that guy. What did I do wrong? He acts like he doesn't want me here."

Marley, too, had noticed Richard's cool demeanor toward Brant. Was he upset that with the arrival of her fiancé their time together would be limited? The idea intrigued her. If true, she'd have to break off this engagement as soon as possible.

"It's your imagination."

With only a raised eyebrow at her, Brant

opened his luggage and took out several shirts, which he hung in the open closet. "His name suits him."

"What's that supposed to mean?"

"Dick."

"Richard," she corrected.

"You say tomato, I say—"

"It's Richard!"

He shook out one of the shirts. It was in a cowboy style, with decorative blue stripes and pearl buttons. At least he hadn't packed any chambray shirts that looked like ones he'd worn to clean out a barn. "You think this one will do, darlin'?"

Ignoring Brant and his Texas twang, Marley collected a pair of black pants and a yellow T-shirt. She turned to see what he had chosen just as he stripped off his white shirt. "Take a good look, darlin'." He lifted his arms and posed, showing off his bare chest.

Overconfident jerk, she thought. *Thinks he's Mr. Wonderful.*

"You should know, in case someone asks, if I have any identifying marks." He sent her that toothy smile that gave her the shivers. "You can tell them I had my appendix out." He pulled down on the top of his pants to display a flat stomach with a tiny scar.

"I'll keep that in mind when it becomes necessary to identify your body." As she passed him on the way to the bathroom, she added, "And the time could be very close, if you keep using those annoying accents." She shut the door after her before he could reply.

Her attempt to tame her hair into a French twist didn't work too well. Curls kept popping out. When Brant began knocking on her door, she finally gave up and came out. Richard had arrived. She looked toward him for approval, disregarding Brant.

Richard gave her an appreciative smile but neutralized it when he glanced at Brant. "We better get going." He turned toward the car.

Brant clasped Marley's arm and stopped her just as she reached the door. "You could have told me, you know." He had fire in his eyes. She'd never seen him angry.

After shaking her arm free, she maneuvered away from him. "Told you what?"

"How you and Richard had a thing going. No wonder he can't stand me."

Feeling coquettish, she smiled at him brazenly. "Jealous?"

Brant yanked her back into the room and shut the door. "Just what kind of role am I playing here? Are we following through with this engagement, or do I collect my ring and head back to Arizona? Because if you'd rather be with pretty boy over there—"

"I like him, okay? If I'd realized he'd be here—"

"Wait a minute. Did you know him before this wedding?"

"Yes, in college. And, no, I never made the connection between his brother marrying my sister and him."

A horn blew.

"But if you had?"

Marley planted her fists on her hips and glared at Brant. "I wouldn't be trapped in this damned engagement."

He duplicated her stance. "What's it going to be? Do we change the game plan now, break up so you can be with Rick or stick with the script?"

She sighed and dropped her arms. She hadn't thought things through. Brant's sudden appearance had her still mulling her choices. How would she explain any of this to her family? "No changes."

Brant took a deep breath. "Okay. Keep in mind you're engaged to me."

"What's that supposed to mean?"

"Figure it out darlin'." Brant pulled the

door open with one hand and wrapped his arm around her shoulders with the other. He planted a kiss on her cheek, one that she wanted to wipe off but couldn't in front of Richard. Brant whispered against her ear, "I realize it's difficult, but we really should pretend to like each other."

BY THE TIME Brant reached the car, Richard had already taken the front seat, so he'd sit next to Marley. Brant mouthed a rude version of Richard's name to her over the top of the car before he opened the door to the rear seat.

"My brother will remember this night long after his honeymoon's a dim recollection." Richard chuckled as he got into the car, then a few moments later he chuckled again, for no particular reason, giving Marley a sense of well-being.

She felt comfortable with Richard. Relaxed. No heightened sense of dread the way she did when dealing with Brant and the unknown. With Richard, she knew what to expect, for the most part. With Brant, anything could happen. Being with Brant was like standing on a precipice and hoping the wind wouldn't blow you over.

When she glanced at her nemesis through

the rearview mirror, Brant seemed preoccupied. At least he wasn't winking or blowing her kisses. For some reason, the thought left her unsettled.

As Marley drove into the restaurant parking lot, Lindy rushed out to meet them. She looked stressed. With a growing sense of unease, Marley parked the car.

Lindy flung open the car door and pulled Marley out. "We've got to talk."

"What's the problem?"

Lindy grabbed her elbow and directed her to a spot several parking spaces away. "That juice Michelle spilled on my wedding gown is the problem." She spoke angrily only inches from Marley's face. "The cleaner's not sure if it will come out." The memory of the event still made Marley wince.

Lindy glanced apprehensively at Brant before continuing. "If one more thing goes wrong..." Her voice rose even higher. "I'm seriously thinking of calling this whole thing off."

Glancing at Brant again, Lindy said, "Who's that?"

Brant leaned against the Toyota, his arms crossed, one boot propped on the bumper. He looked totally unconcerned by the drama unfolding around him.

"My fiancé, Brant Westfield." Brant turned toward them when he heard his name and started to walk over.

"Oh." Lindy cheered up a bit. "He really does look like a cowboy." She offered him her hand. For a moment Marley thought he might bend over and kiss it, but he only held it, enclosing it in both of his. "Nice to finally meet you, sis. Marley's told me quite a bit about you."

"Well, she hasn't told me nearly enough about you."

Oh, my God, Marley thought, *they're flirting.* They finally stepped away from each other when Dennis approached. "You're a lucky man," Brant said after an introduction. While shaking the groom's hand, he added, "Lindy's a lovely bride."

Lindy promptly burst into tears, and Dennis escorted her back to the restaurant.

Brant casually shuffled over to stand by Marley, his thumbs in his pants' pockets. "Are all the women in your family loony tunes?" He turned abruptly and headed back to the car.

Before she could come up with a reply,

Richard approached, totally agitated. "What's your sister's problem, anyway?"

Marley sighed. "Wedding jitters." She averted her gaze, wishing she could provide more of an explanation. However, none of the other brides she'd known carried on like Lindy. Could it be more than nerves?

"She better not get Denny upset. It won't be much fun tonight if he's preoccupied."

Having witnessed the extent of Lindy's aggravation, Marley didn't bother to keep the annoyance out of her voice. "I'm sure once he's in his party hat with a drink in hand, he won't remember his name let alone poor Lindy."

"Don't you think Denny deserves one last time to howl?"

"I think the whole idea is stupid. Getting wasted so he'll be useless tomorrow at the bride's dinner." Marley turned away in disgust. "And I suppose you invited my father. It's the type of thing he'd really go for."

"No, I didn't think of it. All your brothers-in-law are attending, though. Maybe they'll bring him along." He paused, then added, "You're not giving him a chance. He's not such an ogre. Denny introduced us a while ago, and he seems like a regular guy."

"Oh, he can be charming."

"Didn't all your problems with him happen back when we were in college? Maybe it's time to forgive and forget."

How could anyone expect her to forget all the pain of the past? Still…"He's not the way I remember him. He's so…so old. I hardly recognized him." The few moments with her father had been uncomfortable but not a total trauma. Marley hardened her resolve. Red Roman may have changed physically, but his attitude and values remained intact. How could she forgive a man who didn't acknowledge his mistakes or attempt to correct them?

Marley turned to look for her sister. "Where'd they go?" she asked, twirling one of the tendrils that had escaped her French twist.

Richard walked over to her and tucked the section of hair behind her ear. "Did I mention how nice you look?"

Being with Richard felt so pleasant, personal and intimate, something she'd love to continue. Pivoting, she became aware of the sincerity in his eyes. He held eye contact for several seconds. "I sure wish you weren't engaged," he whispered.

Lindy and Dennis returned, giving Marley no chance to respond. And she wanted to. She wanted very much to tell Richard she wanted out of her engagement.

Dennis became the center of attention as his groomsmen arrived, offering their congratulations. A few picked Lindy off the ground and gave her a kiss before setting her back on her feet. They kidded around, a punch in the shoulder, a slap on the back, and made remarks running the gamut from what a lucky guy he was to what an idiot for giving up his freedom.

Her father had arrived, as well. Although he smiled in Marley's direction, she didn't acknowledge she'd seen him. Brant joined the mix, accepted congratulations on *his* engagement and introductions from all her brothers-in-law. He followed them into the restaurant, leaving Lindy, Dennis, Richard and Marley on the sidewalk.

"Here are my keys," Denny said, handing them to Richard. "I won't be in any condition to drive."

"We'll take taxis home. You want the keys, Lindy?" Richard dangled them in front of her.

"No. Leave the car here. I'll go home with Marley." She whirled on her heel and headed for Marley's car, obviously trying her best not to cry.

"But…" He looked after his future sister-in-law in total bewilderment, while Denny stayed close behind her. Once Lindy got in the car, Denny leaned on the door and spoke to Lindy through the open window.

"Call me if you can't get a taxi," Marley said.

Richard placed the keys in his pocket and wrapped an arm around Marley, drawing her to him. "Since I don't have my car, can you pick me up sometime before the bride's dinner tomorrow night? I can get my car at your parents' afterward. I should be sober by then."

He leaned down, pulling her closer, about to kiss her, if her instincts were correct. She ducked to the side so his lips pecked her cheek. "Not even a little one for old times' sake?"

Marley spun out of his arms, not certain why this sudden familiarity felt so wrong. Wasn't it what she had wanted? Something intimate to develop between them? "I'm engaged, remember?"

She stood there for several seconds after Richard backed away before she noticed Brant, standing on the steps. He gave her a thumbs-up before heading into the restaurant. *Exactly what does he mean by that?* He'd obviously seen the attempted kiss. Did he approve of her lack of response, or did he consider this yet another example of her pathetic ability?

Dennis walked over. "Everything okay with Lindy?" Richard asked.

Dennis smiled, something akin to a painted-on Halloween mask. "Oh, Lindy's fine. I'm the one with problems. I'm insensitive, insincere, and an idiot. If you don't mind, brother dear, I'd like that drink quick before I punch someone." He pushed past Richard and went into the restaurant.

Richard gave Marley an "I told you so" look before following Dennis. She headed for the car, unable to shake off the depression that cloaked her. She'd have to. Lindy needed all the support she could muster.

How was he going to get through this night? If one more person asked another question about his wedding plans…What should he say? Would it contradict anything his "fiancée" had made up? He didn't know anything about her job, her hobbies, her achievements. And he was starving.

Brant managed to get a waiter's attention and ordered a cheeseburger. At least when Marley had created her fiancé, she hadn't made him into a vegetarian. He hoped.

"Hey," Dennis said as Brant brought the cheeseburger to his lips. "I wanted to ask a favor. My best friend can't make the wedding. I was wondering…"

Brant took a bite and waited. After chewing a moment, he could swallow. "Yeah, what?"

"You mind being the best man?"

"Me? Why not someone in your family? Your brother, for example."

"Oh, he'd love being paired off with Marley, but I figure—"

"Sure. Happy to." Brant held out his hand and the two shook on it. No way would he give Richard a chance to have more time around Marley. He savored the moment, remembering how she had rebuffed Richard's attempt to kiss her.

Dennis reached into his pocket and pulled out a card. "Everyone's already been fitted for a tux, but you can get one if you go before one tomorrow afternoon. Here's the address. Thanks a million. You're now officially one of the Roman Warriors."

"I'm what?"

"That's what we call the guys who marry the Roman girls. We're the Roman Warriors, a private organization of husbands designed to protect them." He turned his attention to the man approaching. "I guess this is where I get drunk and make an idiot of myself."

Richard came over to his brother and handed him a beer. "Entertainment will be here shortly." He glanced at Brant. "Can I get something for you?"

"No thanks." He stuffed the remainder of the cheeseburger into his mouth. "I can get mine."

Brant had no intention of drinking anything stronger than a virgin Bloody Mary, but he didn't want Richard aware of that. Dennis, the guest of honor, looked as though he wanted to disappear, and Brant figured he knew exactly how that could be accomplished. He motioned for Dennis to follow him to the bar.

"So what's your drink of choice?" Dennis hadn't touched his beer.

"Nothing, really." He placed the glass against his lips and put it down again before taking a sip. He appeared so forlorn. "I wish I could go back to Lindy."

Brant faced the bartender. "Two virgin Marys, and make them look authentic." He stuck a large bill in the jar on the bar. "And keep them coming." The bartender glanced that way and got to work, topping the tomato juice mixture with a celery stick. Brant turned to Dennis and handed him the drink.

"Work on this through the night and follow my lead. You and I are going to become the worse drunks this crowd has ever seen."

Dennis chuckled. The first smile Brant had seen. "So how well do you know Marley?" Brant asked, determined to find out more about her.

"Just met her, but Rick knows her from college." Dennis took a sip of his drink. "Hey, not bad. And there's no alcohol?"

"None. How did they meet?"

"Dancing. She was teaching ballroom dancing at a studio and—"

Brant straightened, his attention riveted on Dennis. "She taught dancing?"

"Yeah. Haven't the two of you…?"

"Of course." *Right.* They were engaged. He should know she could dance. "She's great at it. Never knew she taught it, though."

"She's been trying to teach me, so I won't make a fool of myself at the wedding. Two left feet."

What more tidbits could he find out about Marley? "So have you ever heard her play the guitar?" Brant's attention shifted to the elderly gentleman who joined their group.

"Hi. We haven't met. I'm the grandfather. Everyone calls me Poppy." He held out his hand. "Her guitar playing is a real treat. I'm sorry she wasn't able to bring it this time. We could have used the entertainment." He glanced over to the man and woman who were talking with Richard.

"I'm not sure my heart will be able to handle what Rick's concocted." He turned back to Brant. "Nice meeting you, son, but I think I'll take my leave." He playfully punched Dennis in the shoulder, then headed for the door.

CHAPTER TEN

SITTING IN THE MOTEL ROOM an hour later, Marley gave up trying to console the weeping bride-to-be. Intermittently, Lindy dabbed at her eyes with a towel. "Daddy thinks I'm too young, and it's best if we wait."

Marley took in a deep breath, held it and let it out slowly. "So Daddy put this idea in your head?" She refrained from saying "stupid idea" although the words nearly fell off her tongue.

Lindy sniffled. The volume and intensity increased as Marley remained quiet. "He didn't suggest it. We got talking and well…I kinda suggested we should wait a few more years. Maybe live with each other first." Marley clamped her lips shut, not wanting to say anything that would create more problems. "You figure Mom will let Denny move in if we're not married?"

"I thought he already rented an apartment."

"Well, yes, but we could save so much more

if we lived with Mom and Daddy. The whole second floor is free."

"Wait a minute. Is Red going to live there with Mom?"

"Well, yes. When they get married again." That last statement knotted Marley's stomach and produced another gush of tears from Lindy. "It's so wonderful they're still so much in love." Marley walked over to the bed and sat down on the edge next to her sister. She couldn't believe what she was hearing. Her parents were actually getting back together for real?

"What if Denny and I aren't really in love? What if all this is a mistake?" Lindy huddled on the bed in total distress. Marley cradled her sister in her arms, something she hadn't done in a long time. While she rocked her, Marley pushed Lindy's blond hair from her face and hummed.

If only she'd brought her guitar, she mused for the umpteenth time. The tune "She'll Be Coming 'Round the Mountain" was one she'd learned at camp the summer before her parents' breakup. She'd used it to soothe Lindy and the other children while her parents hurled words and pottery at each other. The strumming had comforted Marley and given her the strength to calm the other children.

"I've missed you so, Marley," Lindy whispered.

"How could you miss me when you had that whole crew?"

Lindy sat up and dried her eyes. "I did. I was lonely after you left. And you came home so rarely. Only when someone got married. Why did you have to go so far away after graduation?"

Marley stood, walked several feet away and began twisting her hands. "I needed to get away."

"From me?"

Marley whipped around. "Of course not." She dropped to the bed again and clasped Lindy's hands. "I couldn't handle my problems, and I ran away from them."

"What problems?"

"I...I couldn't stand Daddy involving himself with us again. After making all my own decisions, I resented him telling me what to do."

"I kind of liked it," Lindy said as her first smile of the evening lighted her swollen face. "I felt he finally cared enough to come back to us. When he left right after you, it was a double loss. You could have returned when he left."

"No." Marley glanced away, unsure if she should risk disclosing more. "I was in love, and I handled it badly."

"You were?" Lindy squealed in delight as she moved closer. "I never knew that. What happened? Who was he? Anyone I know?"

Marley hedged. "You were too young."

"Oh…" Lindy pressed her hands to her mouth. "You weren't pregnant, were you? You didn't run off and have a baby?"

Marley nearly jumped off the bed. "Of course not. I realized we were wrong for each other and moved to another state so I wouldn't run into him again."

"And did you?"

"Did I what?"

"Run into him again?"

After a deep breath, Marley said, "Yes." Lindy knelt on the bed, her tears and heartache apparently forgotten.

"Were you still in love? Did he sweep you off your feet?"

"No." Marley glanced at her ring. "I was already involved with someone else."

With a dramatic sigh, Lindy fell back on the

bed. "How romantic. To have two men fighting over you."

"They never fought over me. Is that what you want? Someone beating up Denny?"

"No, of course not. It's just..." She looked close to tears again. "I've only known Denny. And I'm going to promise to spend the rest of my life with him. What if I marry him and another person comes along who is the real one for me? What if you had married that first guy before you met Brant?"

"We could play 'what-if' all night. Consider this. What if you let Denny go and no other Prince Charming shows? What do you do then?"

"You know, you're right," Lindy said, sitting up. "Look at you. You had to wait, what, ten years or more for the second one. We could be divorced by then."

Marley pressed her fingertips to her temples, excused herself and went into the bathroom. Behind the closed door she shook her fists at the ceiling, then in Lindy's general direction. Maybe Richard should send Dennis to the Antarctic, or better yet the moon, to save him from a life with Lindy, Marley thought before she began to calm down.

No, Lindy needed Dennis. A life with him

would provide love, security and a healthy, nurturing environment. The mere fact that her father opposed this joining made Marley resolve to do everything in her power to make the wedding happen.

She wanted breathing space, a few minutes to herself out of the claustrophobic motel room, so she could counter the problems her father had created. What possible reason did he have for creating all these difficulties? While running a bath, she went back in the room to collect a bottle of bath oil. She'd borrowed it from Richard's place when she'd packed up Lindy's things.

"Why don't you watch some TV while I take a bath? I'll be out in a little while."

In the bathroom, she stepped into the warm water and let it envelop her. What a wonderful relief. The water had just started to cool when she heard a commotion in the other room. Quickly, Marley got out of the tub and dried herself. A harsh rap on the door startled her, and she wrapped the towel protectively around herself.

"Marley, you in there?"

"Richard?" she asked moving toward the door. "What are you doing here?"

When the doorknob rattled, she shouted,

"What do you want? I'll be out in a minute." She redressed in her pants and T-shirt, all the while muttering. *It wasn't even ten o'clock. Why on earth would Richard leave his precious bachelor party?*

With a quick intake of breath, Marley prepared for catastrophe. Something terrible had happened. She opened the door to see Richard, Dennis and Lindy sitting around the room on the bed, chair and desk. Richard had been scowling at the floor but came to instant attention the moment she entered. She looked away from his murderous glare to Dennis, who sat batting a fist into his other hand. His attention rested on Lindy, who appeared close to tears again.

"What's the problem?" Marley asked.

Richard rose from the desk and started toward her. "Where would you like to begin? Problem one, two or three?" Before she could answer, he continued, "Problem one is sitting over there," he said, pointing at Lindy. "Dennis hasn't been able to think about anything else since we started the party. He wanted to leave from the first, but it might still be going on if problem two hadn't grandstanded with the stripper."

Visions of her father improvising something

foolish flashed through her mind. "His performance brought the house down," Richard continued as he paced the room. "The, uh, *dancer* hadn't gone far enough, so he decided to help remove more of her layers. Her bodyguard punched him out...which created problem three. We were kicked out of the restaurant."

"Where's my father now?" She saw him bloodied, taken off in an ambulance to a hospital, and the mental picture distressed her. Quickly, she shook off her unwanted anguish. He probably deserved every broken bone. But her mother would be devastated. The whole wedding could be postponed. Marley's distress returned tenfold.

"Your father? Marley, why is your father the main topic of every conversation we have?"

"Well, who are you talking about then?" she said, as flustered and irritated as he.

"Brant, your betrothed, the pain-in-the-neck problem. He passed out in Denny's car."

"How come you drove it here?" she asked, deciding to go on the offensive. "I thought you were taking cabs home rather than driving drunk."

"Drunk?" Richard pounded his chest. "This is not drunk. This is angry. This is mad. That," he said, pointing toward the door, "is drunk.

And that is dead," he continued, shaking his fist, "if he gets sick in your car." He stood several feet from her, breathing deeply, his face a play of emotions. Mostly she saw pain and disappointment.

"My car?"

"I put him in there. It's a rental. Let them detail it."

Marley closed her eyes momentarily and grasped her head in her hands.

"What the hell do you see in that cowboy? You give up on me and fall for…" Again he gestured toward the door. With a defeated expression, Richard dropped into a chair and placed his face in his hands. "I'll never understand women."

Marley watched him, unable to come up with any coherent thoughts. What had Brant done? She felt a disappointment she couldn't understand.

After a short respite, Richard got up, walked over to Lindy and dropped onto the bed next to her. "I'm sorry I blew up like that, sis. You okay?" She threw her arms around him and bawled. For several moments Richard hugged her, patting her back while glancing around the room. Marley took that opportunity to head for the door. While Richard was occupied, she could check on Brant and possibly minimize any damages. Just as she was about to exit, however, Richard said, "Here, Denny. You take over. I think you're better suited for this."

As he was getting up, Lindy wailed, "I'm cancelling the wedding."

CHAPTER ELEVEN

EVERYONE IN THE room pivoted to face her and shouted in unison, "You're what?"

"Daddy said I should wait."

"But, honey…" Dennis rushed to her side, but she turned her shoulder toward him and avoided any embrace. He slowly backed away.

The three adults watched Lindy, waiting for more explanations. When she didn't explain further, Marley took a seat next to her on the bed and wrapped her arms around her. "It's wedding jitters."

Inconsolable, Lindy declared, "Call it whatever you want, but the wedding is off."

Richard threw his hands in the air and walked over to the door. "Women!" he said and went outside.

Dennis stood only inches away, looking as though he wanted to take Marley's place. "Give us a moment," he said. Marley agreed. When she got up, Dennis took her seat and wrapped Lindy in his arms.

With one last look at the couple, Marley closed the door behind her and joined Richard on the walkway that connected the motel rooms.

"What about your impending marriage? You think it has a chance in hell with that leech?" Richard asked. "You should see your fiancé in action. He's the worst drunk and skirt chaser I've ever seen."

Now *that* was something that did require her attention. She hadn't even checked on Brant's condition. She started to walk over to the car. "How did he get drunk?"

"He downed those Bloody Marys."

"With vodka?"

Richard shrugged. "Of course with vodka. Why? Do they make them with something else out in Arizona?"

"But Brant said he didn't drink." Why hadn't she asked Brant why?

"He lied."

No. She didn't know much about Brant, but she doubted that he'd lie about such a thing. Had someone switched his drinks? Further conversation with Richard was useless until she could talk to Brant.

When she placed her hand on the car handle,

he asked, "What do you want me to do with him? Should I drive him to your mother's?"

"Let me talk to him."

Richard threw his hands in the air and headed back to the motel room, muttering.

Brant lay sprawled across the backseat with one black lizard-skin boot braced against the window. "Get up," she said, knocking on the glass. When he didn't budge, she opened the door. Once his leg lost support, it fell as though unconnected to the rest of his body. It jarred him, and he slowly sat up, squinting at the bright parking lot lights that played across his face.

"What happened?" Marley said to the figure in rumpled clothes.

"Marley?" he asked, looking at her with soulful eyes. His whole countenance had a wrinkled quality to it.

"Are you all right?" she inquired in a stage whisper.

"Oh, Marley," Brant said as he reached for her. "I've been dreaming about you." He grasped her hand and pulled her against him with a strength she hadn't expected. When she tried to get away, he twisted her around so that she was across his chest, nearly sitting on his lap. He tangled his hand in her hair and drew her toward him.

As his lips played across hers, she tasted Tabasco. So he *had* been drinking Bloody Marys. When he didn't draw her closer, she took a breath and returned to taste him again. She'd prove to him she could kiss. Prove it to herself.

"Nice," he said against her lips.

She pushed against his chest and managed to put several inches between them. "Brant, we have to talk."

"I like the conversation we're having." When he tried pulling her back into an embrace, she placed her fingers against his mouth. He began kissing them.

"Brant, please." What was she going to do with him?

"I'm a little drunk."

"A little?"

He started to giggle. In slow motion he sank back against the seat, releasing her. "My head hurts, and I'm tired. We'll talk like this again later."

Nice. Very nice. Brant felt quite content and didn't want to jeopardize his luck. She'd kissed him. And it was better than nice. Definitely a different side of Marley. She actually acted concerned for his welfare. Instead of going ballistic because he had created problems for her cherished Richard, she'd offered an empathy he hadn't expected.

Maybe he should let her know he really wasn't drunk, hadn't touched any alcohol. The virgin Marys had fooled everyone, including Richard. Then again, maybe Brant should keep his mouth shut. She probably only responded to him at all because she thought he was incapacitated. More than likely she'd punch his lights out once she knew the truth.

MARLEY GOT OUT of the car and folded his long legs on the seat to try and make him comfortable. She closed the door, prepared to leave him there for the rest of the night until he sobered up. Heading back to her motel room, she felt more frustrated and upset than she'd ever felt in her life. Once everyone left, she'd have to slip Brant into the motel room. But what should she do till then?

Richard opened the door when she knocked. He ushered her in with a quick, questioning look at the car. She ignored it, unwilling to let him draw her into any conversation about Brant. A furtive glance around the room indicated nothing had improved in these quarters.

Lindy sat cross-legged in the center of the bed, glaring at the bedspread. Dennis sat in one chair. Richard went for the desk, and Marley headed for the bathroom. Her face felt flushed, her lips pleasantly bruised. Sure enough, when she checked the mirror, the evidence showed. She sighed. *It had been...unexpected... lovely...Wow! And they had several more days together before she went back to Phoenix and Brant went on to New York. But would Brant even remember?*

After some repairs, Marley returned to the room. With no other seats available, she had no choice but to sit on the bed next to Lindy.

"I could go for some pizza," Marley said, when the quiet became too much to bear. "Would Molino's still be open?"

No one answered, but Dennis stood and stretched. "Why don't you and Richard go get some? Lindy and I still need to talk."

Marley checked with Lindy to see if she went for the idea. Her impassive posture remained the same. When Marley got off the bed, she made eye contact with Richard, only to look quickly away. She read too many questions there that she didn't want to face.

"Don't bother with pizza for us," Lindy said in a surprisingly harsh voice that caused everyone to jump to attention. Obediently, Richard and Marley made for the door.

"What do we do now?" Richard asked as he escorted her from the room.

"I'm not really hungry."

"Me, either. Maybe lover boy could use some food."

"Didn't he eat?" she asked, giving Richard a worried look.

"Just the celery in his drink."

Brant had been starving when she'd left him. Vodka on an empty stomach. No wonder he was drunk so quickly.

"How much time do you figure they'll need to talk?" Richard asked as he opened the driver's door for her. "A few hundred years, maybe?"

The night had worn her out, and she wanted desperately to get some sleep. Marley sighed, not willing to debate it further as Richard walked around to the passenger side of the car. "Let's give them an hour. Shall we go for coffee?"

A glance in back assured her that Brant hadn't changed his position. If only he'd remain that way, in a state as close to comatose as possible. As they pulled into the parking lot of an all-night diner, something hit her in the neck, and she turned to see Brant's face only inches away. "My knees don't work. You'll have to carry me."

She looked beseechingly at Richard, hoping he might provide some assistance. However, the black storm that raged across his face offered little chance of that in this lifetime. He went out his door and took off without waiting for her.

"Men," Marley muttered. Right now she'd like to smash both their heads together. The moment she reached Brant in the backseat, he threw an arm around her shoulder along with most of his weight. She grabbed on to his arm and struggled to maintain her balance. When he slathered a kiss across her forehead, she nearly dropped him.

"Come on, Brant," she said, slipping her arm around his waist. "Save that for later." The remark was made in case Richard was close enough to hear, yet Brant showed a definite interest.

"Later," he said, running his lips against her cheek.

He took a few trial steps and quickly learned the process. By the time they reached the diner's door, he was nearly supporting himself. He had kept up a babble of endearments, referring to her on several occasions as sweetie, Marley or Carla, some woman she didn't even know.

At least Richard obliged them by holding the door open. The moment they found a vacant booth, Marley dropped Brant onto the bench and pushed him in so she could scoot in after him. Through it all, Brant kept up a besotted babble about how he couldn't wait to get her alone. None of his actions resembled the Brant she'd come to know. When Richard slapped the tabletop resoundingly, Brant finally settled back in the seat.

"He's usually not this way." Did her voice show the panic she felt?

"Didn't you know he had a drinking problem?"

"I got no problem," Brant informed them, but they ignored him. "I don't drink."

"It's never been a problem." Under the circumstances, what else could she say?

"When a guy avoids alcohol and slips out of character the moment he touches it, it's a problem."

Brant propped his head in his hand, supporting the weight on a wobbly elbow. "I got no problem. Just a little headache. Zat's all."

They ordered coffee. She waited, tensing and releasing her fists under the table.

Their coffee finally arrived. Since the air-conditioning had cooled her overheated body, Marley picked up the warm brew and wrapped her hands around the cup to absorb its heat. A little chill radiated along her spine, possibly caused by the deep freeze emanating from Richard.

Slowly she sipped her coffee, wishing she'd asked for decaffeinated. She wanted a good night's sleep and didn't need additional stimulation. At first Brant bent over and slurped his, but by his second cup, he could hold it in an upright position without spilling it all over himself and the table.

"You feeling better?" she dared to ask when he put the finished cup down.

"Yeah. Where's the men's room?" Marley got up from the bench seat. He scooted over and gave her a kiss on the cheek before heading toward the rear of the diner. At least he didn't require her assistance to walk anymore. She sank back on the bench.

"When do you plan to marry?" Richard asked after Brant disappeared.

"Soon," she said, surprised at his question.

"A big wedding with all the relatives?"

"I suppose so. Why?"

"Because technically, if and when Denny

and Lindy tie the knot, I'll be part of the family." Richard got up and tossed a few bills on the table. "Don't bother to send me an invitation."

Richard was already in the driver's seat when Marley and Brant reached the car. Marley didn't bother to say it was her rental, and she should drive. *No more arguments tonight.* "I'll sit in the back." Brant had his arm around her and maneuvered her so that she had no other choice. The strength of the man shocked her, and he still wasn't even fully coherent.

She had zero hopes of controlling Brant as the war waged on. When he started slapping her hands in a comical patty-cake rhythm, she dug her nails into his wrist and swatted his hand. He continued to slap, slap, slap. He was wearing her down. She dug her nails into his wrist again. If only she could extricate herself from this nightmare.

Brant reached for her hand, but before she could swat him away for the umpteenth time, he said, "Nice ring." *Oh, great.* Now he was about to say something to bring the whole farce into the open. Although she already felt like an idiot, so far the onus for the evening's debacle was on him. If he exposed the bogus engagement, though, she'd really look like a fool.

"You gave it to me, remember?" He placed a hand on his face.

"I did? Where did I get that kind of money? Am I rich?" He picked up her hand again and brought the ring closer. "I must be. Oh, but, Carla, you're worth it. Every million dollars I spent on it." He dropped her hand. "I can't think. My head hurts." He put his head on her shoulder and said, "I'm so tired, Carla. Take me home with you."

Who was Carla? Before Marley could push him away, he had fallen asleep, producing a soft snore with bursts of air blown against her neck.

Richard pulled into the motel parking lot and turned off the engine. He didn't move, and neither did she. Brant continued his low irregular chorus of snores. After a few minutes, Richard placed his arm on the back of the seat.

"What do you plan to do with him?" he asked.

"I guess he'll be staying with me."

"There's only one bed in the room."

"I'm aware of that."

Richard quickly faced front. "I'll check and

see if Lindy and Denny are ready to leave. His car's still here."

Marley watched him exit the car and stride determinedly to the motel door. His bearing indicated total distaste for Brant and her decision to keep him in her room. As if she wanted to deal with an intoxicated Don Juan with intermittent memory loss. As if she had any choice.

Richard returned, opened the back door and indicated she should join him. Slowly, she moved away from Brant and laid his head on the seat. Her shoulder was hot and sweaty where his flesh had touched hers. It was the first spot to cool when she got out of the car and into the evening breeze.

"There's a do-not-disturb sign on the door-knob," Richard whispered.

"Oh, great!" Marley fell back against the car and closed her eyes. "What do we do now?" The breeze had turned chilly, and she began to rub her arms. Her shirt and pants were summer weight and not much use against the change in temperature. Her entire wardrobe was behind locked doors ten feet away. It might as well be in Arizona for all the good it did. She opened her eyes as Richard slipped his jacket over her shoulders.

"Thanks," she said, pulling his personal warmth around her.

"I guess the wedding's back on."

"Unfortunately."

Marley bristled. "They're in love. They should get married."

Richard whipped his hand through his hair and glanced in the rear of the car. He looked back at her. "Great chemistry does not a marriage make."

"You should know, I suppose."

"Right. I'm the expert." Richard pressed his hands against the small of his back and arched into them.

She saw the strain in his face as he manipulated the muscles there. "Your back bothering you?" When he nodded, she said, "Maybe you should go home and get some rest."

The door to the motel opened and Dennis slipped out. "I heard you talking," he said. "We're staying here. Lindy finally fell sleep, and I don't want to disturb her."

When he turned and started into the room, Marley said, "Could you get my suitcase and Brant's?" He nodded and came back almost immediately with both suitcases and Brant's shirts over his arm.

"What now?" Richard asked. "The novacancy sign is flashing, so you can't stay here."

"My house, I guess. As long as Lindy's sleeping here, we can use her room." She felt too tired to think of any other possibility. She slipped out of his jacket and returned it to him. "You'll be able to pick up your car."

"Sounds like a plan," he said without a drop of enthusiasm.

CHAPTER TWELVE

"HAS HE GONE?" Brant asked, sitting up in the backseat.

"Yes." Richard had retreated to his own car and driven away before Marley could get out of the passenger seat and onto the driveway. His swift departure had given her no chance to discuss the multiple problems of the night, and she'd wanted so much to have a sit-down talk with Richard.

After watching his car until it disappeared behind the bend, she went back to her Toyota to get Brant, but he was out and on the drive-way before she reached the back door. The rain had completely stopped a few hours before. Country scents of damp earth and flowers filled the air, and insects hummed nonstop in the background.

"We staying here?" Brant stood, hands on hips, surveying the rambling house with its huge front porch.

"We'll use Lindy's room, but be quiet. I

don't want anyone to hear us." She went to get the suitcases, but Brant already had them.

"You take the shirts," he said. "I'll take these." He grasped one bag in each hand and started for the house, avoiding the puddles of water that remained on the path.

She grabbed his shirts from the backseat and turned around. For a moment, she studied him. Something didn't seem right. This sudden energy and coordination. How could he be drunk one minute and totally sober the next? She rushed up to him and swatted his arm. "Were you only acting drunk?"

He stopped and grinned. "An award-worthy performance."

"Ooooh!" She threw his shirts onto the wet grass. "You…you…you…actor!" Right then she couldn't think of anything more insulting. And after she'd been so concerned and worried about him. And so willing to spend extended time kissing him. How could he add to all her frustrations?

"What are you doing?" He dropped the suitcases and rushed to his shirts, which lay in a puddle of water. "I ironed these." As he stooped to pick them up, Marley used the pent-up emotions she'd suppressed all night and pushed. Brant went sprawling onto his back on the wet grass.

"I hate you," she said, dropping to smack him. Except he moved quickly out of reach. Her knees hit the saturated earth first and then she fell flat on her stomach, soaking herself.

Undeterred, she lifted herself by yanking on his shirt. The pearl buttons popped, and his shirt snapped open. Brant captured her wrists. For several seconds he immobilized her; then he rolled her onto the wet grass, got up and stood over her. "Are we done now?"

After a few seconds, he held out his hand. She took it and allowed him to pull her to her feet. For a moment they stood facing each other, both breathing hard, until Brant bent to pick up the shirts. He stayed clear of her, though, so there was no possibility of her knocking him over again. He handed them to her. "I'll get the bags."

She headed for the house. The chill of the night oozed through her wet clothes, and she was freezing by the time she reached the porch. She hoped no one had witnessed their tussle. She couldn't handle one more embarrassment.

She took out her house key. She paused when Brant asked, "Is there an alarm?"

"No, only a big dog. Buster won't do anything if I go in first." She gave Buster a rough brush with her hands when he greeted her inside the living room. "Nice boy." One lamp gave a soft glow with plenty of light to maneuver between the large pieces of furniture. She glanced at Brant making friendly with Buster. When Brant looked up, she placed a finger over her lips before heading for her grandfather's side of the house. As long as Poppy hadn't worn his hearing aids to bed, they'd be able to sneak up the staircase without waking him.

At the top of the stairs, Marley flipped on the hall light and walked quietly past her room, where Aunt Effie snored. Hundreds of eyes stared at her as she entered Lindy's room. Brant, behind her, sucked in his breath. "This belongs to the adult who's getting married Saturday?"

Marley considered commenting, but decided against it. She was past defending her sister. "You can use that bathroom." Marley pointed to her left, then tossed Brant's shirts, which had by now lost their hangers, over several stuffed animals. "I'll take the bathroom across the hall."

"That my bed?" Brant said, indicating the canopy bed, the only one in the room.

"Whoever gets to it first."

Brant let the suitcases go, discarded his shirt and dropped his pants, revealing baby blue boxers. In seconds he was sitting on the bed, struggling to get his boots off at the same time.

Too tired to even think straight, Marley went over to her suitcase and pulled out a summer nightshirt. When she looked up, Brant was down to his boxers. His near nudity didn't seem to bother him, and she was not about to remark about it.

"Where you sleeping?"

Marley pointed to a corner of the room. "I'll get a sleeping bag." By the time she washed, dressed in her nightshirt and collected the camping gear from the hall closet, Brant was sound asleep, sprawled across the top of the floral bedspread on his stomach. She stopped and watched him for several seconds before sighing and heading to the corner.

Marley kicked several animals to the side and collapsed onto a thin mattress and a down-filled sleeping bag. She grabbed a stuffed bear for a pillow and was asleep the moment her head hit the bear's belly.

MARLEY AWOKE TO an annoying tickle on her face. She brushed it away, but it kept coming back, first on her nose, then her forehead and finally her chin. She opened one eye and looked at Brant. He tapped her nose with a whiskered calico cat before tossing the stuffed animal off to the side.

"Good morning, Sunshine. Did you sleep well?"

"What time is it?" She turned over onto her stomach and considered going back to sleep.

"Time to get up. I already showered and shaved." Brant bestowed a resounding slap on her rear.

"Stop manhandling me." She flipped over and sat up.

Brant leaned against the bureau with one of the bed pillows behind his back. His arms were locked around his bare legs. He'd changed into khaki shorts. At least he hadn't worn his threadbare cutoffs. "Shall we clear the air?" He paused, but not long enough that she could reply. "I'm not the only man handler in this room. Look at these bloodied wrists."

She turned and faced the other direction. "You deserved that and double. You weren't even drunk when you began getting friendly."

"Don't recall any complaints." He chuckled.

"Okay, I'll give you that one, but knocking me over?" He leaned closer. "You appeared ready to scratch my eyes out last night. Lucky for you that ground was soft and wet, or you'd be facing a big lawsuit. I could have broken something."

She looked back at him. "Your neck would have been a nice touch."

He picked up one of Lindy's tiny pandas and tossed it at her. She knocked it away.

"I could use a cup of coffee." Marley yawned and stretched her arms over her head. She brought them down immediately when Brant's eyes flicked with too much attention in her direction.

"I smell bacon. Sounds like your family's up. Should we join them?" He started to get up.

"No!" She placed a hand on Brant's knee, trying to soften her quick rejection. "I mean, we do have a lot of things, personal stuff, to discuss, and we can't do it with everyone else around."

"Come on." He took her hand and pulled her to her feet. "Should we slip down the stairs unbeknownst, or tell your family we stayed in this room last night before we leave?"

"Let's see if slipping out works." She extracted a pair of green shorts and a matching sleeveless top from her suitcase and took them to the bathroom to dress. When she returned, Brant had his suitcase on the bed.

"I'm kind of in a predicament. All my shirts are filthy and my one pair of pants is covered with mud." He looked up at her. "You have a laundry handy?"

"What about shoes?" Marley asked. She had a dreadful vision of him wearing his black boots with his shorts.

He drew out his sandals and waved them in the air. Marley turned and rummaged through Lindy's closet. "Here." She handed him an oversize T-shirt in faded navy blue with *PITT* emblazoned across the front in a dull gold. "I used to use this as a nightshirt before I gave it to Lindy."

"Great. I'm reduced to wearing lady's jammies. Should I be concerned about this?" He pointed to the letters. "Does P-I-T-T refer to pit bulls, or is it some kind of homage to Brad Pitt?"

"Neither," Marley said with a chuckle. "It's my college logo for the University of Pittsburgh. Did you attend college?"

"Yes, Y-A-L-E."

She looked at him, furrowing her brow in disbelief. "Yale?"

"My goodness, she can spell!"

"Yale," she repeated. "I pictured you more as a community college type. Say, majoring in horse manure."

Brant started to laugh, and he didn't stop until they began sneaking down the stairs with their dirty clothes and their suitcases.

OVER BREAKFAST, MARLEY told Brant about all the drama he'd missed while doing his drunk act. They had deposited their clothes at the laundry, and the proprietor had promised to have them ready before noon. Since they had time to waste, they relaxed and talked in an outdoor café. With no more rain clouds in the sky, the sun began burning off some of the humidity.

"What is it with you and drinking?" she asked.

"You see how stupid I was when I was acting drunk?"

Marley nodded.

"Well, that's how I am when I drink. Stupid. No control. Can't remember a thing and wake up with a splitting headache." He looked up. "The first and only time it happened was in college. Something no one would let me forget so...I limit myself to one drink and nurse it most of the night. I need to be in control and won't ever let that embarrassment happen again."

"You ever consider your drunk performance could backfire and give you the same embarrassment?"

Brant took a sip of coffee and glanced up at the sky. "No. But that's something to consider. I'll have to think about it. Last night, I kept away from the liquor completely."

"No. You had at least one Bloody Mary. I know."

A smile was starting. "Really. How would you know that?"

She leaned across the table and whispered, "I tasted Tabasco."

"And didn't it taste good?" Brant moved closer. "I had a virgin Mary. No vodka."

Marley felt a heightened awareness, quite different from the comfortable feeling she'd had with Richard. Somehow sipping coffee while talking to Brant was the most natural thing to do, but on a heightened scale. She sat back and changed the subject. "Why Yale? I didn't take you for Ivy League."

"You didn't take me for anything better than a bargain-basement hobo."

If he wanted a denial, he was out of luck.

She waited for him to readjust in his seat, lean on the table and continue.

"My father's family were some of the original settlers in Arizona, but my mother came from Connecticut. We used to stay with my grandparents outside of New Haven, during the summer. I got to really like the beaches and thought acting would be a lot more fun than horse manure at some community college." He paused. "And of course there was a girl, a neighbor of my grandparents."

"How did that work out?"

He glanced at her. "It didn't," he said before taking another sip of coffee.

They sat silently for a long time watching the activity on the street, then Marley asked, "Are you able to make a living as an actor?" Quickly, she amended her remark. "I mean, why Phoenix? Why not Hollywood or New York?"

"I've acted on TV, movies and the stage, but for the most part I'm a narrator."

"You lost me."

"You've seen commercials with only a voice in the background? I do that and things like promotional material, pretty much what the Civic Center hired me to do. Phoenix is home, but I go wherever I'm needed. As you know,

Sky Harbor is an easy commute from our apartment complex, so I can get an airplane anytime. What I hope to expand into is more books on tape. I have a friend from college who writes mysteries, and I read them for a recording company. His latest has several dialects that I'm practicing to perfect."

"The accents?" There had actually been a purpose to all those annoying flips from Texas cowboy to British count? Maybe if she'd known...

"Sorry I was driving you batty with it, but my voice is my meal ticket. It pays the bills. What about you?"

Her life couldn't be more dull compared with his. "I manage an accounting department for a large company in downtown Phoenix."

"You like doing that?"

She sighed. "It pays the bills." Again they had a long pause with no need to rush into conversation. All this time she'd avoided Brant. Who would have thought he was actually an interesting person to talk to as well as someone she'd like to know better?

"What made you decide to follow me here? You could have left a message for me to call you about the ring."

"Would you have called me back?"

Marley cocked her head. "Probably not."

"When I phoned and got your mother, my only concern was returning the ring. But I couldn't tell her that. We got to talking and I played the part of the fiancé, distressed because we were apart. That's when she invited me to the wedding. What could I say?" He looked at Marley, his palms in the air. For the first time she noticed his eyes were a dark blue, not black the way she'd thought at first.

"I said, why not? It sounded like fun. I figured you'd be so ticked off, since you gave me the evil eye every time we met, and I wanted to see your reaction. But," he said, raising a hand to silence her before she could reply, "my sisters got hold of me and..." He pointed to his hairless face and the attractive haircut.

"I had kept the hair long after I finished my last movie, and it suited my hobo disguise. But I figured you'd prefer this."

She shrugged. "I didn't dislike your hair." He looked presentable, something her family might appreciate. "But I admit, I'm not fond of beards."

"I don't like them, either." He rubbed his smooth cheek. "They itch."

A waitress approached and asked if they'd like anything else to eat. "Yes," Marley said, happy to change the subject. "French fries and gravy."

Brant grimaced.

"A Pennsylvania treat."

He glanced away, still looking as though he had tasted something foul.

"So you have sisters. Any brothers?" she asked.

"No. Three sisters, and I'm the baby so I'm henpecked to death."

Marley considered this. She'd always wanted a brother. How would she have handled one?

"They know, by the way, that this engagement is all an act. And they were against me doing anything that might embarrass you or your family."

"I hope I'll have the opportunity to thank them. You clean up well."

He sighed and concentrated on his hands, examining the palms. "I have a little confession."

"What's that?" Perplexed, she waited for some revelation and hoped it had nothing to do with last night's kissing.

He regarded her for a long moment before speaking in a barely audible voice. Marley leaned forward, even more interested. "I missed that."

He adjusted his seat and bent over the table. "You really shook me up when you offered me money."

"I'm sorry. I—"

"Don't be." He reached for her hands and gripped them. "You were right. The women in my family have been after me to invest in better clothes. I probably didn't just to spite them. Sometimes it really rankles having the equivalent of five mothers." When Marley appeared confused, he added, "Three sisters, a mother and grandmother, all telling me what to do as if I were still ten years old." He released her hands and sat back. "That's why I prefer living on my own in Phoenix instead of at the ranch."

Marley had enjoyed the connection and wished he still held her hands. She brought her own to her lap, not knowing what to do with them. "I can relate to your sisters." When an eyebrow went up, she reached over and touched his hand, half expecting him to pull away. He wrapped his fingers around hers.

"As the oldest, I've always been the second mother, making sure homework was completed, baths were taken, entertaining my sisters when our mother was too busy. I managed to escape, like you, yet they forever pull me back. Help me here—what do you think about this boyfriend, should I cut my hair? I am so happy this is the last wedding I have to be involved in."

Brant took her fingers to his lips and kissed them, watching her all the while. "I guess the firstborn gets all the responsibilities, while the babies like Lindy and me take advantage." He placed her hand back on the table but didn't release it. "Being the only boy comes with its own set of problems."

"Like what?"

"My father wants me to take over the ranch."

"And give up acting?" Marley could sense this wasn't something Brant wanted.

"Nothing that specific yet, but he did want to talk to me while I was on hiatus. Another reason I wanted to follow you here. I wish he'd sign everything over to Elaina, my oldest sister. She's better suited to ranch life."

"But if you don't take over, you can't say you own a ranch."

He shook his head. "I can always say that. So far no one's challenged me on it."

After another comfortable pause, Brant broke the silence. "So when did you and Richard first meet?"

"In college. I was a junior and he was a se-

nior. We dated for several months and it got…"
She stopped, then added, "Personal."

"Who broke it off?" He held up his free
hand and said, "Wait. I know. It was you."
Brant pointed his index finger at her and shook
it. "He has this wounded puppy-dog look like
he can't understand what he did wrong, and
I'll bet you never told him."

Marley sighed and slowly began to pull her
hand away. "He reminded me too much of my
father."

"And that's a bad thing because…?"

"My father…" How should she start? "You
met him last night, didn't you?"

"Yes. He seemed very pleased that you're
settling down and warned me to treat you
properly or he'd come after me with a shot-
gun. Sounded serious."

"He doesn't…" Marley felt a tightness in
her throat. Without giving the words much
thought, she blurted, "He likes women, and it
never mattered that he was married."

The waitress returned with a plate of French
fries and set it on the table. Brant looked at the
fries but didn't take any. Marley, feeling grateful for the distraction, took one and scooped
up some gravy before putting it in her mouth.

When Brant still didn't look as though he might try one, she said, "Coward."

Brant took a fry, dipped it in the gravy and ate it. For a moment he appeared nauseous, until his expression changed and he reached for another one. "Not bad, but definitely an acquired taste. I prefer mine with vinegar, something I picked up when I was in England."

He brushed off his hands and pushed the plate closer to her. "So why did your father's fooling around affect you and Richard?"

"I was afraid Richard would do the same, leave me when something better came along. I've seen the pain my mother experienced, and I couldn't tolerate that." After turning so that she faced Brant straight on, she gazed into his eyes. "You impressed me as being the same type of guy."

He sat back in his chair. "Where did you get that idea?"

"I've spotted you with women, several different ones, in fact, taking them home at night, seeing them off in the morning."

Brant bent over the table and decreased the space between them. "I'm flattered."

"I didn't mean it as a compliment."

"No. I'm flattered you paid so much attention. I never knew you cared."

"I don't. It doesn't matter to me what you do. We're not involved and never would be because..." A sudden sadness enveloped her. On one side, there was Brant. She'd begun to like him as a person and a possible friend. And this scared her. How could she expose herself to someone who admittedly enjoyed playing the field?

On the other, there was Richard, a man she'd once loved. What if he still cared for her? He'd already showed it several times. Wouldn't it be foolish not to explore that possibility? She had to give up on one of them.

She needed out of this arrangement with Brant—a chance to be with Richard. Marley took a deep breath. "I want to break our engagement."

"What?" Brant half stood. Was he acting again? The look he gave her of hurt and disbelief disappeared so quickly she wasn't sure if she'd just imagined it.

"You heard me. I think something could develop between me and Richard again, and it can't get off the ground if I'm engaged. I'll tell everyone we had an argument, and you left for Arizona." Marley slipped off the ring and pushed it across the table. The easy camaraderie between them had disappeared. "Here.

You can return it when you get back, and if there're any additional costs—"

"No can do." Brant regarded the ring for a moment. Then he grabbed her hand and kept it and the ring from coming closer to his side of the table. He released her, got up and began running his hand through his hair, looking in every direction except at her. Finally, he sat down and fingered the ring.

Brant grasped her hand again and put the ring on her finger. "As of last night, I'm in the wedding. Denny's best man, his army buddy, couldn't make leave, and he asked me to fill in for him. Denny gave me a card for the tuxedo place." Brant dropped her hand and reached for his wallet. "I have to be there before one today to get fitted." Brant placed the card in her hand, then sat back.

"How can I be in the wedding if we break up?" he asked. "How can I get out of it and not upset everyone who's counting on me?"

Marley collapsed on the table, pressing her face into her hands. When would this nightmare end?

Brant patted her on the top of her head. "Cheer up. I'll let you dance with Richard at the wedding." Marley dragged herself up and glared at him.

"You'll let me!" She stood and leaned on the table. "This engagement is fake. Stop acting like you own me and can dictate what I'm supposed to do or how I should behave."

"As though you'd allow that even if we were engaged." Brant stood also and tapped his index finger on the table. "Stop going schizo on me. One minute you act like a human being and the next thing, you're off the wall. I don't get it."

Marley dropped back in her seat and tried to control her quivering chin. She didn't look at Brant. She'd no intention of crying. Compressing her lips, she tried to focus on what she should do next. They needed their clothes. "The laundry should have everything ready by now."

She got up and started in that direction. She'd gone only a few feet, when Brant grasped her arm and turned her around. Before she could muster any more control, Marley began sobbing into the *PITT* emblem inscribed on his shirt.

"Let it all out," he said, resting his chin on her head. He ran his fingers through her hair, gently pressing her against him. The closeness, his strong arms holding her, made everything worse. The tears nearly exploded inside her.

Brant had somehow managed to infiltrate all her defenses. She never felt so vulnerable, and deep down she wanted his comfort, his companionship and...

But he was Brant, an actor, someone who could turn on the charm without meaning any of it.

CHAPTER THIRTEEN

MARLEY HAD CALMED down by the time they reached their motel room. Lindy and Dennis had left and returned the key, so they had to get a different room. "I'll take care of it," Brant said as they walked into the office and over to the counter. "A suite, if you have one."

"A suite. No, that's too expensive."

Brant turned to her. "In case you haven't caught on, my dear, my Goodwill wardrobe is mostly for disguise. I can afford it."

"One king-size or two queens?" the manager asked.

"Two," Marley said quickly.

Brant gave her a sidelong glance before returning his attention to the manager. "Two beds, for two nights and no smoking. Put it on this." He handed the man a credit card. While Brant filled out paperwork, Marley went outside to wait, thankful that she didn't have to add more to her own credit card.

To keep this farce going, they'd have to

share the same room. Two nights, two beds. How was she going to handle the next forty-eight hours? In emotional time, that had the equivalent of two centuries. She'd already fallen apart. Breaking down in tears was a new thing for her, and, she had to admit, it had felt good. Right up until it had felt too good. Brant's attempt to comfort her, his closeness, his fresh shower smell, his—

"You ready?" he asked as he came out of the office. "I'll get the bags." She followed him with their clean laundry, neatly washed, pressed, hung on wire hangers and wrapped in plastic.

This motel room had a living room with a large sofa and matching chair. The two queen beds were located in a separate room. Brant went into the bedroom with the bags. When he emerged, the PITT shirt and his shorts were gone and he was wearing one of his long-sleeved Western shirts and black pants.

Marley sat on the sofa and flipped on the TV. Brant flipped it off.

"We have to talk."

With her arms folded across her chest, Marley stared at the blank TV. "I'm sorry I lost it earlier. I don't usually have crying fits."

"You're wound way too tight. A good cry

can be very beneficial. My sisters do it on a regular basis."

She glared at him. "If you so much as mention PMS, Brant Westfield, you will be smothered in your sleep."

"Oh, will you quit it with those idle threats." He grasped her hand and pulled her from the sofa.

"They aren't idle—"

He kissed her.

It was so quick and unexpected, very much like his kisses last night. When he was through, Brant held her arms so she couldn't move away.

"Now, have I got your attention?" He was breathing hard, a dragon with flames about to spew from his nostrils. The raw emotion surprised her. "That seems the only way to shut you up. We are not going off on another tangent of threats, rants or women's liberation. We have only a few hours to prepare for Armageddon." He pulled her to him again. When he merely wrapped his arms around her and held her close, she felt disappointed and a little curious. What was he planning to do next?

"I'm sorry," he whispered near her ear, "for coming off as a control freak. I'm experiencing stage fright. I don't usually, and it scares me to death." He took a deep breath and held her a few inches from him. "I don't want to make an idiot of myself and ruin this for you."

She studied him. Sweat beaded above his lip and his eyes had a wild look she hadn't seen before. "Are you acting?"

Brant closed his eyes and placed his forehead against hers. "No. Lady, you've got this idea I can turn it on and off at will. The only time I wasn't me, the real me, was when I pretended to be drunk."

"And the kiss?"

He moved his head back and regarded her, his lips turning up on one side. "Which time?"

"Either time."

"Just now was totally me, frustrated and desperate." He paused. "Last night started out as part of the act. It changed when you...you surprised me."

He released her, and Marley headed for the sofa again. She felt his hands on her shoulders, and she froze. He reduced the space between them and murmured, "I'm not going to strangle you. Relax." He began massaging her shoulders. "You have any special way to relax? A mantra or something?"

"I play my guitar." She sighed and added, "Which I left back in Phoenix."

"You have to understand, Marley," he said as he worked the kinks out of her shoulders, "I have to be prepared, know my lines and have a general idea of what I should do. I can't improvise in a vacuum." His manipulations worked, easing much of her stress, and Marley began to relax. "We need to sketch out this engagement, how it plays. Right now, we have me coming off as Danny Zuko from *Grease* and you as a witch from *Hamlet*. The two don't play as engagement material."

"Awwho," Marley said when he dug deeper into her shoulder. She moved out of his grasp, flipped around and placed her hands on his back.

"The witch wants her turn."

"I was speaking figuratively."

She could feel the tension in his shoulders and found it disturbing. All the time she'd known him, he'd seemed lighthearted to the extreme. Who would have guessed he was so uptight?

Marley glanced around for a straight-back chair and spotted one at the desk in the other room. She pushed him toward it and ordered him to sit. "Face the back so I can work on these muscles."

"Wait." Brant snapped the pearl buttons on

his shirt and pulled it off, all the while watching her. She kept her expression neutral as he undid the cuffs, not wanting him to know how much she liked the way he looked.

"I figured out why you wear these Western shirts. They make it so easy to expose yourself."

He grinned.

"All those hours of struggling with Pilates finally paid off?"

"Wondered when you'd notice." He winked. After laying the shirt neatly on the bed, he sat down and placed his arms on the back of the chair. "Do your worst."

She worked on his shoulders for several minutes, enjoying his grunts of pleasure and complimentary comments. When she was through, she gave him a light slap on his arm and sat on the bed across from him.

"You're good. Where did you learn that?"

"I had a roommate who was into sports, and I learned a few techniques to relieve the aches and pains."

"What did she play?"

"*He* was on the basketball and track teams." She smiled at his shocked expression. "He played football, too, but I met him after football season. He graduated that spring semester."

Brant put his shirt on, but he did up only a few of the bottom buttons. He didn't bother to tuck the shirt into his pants. "Surprise, surprise," he said rolling up the sleeves. "I take it this guy wasn't Richard."

Marley placed her hands behind her and leaned back on the bed. "Could we have one agreement between us? Stop talking about Richard."

Brant did a little finger dance, indicating she should get to her feet and come to him. She did, and they stood almost toe to toe. Was he about to kiss her again? she wondered. She hoped.

"I agree, although it will require an equal commitment on your part." He took her hands and gazed into her eyes.

"We need to get into character. We are engaged. I think you're the most beautiful, wonderful woman in the world. I want you to have my children." He paused. "And if you don't stop laughing, I'm going to kiss you silly."

"Promises, promises," she said, then quickly moved away from his reach.

Brant flung himself face down on the bed. "Marley," he said, his voice muffled in the pillow. He continued to say her name while he smashed his fists into the bedspread.

Marley had a sudden fit of conscience and moved closer to comfort him. "I'm sorry," she said and sat on the bed next to him. "I've never been engaged before. I don't know how to act."

"You've got to at least pretend to like me. Everything and anything I say appears to make you mad or send you into hysterics. Help me! What can I do to make you like me?"

She stared at him. "But I do like you." She did. And the idea of her liking him surprised her as much as it appeared to surprise him. "Okay, so I didn't think I ever would." She folded her arms protectively across her chest as he sat up beside her. "You come off as very annoying, full of yourself and like you think the world should revolve around you."

In a sudden move, he dropped onto his knees in front of her and clasped his hands on her lap. "I'm what?"

"Stop it. You're too much...I don't know." She grabbed his hands and tried to push them off her lap. "I can't take you seriously. And you make me nervous."

He got up and began walking around the room, scratching his head. He turned and said, "Pretend you're practicing your guitar chords."

Taking a seat next to her, he said, "Don't go into a hissy fit, but I heard you play. Listened to it, in fact, sometimes for hours."

Her face fell. "I'm sorry. Why didn't you tell me? I would have stopped."

"Precisely why I didn't say anything. I didn't want you to stop. You're really good, and I found it relaxing, as well." He pushed her back against the bedcovers and lay beside her. "Loosen up. Pretend you're strumming the guitar."

Marley closed her eyes, but she couldn't concentrate on her guitar. Not with Brant so close. "When did you hear me?"

"The first time I was on my balcony, resting on the lounge. You came out on your balcony and began playing. I figured if I said anything or made any sound, you'd take off. So..." Brant reached over and pushed a section of loose hair from her forehead. "I started these fantasies in my mind. You and me playing our guitars together."

"You play?" she said, opening her eyes.

When his lips were a breath away from hers, he said, "I thought it was something we could share—a mutual interest in music." His lips brushed hers. "I know all the songs you were playing. Wouldn't it be fun?"

Every part of her soared, and she didn't want it to end. When Brant finally pulled away, she asked, "Did they teach you how to kiss like that in acting school?"

"Marley! What is it with you?" Brant fell back on the bed, his eyes scrunched into painful slits as he pulled at his hair. "Is your goal emasculation? Because I really can't take any more of your insults."

She sat up and looked down at him. "It's just I—I've never been kissed like that." He didn't move, so she continued. "I like it."

He opened one eye.

"I'm merely saying you're a good kisser," she continued. "I wondered if it came naturally or you had to learn it."

Brant sat up and stared at her. Slowly he got off the bed and walked over to the door. Turning around, he began to chuckle. "If I didn't know that hair color was real, I'd swear there's a ditzy blonde under that red mop."

When she didn't reply, he came back over to the bed. "What? No retaliation? No defense for all the blondes in your family?"

"I'm clinging with all my might to my warm and fuzzy side. Don't push it."

Brant pulled her to her feet. When she was in his arms, he said, "I don't know if it's learned or natural. But I'm ready and willing to teach you everything I know. You game?"

Marley placed her hands around his neck. Without saying a word, she showed him she was definitely ready to learn.

A while later, Brant said, "We better stop." He pushed her away and directed her to the chair. "It's getting harder and harder for me to remember we're only pretending to be engaged."

"Right." Marley caught a glance of herself in the mirror. She was smiling, a very happy and contented smile.

Brant stretched out on one of the beds, pulled the pillow over and whacked it a few times before putting it under his head. "What is it about music you find relaxing?"

Marley concentrated on a water spot in the ceiling. "I don't really know. It's something that makes me all—" she motioned around her body before tossing her hand in the air "—cozy inside."

"Just guitar music?"

"No. Not at all." She looked back at him. "I love jazz. Not the improvisational kind so much because I appreciate a melody I can follow—probably my math background where I'm into order."

"And..."

"Concerts. I go whenever I can. I've met many of the music teachers at the Maricopa Community College where I teach at night, and they have wonderful presentations by the students. One young fellow I've been jamming with at the condo has been doing very well in the guitar program."

Marley could barely control her enthusiasm, and since Brant didn't interrupt, she continued. "I like rock and folk and I especially love the words in songs that describe feelings. You can pretty much figure out a singer's entire life from the songs he writes."

"Only male singers?"

Marley shrugged. "Women may write beautiful songs, too, but the real turn-on for me is to hear a man singing to me alone. I feel good when I listen to the lyrics."

"You like any other instruments besides the guitar?"

"Yes. The saxophone and of course drums, all kinds of percussions...and violins. Especially in Irish music." She paused. "What about you? Any particular music you enjoy?"

"I love listening to you play, and I've collected a few different string instruments. One day I'd like to learn how to play them."

"Isn't that the most fun, learning something new?"

Brant nodded. "Anything you don't like?"

Marley became thoughtful. "Nothing I can think of. Music is my passion."

"You've mentioned nearly everything but the piano."

"Oh, I didn't mean to leave that out. I often play my guitar while listening to piano music. It's one of my biggest pleasures." Her expression turned dreamy. "One of these days I'm going to learn to play the piano."

"Me, too."

She looked at him. "You, too, what? Music affects you the same way or you always wanted to learn how to play the piano."

"Both." Brant sat up, reached over and grasped her hand. "I feel the same way you do about music, an enjoyment I think of as an afterglow. But the only time I prefer a song written by a man is when I can sing it to a woman." That smile again. *Does he ever turn it off?*

Marley looked away. And then she had a thought. What about all those women she'd seen with him? Did he delight them in the same way, touch them so that their lips longed for more?

She shook her head. "So, were you engaged before?"

Brant got off the bed and sat on the desk, his legs dangling. He held on to the edge with both hands. "Yes," he said in a flat voice. "We never married."

"I don't mean to pry, but maybe you can give me some hints. What am I doing wrong?"

"It's body language, mostly, but you've improved. No more flinching when I touch you." His eyes beamed down on her, and she felt a flutter in her midsection.

After an uncomfortable pause, Marley asked, "Was it your grandfather's neighbor?"

Brant nodded and cleared his throat. "We were supposed to marry when I graduated. She died from leukemia, a debilitating cancer, in my sophomore year." He looked down at the rug and kicked his feet a few times before glancing back at her. "It taught me one thing. Don't waste time waiting." He sighed.

"What about you? Why didn't you marry the jock?" When she appeared confused, he added, "You know, the roommate back in college."

"Oh, Phil." She smiled. "He was one of many. Several of us rented a large apartment, and we had our own bedrooms. I was in the wedding party when he married our other roommate."

"Which just goes to show how little I know about you. I need more info. We're supposed to be intimate. You have any scars, birthmarks or tattoos I should know about?"

"No. What about you? Anything more than that tiny pinprick below your waist?"

He looked wounded by her remark. "I'll have you know that was a near-death experience. My appendix ruptured while I was riding and—"

"Riding what?"

"A horse, of course. I was riding at my parents' place when it happened. A total disaster and—"

"Oh, I should know about your parents."

"You're not interested in how I had to be rushed to the hospital?" He glanced at the ceiling. "Another time. Okay, let's see. My parents recently celebrated their forty-seventh anniversary. My oldest sister, Elaina, is forty-five, Jacqueline is forty-three, Roberta is thirty-nine and I'm thirty-seven. My parents gave up having children once they had me. Finally had their boy." He leaned toward her, still holding on to the edge of the desk. "You realize I'll be giving a test later to see how much of this you absorbed."

"I might remember the numbers, but I've already forgotten the names. Any of your sisters married?"

"All of them, but we don't go for the traditional wedding your sister is having. Every one of my sisters, including my parents, took a trip to Las Vegas. That's our tradition. As my fiancée, I'd expect the same."

Thank goodness their engagement wouldn't go that far. "You're full of it. Vegas? Really? My mother would have a heart attack."

"So, how old are you?"

"Thirty-four. I was twelve when Lindy, the last sister, was born. My father divorced my mother right after that. Not exactly a happy time in our lives. Certainly nothing that would endear me to my father." Marley focused on the crumpled bedspread for a moment before continuing. "I'm the oldest then comes Chloe, who's five years younger, then Jen, Franny, Morgan and of course, Lindy. You'll get to know everyone tonight at the dinner party. They're all married and there are six grandchildren. Including Michelle, who considers me her favorite aunt."

"Will the kids be there, too?"

Marley nodded. "What else should we know?" She got up and walked past him. "We need to stick as close as possible to the truth. And..." She came back to stand in front of Brant, her hand over her mouth. "I've lied. I never expected to see you here so I created this person I thought my family would like."

"They wouldn't like the real me?" He hesitated. "Or you don't like the real me?"

"What is the real you? I have no idea. But all my sisters married very nice guys, and I'm the last to go. I wanted to impress them, and, frankly from what I'd seen of your wardrobe, I needed to get creative.

"I'm the only one in my family who ever finished college, so Yale's good." She began pacing in front of him, ticking off the different points on her fingers. "My grandfather thinks you're doing well, owning a horse farm."

"Ranch."

"Everyone thinks you're rich, especially after seeing this gorgeous ring." She flashed it at him, and he took her hand. "My sisters like the idea of a cowboy, and you fit that bill. Their husbands, on the other hand, like sports."

"I've been to a few Cardinal games."

"That would do."

"So I shouldn't tell them I keep in shape by dancing?"

"No way." She considered a moment, then asked, "You dance? You're not into Pilates?"

He shook his head, got off the desk and did several spins across the room, reminding her of moves in her early ballet class. "Don't you dare! I don't want them turning redneck on you. And no reference to any kind of acting. I want them to be impressed."

"How about I mention a scholarship to Oxford?"

"No. Don't go making up more things, Brant. We need to keep the story simple and truthful."

He stared at her but didn't comment. She placed fingers on her temples, trying to think of what else they needed to know about each other. "Hobbies. Do you have hobbies? Hunting, fishing?" She plopped down on the bed.

He shook his head. "What about you? You go around shooting Bambi with your redneck relatives?"

"Not me," she said, shuddering involuntarily, "but the men in my family like to hunt. They might try to offer you some venison. You can tell them you're a vegetarian if you don't want to eat it."

Brant came over and sat next to her. "I thought we were sticking to the truth. Just because I don't care to kill it, I'll still eat it. The cattle we raise go to a butcher in town, and I'm very fond of red meat. What about you?"

"I like steak."

"I mean, what are your hobbies besides playing the guitar?"

"When I'm not involved in music, I take classes in things to better myself."

"Like what?"

"Math." She glanced at him. "I know it makes me a number one geek, but when I moved to Phoenix, I taught math in high school. Then got my master's so I could teach it at a college level."

"But you're an accountant, right?"

"Yes. Teaching didn't pay well, so I had to find something else. I took courses in book-keeping and accounting, along with Spanish, so I could be bilingual. Very handy when you live in Phoenix."

"Definitely. Spanish is the main language at the ranch. You need a hobby, something more physical like horseback riding. I know this great place where—"

"Brant? You in there?"

Marley and Brant looked at each other and

mouthed, "Richard?" As Brant got up to answer the door, he buttoned his shirt. Marley was right behind him when he opened the door.

CHAPTER FOURTEEN

RICHARD SWUNG THE GARMENTS he'd been carrying off his shoulder. "You were supposed to
get fitted before one this afternoon. When you
didn't show, I took these. Let's hope you're the
same size as the original best man." He tossed
the black tux and white shirt into Brant's arms.
Richard looked in Marley's direction and gave
a curt nod of recognition.

"Rehearsal is at six in the church. The
bride's dinner is at seven at the same restaurant
as last night's fiasco. The maître d' has agreed
to let you come, providing you don't drink. I'm
making it a point to break both your arms if
you so much as look at the bar." When Brant
didn't supply any rebuttal, Richard added,
"And if you don't think that's possible, every
one of the groomsmen has volunteered to hold
you down while I do it."

"Thanks for bringing them over," Brant
said, adjusting the assortment.

Richard glanced at Marley, his expression softening. "I'll see you later."

Before she could say anything to Richard, Brant closed the door and blocked the exit with the tux, shifting back and forth every time she made a movement to pass him. Marley clamped her jaw and fumed. By the time Brant let her get around him, Richard had already left.

"That went well," Brant said and headed to the bathroom with the garments. "I'll see if these fit."

Marley followed him. What had gotten into him that he was acting this way?

He hung the garments on the shower curtain rod and began popping his shirt open again. "My, my," he said, gazing at her. "You want to watch me dress?"

Marley turned on her heel and shut the door to the bathroom. "Oooh, that man infuriates me." She grabbed her purse and went out of the motel, giving the door a violent slam.

WHAT DID HE DO? Brant leaned on the bathroom sink and stared in the mirror at the idiot staring back at him. He had finally made headway with Marley, and he'd blown it. What was it with him, anyway? The girl of his dreams...

He backed away. Not just his dreams. This was *the* woman, the one person with whom he wanted to share his life. They had so much in common. A love of music, dancing— He could imagine her dancing like an angel in his arms. He'd love to spend the next fifty years dancing with her, or playing their guitars together. And she wanted to learn how to play the piano. He'd teach her that, and she could help him become more proficient with the guitar. Perfect. He wanted this engagement for real.

Not that he had a chance. He'd acted like some immature juvenile blowhard in high school. He couldn't help himself. The moment Richard had shown his face, Brant had wanted to destroy it. Instead he'd probably thrown Marley into his waiting arms.

Disgusted with himself, Brant decided to try on the penguin suit. He slipped into the shirt and jacket. Fit okay. Not as good as the tux he had hanging in his closet in Phoenix, but it would do. He tried on the pants and burst out laughing. How tall was Dennis's friend? Four feet? The pants ended mid-calf. No way would they work.

And Richard was responsible. Brant could understand the hostility. He certainly shared it. But why ruin his brother's wedding? Brant rehung the pants and decided to discuss the matter with Dennis when he saw him at the rehearsal.

That is, if he ever made it there. He expected Marley to pick him up, but quite possibly she wouldn't after his earlier behavior. He decided to shower and get ready anyway. He still had the pertinent wedding information on his tablet. If she didn't show, he'd call a taxi. He wasn't about to give up on Marley, not now that he knew she was the one he wanted as his wife.

LINDY GUESSED THERE were problems the moment Marley walked into the house. She grasped her hand and drew her through the throngs of relatives in the living room right up the stairs into the menagerie of stuffed animals. "We can talk here," Lindy said, grabbing a chair and dumping a group of teddy bears onto the floor. "Being engaged is sometimes the pits. Take it from someone who knows."

Marley sat in the offered chair and tried to filter through fact and fiction. What could she say about Brant and her engagement without spilling the truth? "Men can be absolute animals," Lindy continued. "Has Brant hurt you, physically, emotionally? You let me know, and

I'll have Denny bop him one. He has no right to hurt my best friend and sister." She gave Marley a hug before taking a seat on the bed. Whatever problems she'd had the night before were gone.

"He's not trying to get out of the wedding, is he? Because that could create trouble. We don't want one of the bridesmaids without an escort."

"No, it's not that. Richard brought the tux over and—"

Lindy's blue eyes popped, and she put her hand over her mouth. Her squeaky scream sent shivers down Marley's spine. Lindy jumped off the bed and started a crazy dance in front of her, stomping her feet and waving her arms. Buster, who had followed them up to the room, began to howl. "He's jealous. I knew it. Rick came onto you, and Brant's jealous. How romantic!"

Retaking her seat on the bed, Lindy curled her legs under her. "I know all about it. Denny told me. You and Rick had a thing back in college. Now you're engaged to Brant, and Rick wants you back."

Marley could only watch in shocked dismay. The moment she thought of something to say, Lindy started on a new tangent that left

Marley speechless. Finally, Lindy caught her breath and sat back, as though waiting for an explanation.

"How did Denny know?"

"Oh, Rick told him. He was so shocked to find out Denny was marrying the sister—me," Lindy said, pointing to herself, "of his college girlfriend. He said you didn't, you know. Well of course he'd say that." She paused. "Did you?"

"Did I what?" Marley got up and headed toward the bathroom. "You're way off base, Lindy. Brant and I needed some time alone. He's exhausted and wanted to take a nap."

Marley closed the door and blocked out further remarks. Was Brant jealous? That might explain…Marley let the thought die because he had no reason to be jealous. The engagement wasn't real. Except it was becoming harder and harder to remember that.

MARLEY HAD DEBATED until the last minute whether to pick up Brant or leave him at the motel to stew. Not wanting to cause turmoil with her family, she opted to ignore his behavior. Why had he acted like such a jerk?

Trying to figure him out was destroying her brain. Marley smashed her palm against the steering wheel. That was it. No more. She'd end this engagement. *End this torture.* She'd thrown out the jealous factor that Lindy had suggested. Marley's opinion of Brant had been correct from the start. He was an arrogant know-it-all, and they had nothing in common. So what if he could knock her over with his kisses....

When she pulled up to the motel a little before six, Brant came out as though he'd been waiting for her. He was dressed in another Western shirt in blue-and-white stripes, his black pants and boots. His dark hair appeared damp from a shower. Neither he nor Marley spoke when he got into the car, and they drove in silence to the Lutheran church. He was out of the car the moment she stopped and opening her door before she removed the key from the ignition.

"I have one thing to say, Brant Westfield," she stated quietly through clenched teeth as she got out of the car.

"Only one?"

"If it hadn't been for your drunk act, no one would be angry with you."

"Richard's the only one angry with me. If it hadn't been for my drunk act, there wouldn't be a wedding." He walked swiftly toward the church entrance, not waiting for a reply.

If only she hadn't left her clothes in the motel room when she took off earlier. Keeping up with his long stride was difficult in the three-inch heels she'd had to borrow from her sister. Fortunately, they both wore the same size. All of a sudden she stopped and headed back to her car. "I have to get something," she said more to herself than to Brant. The full skirt of the dress she'd borrowed, in shades of lavender and blue flowers, billowed in the wind, and she pushed it down. The weather was at its worst again, threatening rain. Just what they needed for a garden reception.

Brant followed her.

"What did you forget?"

"A bouquet for the bride. Made up of all the ribbons from her shower gifts." Marley climbed into the backseat and reached for the hodgepodge of color. Her skirt billowed once more, and she felt Brant's hand putting it in place.

"Nice," he said as she backed out of the seat. "The bouquet," he added, but the smile on his face was a little too wicked. Just how far had her skirt gone up?

As they started for the church again, Marley asked, "What did you mean there wouldn't be a wedding?"

Brant stopped. He cleared his throat. "Richard had planned to party all night even though Denny wanted to be with his bride. Lindy was threatening to cancel. You think there'd be a wedding tomorrow if the party had continued through this morning?"

"Richard sounded mad at you. He threatened to—"

"The guy's an idiot. And I'd do it again in a heartbeat." He opened the door to the church. "Bachelor parties shouldn't destroy the groom."

She was about to say more but held her comments as Lindy and Dennis met them in the vestibule. "Thanks for last night," Dennis said, holding his hand out to shake Brant's. "I'd have ended up in the hospital if you hadn't intervened. How does the tux fit?"

"How tall was the best man? The pants are about six inches too short." Brant quickly added, "But it's no problem if I can wear my black boots." He pointed to his shoes.

Dennis appeared confused. "Yeah, sure. That should work." He glanced toward the altar. "I guess we should start. The minister is waiting for us."

Brant looked around, obviously puzzled. "Isn't anyone else coming? I thought all your sisters and their husbands were in the wedding."

Lindy chuckled. "They're with their kids at the restaurant. This is number five. They didn't feel it was necessary to go through a rehearsal again."

Dennis gave Lindy a kiss and hug, whispering in her ear before heading toward the altar. Brant was about to follow him when Lindy caught his sleeve.

"Don't you think you should...?" She nodded toward Marley.

"Sure." Brant walked back and took Marley in his arms. She expected a peck on the cheek after their squabbles, but he kissed her with the same fervor as previously. "Am I forgiven?" he murmured, still holding her close, "for being an idiot?"

He planted a kiss on her nose before following Dennis.

"I like him," Lindy said. "So does Denny."

So do I, Marley thought. And she didn't want to, not when she knew nothing could come of their time together except eventual heartache. They were too different, poles apart.

Lindy and Marley watched the group of men

as the minister directed their positions. A commotion had started between Dennis and Richard, but the women weren't able to hear any of it. After several indistinguishable words, Brant moved and Richard took his spot.

"Who's the best man?" Marley asked.

"It's forever changing. Denny wanted his army buddy, then gave it to Rick when Larry couldn't get leave. Then when Brant arrived, we figured it would be better to pair you two—maid of honor and best man. It seems Rick has it again." She poked Marley. "You don't think they'll end up fighting, do you?"

Marley shuddered. She certainly hoped not. But something niggled at her. Why had Dennis thanked Brant for last night? It made no sense.

"You're up next," Lindy said. She held the assorted ribbons, bows and trinkets to her nose and pretended to smell the bouquet.

Marley glanced around. "Where's Dad? Isn't he giving you away?"

"Sure, but he's only walking me down the aisle. No big deal."

Despite Lindy's blasé remark, Marley could sense the disappointment. "Right," she said, mustering some false cheerfulness. "No big deal."

Without the help of music, Marley chose

to walk the long aisle at a regular pace, all the while watching the four men watching her: the minister, a balding man about her father's age; Dennis, a tall, handsome copy of his brother; Richard, an Adonis with golden hair; and Brant. Her heart skipped a beat when she gazed at him.

Biting on her lower lip to avoid smiling, she focused on the altar. When she got to her spot, she turned to see her sister and noticed that only the minister and Denny observed the bride. Richard and Brant both kept their eyes on Marley. She made it a point not to look at them again and almost missed accepting the colorful bouquet when Lindy handed it to her.

The minister began explaining the ceremony and asked if either the bride or groom had prepared their vows. They had but, in embarrassed whispers, said they'd prefer to wait until the actual wedding. "Be sure and practice," the minister cautioned. "Though I can always step in with the usual if there's any problem."

Finally, the minister said, "Now is when you kiss the bride." Denny picked Lindy up off her feet and kissed her just as Richard took Marley's arm. For a moment, she had a panic attack, thinking he planned to kiss her, too, but instead he followed the bride and groom down the aisle. What would she do if he had kissed her? What would Brant do? She could hear his breathing behind them; he was that close.

"Mind?" Brant said as he caught up with them and took her other arm, attempting to disengage her from Richard. "I'm going to renegotiate this best man business with the groom. I'm the one who will be walking my fiancée down the aisle."

"You will not," Richard said, successfully halting the three of them at the entrance to the vestibule. "Denny's my brother. You don't even know him. How can you give the toast? Yeah, right. How can you give a toast when you won't even be able to drink it?"

Dennis stepped between them. "Stop this right now. You're getting Lindy upset." He glanced from one man to the other. "Work this out between the two of you. If you can't, you can both stay out of the wedding party." With that final announcement, he escorted Lindy to the car.

Totally frustrated, Marley clenched her hands and tried to control her temper. What had happened to Brant? Why had he become this possessive, this horrible… jerk?

Brant faced Richard. "Mind giving us a moment? I'd like a word with my fiancée."

Richard nodded. "Sure. Take your time. We can settle our problem at the restaurant."

When Richard was out of earshot, she said to Brant, "You're an idiot."

Brant started to laugh.

"It's not funny. Whenever Richard's around, you act irrational."

Brant sighed and blew air through his teeth. "You're right. I want to poke his eyes out for looking at you, knock his teeth out for smiling at you and break his arm when he touches you. But I don't." He raised his hands. "I keep my hands to myself." He paused before adding, "And act like an idiot."

"Lindy thinks you're jealous."

"Oh, is that what it's called?" He reached for her hand. "Come on," he said, leading her to a cement bench outside the church. "Let's talk this over."

He sat on one side, and she sat on the opposite. "Have we backtracked? You won't come near me again?"

Marley wanted so much to be close to him, but she didn't know how to say it and could only sit staring at a blade of grass that hadn't been mowed. He had been the one to initiate physical contact. If only he would hold her, kiss her. She wanted to feel that euphoria again.

He sighed. "If you want to break the engagement off now, it's perfect timing. Everyone will accept the fact that we've argued, split up and you're free. You can go off with Rickyboy and live happily ever after." Brant got up and started for the car.

"I didn't—"

He turned. "Or you can be engaged to me for real and marry me."

Marley gripped the edge of the bench until her hands hurt. "You're crazy. You're making me crazy." She got up and considered running for her car. Instead, she sat down again. "You're right. We should break off the engagement. Here's your ring." Without looking at Brant, Marley slipped it from her finger and held it out to him. After a long hesitation, he took it.

"What about the wedding? Should I still be in it?"

"Of course. We can't upset Lindy and Denny. I need to get my things from the motel. I'll stay with my mother."

"Fine," he said without emotion. "Drop me off at the motel."

They drove in silence. Marley's mind was in turmoil. How could she face her family and tell them the engagement was off? Why was the engagement off? The whirlwind Brant created had gripped her somehow and turned everything upside down.

After she'd gathered her things at the motel, she asked, "You're coming to tonight's dinner, aren't you?"

Brant shook his head, still not looking at her. "No. I'll let you handle that one. Pick me up before the wedding tomorrow."

Marley started for the door and stopped. "Why did we break up?" she asked. She felt shell-shocked. "I mean, everything was going right along. I don't understand."

Brant walked over and wrapped his hands on either side of her face. "I love you, Marley. When you and your friend created this crazy engagement, I thought I'd died and gone to heaven." He brushed his lips against hers and continued to circle her jaw with his thumbs.

Marley listened in a daze, spellbound by his soothing voice, his gentle touch.

"Then that ring fiasco…it had to be kismet." He dropped his hands to her shoulders and drew her against him. Marley closed her eyes and tuned into the joy she felt in his arms.

"I want to marry you. I want you to have our children—ten beautiful daughters we can raise together."

Marley's eyes flew open, and she stiffened, yet didn't push away. "What are you talking about?"

"If we go back to being engaged, I want it for real." They stood there for a long time in each other's arms while Marley tried to think. She couldn't. *Marriage? For real?*

"Aren't you going to say anything?" He drew a deep breath before asking, "Or do you still want Richard?"

Hearing the name, pronounced correctly for a change without any overtones, brought her back to awareness. She pushed against Brant's arms to give herself some space. "Why are you and Lindy throwing Richard at me like I have to choose between you? I liked you better drunk than I ever liked Richard sober." She paused. That didn't sound right. "I mean—"

"I know exactly what you mean," he said, grinning.

She kept her distance when he tried to pull her back into his embrace. "You can wipe that smile off your face. Our lives are resting on this decision, and I won't be forced into making it this minute. If you want to marry me,

Brant Westfield, you better…" All her gusto left and she collapsed against him. "Are you serious? Do you really want to marry me?"

"Oh, Marley, if it were possible," he said, pressing her to him, "I'd make it a double wedding tomorrow in front of all your family and friends."

CHAPTER FIFTEEN

MARLEY MOVED OUT of the embrace. "Brant, I can't agree. It's too soon. You prefer not to waste time…and you know how you feel and what you want, right from the start. But I'm not like that. In the short time I've known you, everything's changed. I had this idea about who you were, and you aren't this person. I don't know the real you." When he came closer, Marley held out her hand and said, "Don't you kiss me. Trying to think straight is hard enough without you—"

He put a finger on her lips. "Let's make this simple." From his pants pocket, he extracted a ring loosely tied with a pink ribbon. "We'll stay with the fake engagement, and you can wear this ring." He reached for her hand and put the ring on her finger. "And I'll give you the real one when you agree to be my wife."

Marley shook her head. "No, you have to return the other one when you get back to Phoenix."

"No, I'm saving it for you."

"But it's too—"

"Marley, I can afford it. Like I said, despite what you originally thought, I'm not on the skids." He put his arm around her and pointed her in the opposite direction. "We stay with the original plan. Let's go. I can't wait to meet your whole family." He opened the door and ushered her out, leaving all her things behind.

THEY ENTERED THE crowded ballroom, where a band provided by the restaurant played. After Marley introduced Brant to the rest of her sisters, she and Brant mingled before getting food from the buffet. Marley's sisters made a point of teasing Brant, an indication that they liked him, and her brothers-in-law talked hunting and fishing.

After eating, Brant left her to visit with the grandchildren, who were seated at a smaller table, and he talked to them for several minutes while she talked to her parents. Since her mother seemed so happy and content, thanks to her ex-husband's return, Marley decided to make peace.

"It's a wonderful party, Mom." She turned to her father. "And I'm glad you could be here to share it with us." He wrapped her in a warm embrace, the first she could ever remember receiving from him.

"Thank you," he said.

Her mother dabbed at her eyes and smiled at her tearfully. "Yes, thank you." Before continuing, Nora looked at Red as though asking permission. He gave the faintest nod, and she turned back to Marley. "We're getting married again." Quickly she added, "Don't say anything. We plan to tell everyone tomorrow at the wedding."

Marley made a supreme effort to control her thoughts and not say something she might regret. After a slight hesitation, Marley said, "I wish you the best." She left to find Brant. She needed to get away and focus on something other than the sickening feeling of remorse that gripped her.

"Are you all right?" he asked when she joined him.

Wanting to put her mother's announcement out of her mind, she said, "I'm fine." She glanced around the large ballroom, and spied Dennis. "Come on," she said. "I want to talk with my future brother-in-law."

Dennis greeted them with an easy grin, but it changed to a scowl when she asked, "Why are you grateful to Brant for last night?" She heard Brant clear his throat, and she pivoted to see him nodding at Dennis.

"Well." Dennis kept his eyes on Brant. "He showed me what to drink, how to make it look as though I was drinking the real stuff." He relaxed and turned his attention to Marley. "I didn't want to get drunk—I didn't even want to be there. I wanted to be with my Lindy, and Brant said he'd make it possible." Dennis started to smile. "And he did. He can act crazy."

Immediately, Dennis put a hand on Marley's arm. "Don't worry. He was only acting. Put on a good show, too, and we got kicked out."

When it appeared that Dennis planned to continue, Brant waved dismissively and directed Marley to the dance floor. "So, does he know you're an actor?" Marley asked, placing an arm around Brant's shoulder. They were well into the dance before he answered.

"I didn't tell him." Brant wrapped both arms around her waist and drew her close. "You have any particular reason for hating actors? For the most part, despite the paparazzi propaganda, we're a pretty nice lot. In fact, I know more people in accounts receivable who belong behind bars than I know actors who do."

Marley chuckled and placed her arms

around his neck. "Touché." They glided on the ballroom floor for several minutes, and Marley marveled at how well he danced. He made it seem effortless, something few men of her acquaintance were capable of doing. "You're the only actor I know, and I'm getting an entirely new perspective. I'm really beginning to like actors," she whispered next to his ear.

"I only want you to like one," he whispered back and kissed her ear. "You're a wonderful dance partner. Is it natural or learned?"

"I taught ballroom dancing while in college. One of the many hats I wore to help pay for my schooling."

"But didn't your family help?"

"Except for child support, my father was out of the picture, and I would never have considered asking him for anything. Mom was supporting the family with her catering business, and Poppy was dealing with Nana's sickness. He had a mountain of bills when she died."

"Dancing paid your tuition?"

"No, only contributed to it. I managed to get some scholarships and student loans. What about you? Yale has to be expensive."

"You know that ranch I mentioned?" Marley nodded. "Long before my family ever went into ranching, my great grandfather discovered gold on our property." He shrugged. "I never had to worry about tuition."

Before Marley could comment, her grandfather tapped Brant's shoulder.

"May I have this dance?" he asked Marley. With a nod, Brant stepped away, giving her hand to Poppy.

As they moved around the floor, Poppy said, "I approve. Not that you'd care one way or the other, but I think he's good for the long haul."

"Thanks, Poppy." She placed a kiss on his withered cheek.

Michelle joined Marley and wanted a dance with her. As they circled the floor, Brant came over. "Why are you two beautiful ladies dancing by yourselves?" He picked Michelle up and held her with one arm while he grasped Marley with the other. He stopped. "I don't believe I've had the pleasure of meeting this young lady. What's your name?"

"Michelle."

"And who do you belong to?"

"Aunt Marley."

Brant turned to Marley. "Sounds like you've got an admirer."

"Oh, I don't think so." Michelle glowed as she looked at Brant with total admiration. "I think this little princess just zeroed in on her prince."

For a fraction of a moment, Brant eyed Michelle with concern; then he switched back to his devastating smile. Boy, he could turn that admiring look on anyone. Michelle appeared enchanted.

"Aunt Marley, do you mind if I take the princess for a spin?" And he was off, in perfect step with the music, leaving Marley on the sidelines.

Chloe approached her. "I'm going to leave, but I'd hate to spoil it for Michelle. She's quite smitten with Brant. Could you watch her the rest of tonight? I need to rest so I can participate in the wedding."

Marley hesitated. She didn't want more pressure on Chloe. She'd never forgive herself if Chloe lost this baby. "Of course. No problem." She'd take Michelle over to her mother's and work out something there. Maybe the camping equipment she'd used the night before.

"I'll have Al get some of her things from home and drop them in your car. Thanks." Chloe hugged her sister and said softly, "Don't squeeze too hard. I'm having a really hard time keeping my food down tonight."

For pretty much the rest of the night Michelle stayed with Marley or played with her cousins. Brant danced with all of Marley's sisters, and Marley had a chance to partner with all her brothers-in-law. Although dodging their feet was difficult because they put plenty of exuberance into their dancing, she felt happy that her sisters had found these men. Even her father had one dance with her before Richard came over.

"May I?"

"Of course." She felt relieved to be with someone else, since she found it so hard to talk to her father.

As Richard drew her into his arms, he said, "I remember when we met. You were teaching dance, and I made it a point to take up as much of your time as possible."

"I did a good job. You're definitely one of the better dancers here."

"Not as good as twinkle toes, though."

When the band began a song with a Latin beat, he hesitated, and Brant cut in.

"You mind, Richard? I'd like to dance with my fiancée."

Thankfully, Richard backed away.

"You're one of the few people here who can actually follow this music," Brant said. "I'll have to introduce you to my dance classes. You'll really enjoy them."

How wonderful, she thought, a man who knew what he should do with his dance partner. Was it because he'd been taught or was it something that came naturally? When they finished the dance, people clapped, and she noticed for the first time they were the center of attention.

Marley gripped Brant's arm. "Chloe isn't feeling well, and I'm taking care of Michelle. She'll be sleeping with me at my mother's."

He broke into a slow grin. "She'll be sleeping with you at the motel. Two beds, remember?" He zeroed in on the men in the band leaving the stage. "I've got plans, and they include both of you staying at the motel."

"What kind of plans?" she asked warily.

He came closer and whispered, "I plan to charm you with what we discussed about music."

Panic. She felt it immediately. "No, Brant. I want to stay at my mother's."

"Where would you sleep?"

"We'll camp. I can use the same stuff I used last night, and we can sleep on the floor in Lindy's room."

Without commenting, Brant reached for

his wallet and went over to one of the guitar players.

How could she make him understand her sister's well-being was more important than continuing their discussion of music?

Marley recognized the two men were speaking Spanish, but she was too far away to hear exactly what was being said. How had Brant managed to find a Latino east of the Allegany? He gave the man a bill and took the guitar. The man looked her way and smiled.

Brant moved in front of the stage, threw the strap over his shoulder and began to strum. Marley, who had begun a conversation with Lindy, stopped. Something close to fear gripped her for a moment but subsided as she began to enjoy the music. Michelle walked over to her, and one of the men offered Marley a chair. She sat down, cradling Michelle in her arms.

"Some things don't come easy," Brant began as he strolled over to her. She recognized the song from one of her favorite albums by England Dan and John Ford Coley, one that she often played while strumming her guitar. Was this one of the songs he'd heard her play?

Michelle turned around in her arms and looked at Marley. "He's singing to us."

"That he is." Did Marley have the same glow as Michelle? "And he's good, too," she whispered against her niece's ear. The girl's soft blond curls tickled her check, and she patted them in place. If the glow wasn't on Marley's face, it certainly was in her insides, turning them to mush. If this is what he planned as charming her by music, it was working.

Michelle squirmed on her aunt's lap, keeping time with the music.

He sang another, "Baby, I'm-A Want You," a romantic love song that she recognized from the group Bread. So he was as familiar with music from the 1970s as she was. All this time he focused on her as though she were the only person in the room. She found it difficult to take a full breath. As he sang, a connection she'd never considered possible began to grow. Who would have thought only days before that Brant Westfield could totally turn her life upside down?

Someone behind Marley said, "Wow, I wish my guy could sing like that."

When Brant was through, he walked closer to Marley. As people around them clapped, he wrapped an arm around her and kissed her on the cheek. "Next time we play together," he said. "I've got to return this." He took her hand, pulled her from the seat and headed over to the bandstand with Michelle holding her other hand.

Even though the person who had loaned him the guitar spoke in rapid Spanish, Marley had no trouble understanding it. After thanks on both their parts, the men shook hands. When the dancing began again, Brant picked up Michelle and spoke to Marley. "He asked me—" Brant started, but Marley interrupted and repeated the conversation in Spanish.

Brant's jaw dropped. "Lady," he said, pulling her tight with his other arm, "never stop surprising me."

"I told you I learned Spanish." The man had asked Brant to join their group for another song. "Why don't you? I enjoy listening to you."

"Will you play, too? I'm sure they have extra guitars."

She felt the color drain from her face. "No. I—"

"I know. You have to have everything laid out, carved in stone before you'll take a chance."

"Are you saying I have no spontaneity?"

He nodded. "I calls them the ways I—"

"Okay. I'll do it."

With an ear-to-ear grin, still holding Michelle, Brant elbowed his way through the crowded dance floor. After a short discussion, Brant placed Michelle on the stage and lifted Marley to stand next to her. Marley and Brant took the offered guitars.

"You okay?" he asked Marley.

"I'll manage."

"She'll do fine. Won't she, Michelle?"

Michelle nodded and glanced shyly around, pressing her body against Marley's leg.

"You know this. I've heard you playing it many times." He announced to the band, "La Bamba," and Marley and Brant began playing the traditional Mexican wedding song. It was one Marley had hoped to play for her sister's wedding, so she was very familiar with it. Obviously, so was Brant because he sang the Spanish words with decisiveness, in perfect harmony with the other man in the band.

The audience was transfixed. Marley managed to keep up with Brant and found it exhilarating. They played several more tunes until their bridal party began to disperse.

The three of them got off the stage to applause as the adults gathered their children. Michelle continued to stick close to Marley, although she never let Brant out of her sight.

The oldest grandchild, Matthew, who was ten, approached Brant. "I know who you are," he said. "You're Comoto."

Brant glanced at Marley and Michelle, then went down on one knee so that he was closer to Matthew's height. "How'd you figure that out?"

"I've got the DVD. Watch it all the time."

Brant stood up and ruffled the boy's hair. "No kidding. You enjoy it?"

"Sure. I'm going to be a komodo dragon this Halloween."

"Good for you," Brant said, and the boy took off. Brant pressed his lips together and glanced in every direction except at Marley. When he did look at her, he sighed. "I was the voice of the komodo dragon, Comoto, in the movie."

"Should I be looking you up on Google?"

"Please don't," he said, wrapping her in his arms. "I've made so much progress with you so far, and I don't want it all ruined." He released her and headed for the band. "I'll be back in a moment." When he returned, he carried two guitars by their necks.

"I borrowed these. We'll finally have a chance to play together alone."

CHAPTER SIXTEEN

MICHELLE'S FATHER, AL, who was six-five, the tallest of all her brothers-in-law, met them at Marley's car. "Here're all her clothes and car seat. We really appreciate this. All the stress from this wedding has both of us worried." Al picked up Michelle and hugged her before placing her in the car seat in the backseat of Marley's car. "You be good for Aunt Marley." After he straightened, Al pulled Marley into a big hug. "Thanks." He kissed her forehead before stepping away.

Although Brant didn't say anything, he had a questioning expression. Al turned to him and shook his hand. "We've only told Marley. Chloe's pregnant, and she needs her rest." Brant nodded.

With the guitars stored safely in the backseat, Marley drove Brant to the motel. Michelle amused herself by singing music only she understood.

"How come you didn't get all out of shape with Al when he hugged and kissed me?"

"You think I'm crazy? He's bigger than me. Probably could take on a sumo wrestler with ease." Brant reached over and moved her hair away from her face, momentarily caressing her cheek with his thumb. "Besides. There's nothing going on between you two." After a short pause, he asked, "Why are they worried?"

Before answering, Marley glanced at Michelle. The little girl had fallen asleep, so Marley felt safe in discussing the details with Brant. "Chloe had a miscarriage two years ago in the early stages. She won't tell anyone she's pregnant until she begins to show." Fearful, Marley took in a deep breath. "Chloe doesn't want to deal with all of us…you know, feeling sorry for her if she loses this one." Marley pressed her lips together. "I hope and pray she's able to…"

Brant placed his hand on hers and entwined their fingers. "Me, too." He glanced around at Michelle. "She deserves a sister or brother." When he looked back at Marley, he asked, "Why do you get the honor of watching her?"

"Does it bother you? I mean—"

"No, of course not. She's an absolute delight."

"You know, she adores you."

"All little girls do."

"Brant, you have the biggest ego." She took a quick look over at him and realized he was teasing.

"Why you? How come you're watching Michelle when there's a grandmother and four other sisters? Is this another thing put on you because you're the oldest?"

"Chloe is the closest to me in age, and I've always had a special bond with Michelle. And Al. He and I used to date before Chloe got her claws into him." She chuckled. "But you're right. There's nothing between us now but friendship."

When they reached the motel, Brant said, "Come in for a moment." He retrieved both guitars from the backseat. "I need to show you a problem I'm having with my tux." When she didn't move from behind the wheel, he added, "It's okay. You're safe. Besides, it won't take long. And you left all your stuff inside."

He headed for the room without looking back.

For several moments, she just sat there. Marley checked on her niece, who was still asleep, and debated what she should do. *It wouldn't take long, he promised and if he had a gen-*

uine problem.... With a sigh of resignation, Marley gently removed Michelle from the car seat and carried her to the motel door that remained ajar.

"I couldn't leave her in the car," she said as she walked into the room.

"Of course not." Brant took Michelle from her arms and placed her on the overstuffed chair. He still wore his western shirt, but had changed into the black pants that belonged to his tux. He held out his arms and asked, "What do you think?" Shocked, she took a gulp of air and placed her hand over her mouth.

"I can drop them," he said, lowering the waist below his butt and exposing his boxers, "the way the juvenile delinquents do in Phoenix. Or I can wear my boots, which come right to the cuffs. Of course, when I sit, the pants hike up to my knees." His expression remained serious. "Any suggestions?"

She walked over to him. "The bride should get all the attention, not the best man and his blue butt." She took out her cell phone. "I'll give Denny a call—"

Brant placed a hand over her phone. "Don't. I've already discussed it with him. These pants probably belong to one of the other men."

"You're kidding. I don't know anyone in the group who's that short."

"Don't worry. We'll trade tomorrow."

Marley clicked off the phone and put it back in her pocket. "So you didn't need my opinion?"

"Not about that." His expression remained neutral. "You surprised me tonight, several times, in fact."

"How?"

"The way you dance." He took her into the dance position he'd used earlier that night, both arms circling her waist. "I usually step on my partner's feet at least once but you—you made it look as though I really knew what I was doing."

"You did know." She placed her arms around his shoulders. "Take it from someone who appreciates a good partner."

"Oh, Marley," he said, hugging her close. "There's so much I need to learn about you." He kissed her cheek. "Stay here tonight. You and Michelle can have one bed, and I'll take the other." When she hesitated, he said, "Or you can have both, and I'll sleep on the sofa."

"No." Marley pushed out of the embrace and started for her niece before her resolve disintegrated. She was about to pick her up when

Brant began strumming a riff on the acoustical guitar.

"You know you want to." He played several more bars. "Admit it. Tonight was the best night you had in a long time. I know it was for me." He walked over to her, still fingering the frets while he strummed. "And it doesn't have to end."

Marley stood with her back to him, her hands by her sides, while she listened to him play. Finally she sighed. "Okay, Brant. You're going to put Michelle on one of the beds."

The guitar made a sickening sound as he tossed it on the sofa. In seconds, he was carrying Michelle back to the bedroom.

Once he had Michelle on one of the queen beds, he dimmed the lights. Marley helped get the little girl changed into her pj's, and Michelle slept peacefully through it all. When she was finally settled, Marley drew out a pair of shorts and a T-shirt from her luggage and headed for the bathroom to change. When she emerged, Brant was already in his khaki shorts and sandals with his shirt sleeves rolled above the elbow.

"Do you prefer nylon strings or steel?" He held the two guitars out to her.

Marley glanced over at her niece. "We might wake her."

Brant directed her to the sofa and closed the bedroom door enough so that the light wouldn't disturb Michelle. "If she's like my nieces and nephews, she can sleep through a rock concert."

Marley accepted the guitar with nylon strings. "Is that what we're going to have here?"

"Absolutely."

Once settled on the sofa, the two of them tuned their instruments. And they played. For the next few hours, they improvised, each delighting in the music they were creating.

"Oh, my God," Marley said when she noticed the time. "I've got to be at the beauty parlor to get ready for the wedding in—" she looked at Brant "—five hours. I'll never get enough sleep."

He stood and stretched, then turned to help her to her feet. "Whew. That could destroy our backs. Next time we get something with less give." He picked up their guitars and placed them on the chair.

Marley walked over to where Michelle slept. Before she could place a knee on the bed, Brant grasped her shoulders and directed her to the other bed. "You'll never get any sleep with Michelle."

She looked over her shoulder at him. "Where are you sleeping?"

"The sofa pulls out into a bed." He shrugged. "Aren't you glad I got the suite?"

"You had no idea when you requested it that you'd need the couch."

He came over to her and wrapped his arms around her, pressing his lips against her neck. "True. But if you don't tell me how grateful you are that I got it..."

She turned in his arms. "I'm totally grateful. It was a thoughtful, generous—"

He stamped her lips with a quick kiss and headed for the living room. "Sleep well."

SHE AWOKE TO grunts and screams emanating from the living room. Marley rose on her elbow and looked at Michelle's bed. It was empty. She scurried to the living room, to see Michelle giggling and kicking, while Brant dangled her above him. He put her down and began tickling the squirming child. "Do you know what she did? Nearly poked my eye out." He continued to tickle, laughing as hard as Michelle.

Brant pushed himself up and gazed at Marley. "You sleep well?"

"Yes."

He turned to Michelle, who was looking at him with love and trust. "I did, too, until this monster started poking me." He began tickling her again.

Marley grabbed her niece and headed for the bathroom. "We have first dibs." She glanced back at him; he'd already lain down on his stomach and gone back to sleep.

She faced her niece. "Let's get ready as fast as we can so Uncle Brant can use the bathroom." Al had included Michelle's toothbrush with her things. Marley placed toothpaste on their brushes from a small tube Brant must have provided, because it wasn't her brand.

Marley sighed. She'd really miss this little girl once she returned to Phoenix.

They'd taken quite a bit of time, enough so that Brant knocked on the door. "Come on, girls. It's my turn." Once the door was open, he picked Michelle up and stood her on the rug outside the bathroom.

Marley quickly put on the dress she'd worn the night before so she could leave it when she changed at her mother's. All the extras she required, including the underwear and shoes were already there. She helped Michelle into the extra clothes Al had provided the previous night.

"You decent? I'm coming out."

Marley was busily folding her clothes and repacking her suitcase when Brant came over. He took her in his arms and rubbed his newly shaved face against her cheek. "You like?" His breath smelled minty fresh from the same toothpaste they had used.

She caressed his chin and murmured, "Yes."

She was about to kiss him, when someone knocked on the door. Marley caught her breath when Brant tensed. "It better not be Richard."

Still gripping Brant so he couldn't get past her, Marley shouted, "Who is it?"

"Al. I'm here for my daughter, and I have Brant's pants for the wedding."

Brant broke away from her and stopped at the door. He pulled it open and stood on his toes to look around Al. "You alone?"

"Yeah. Who else did you expect at this hour?"

Brant tugged him into the room. "Richard. He has a habit of showing up. Can't get it through his pea brain that Marley's off-limits."

Al chuckled. "He's probably the one who got you the wrong pants. Here. These should fit."

He turned to his daughter, who ran into his arms. "You have a fun time with Aunt Marley and Uncle Brant?" Michelle pressed her face shyly into her father's neck.

Brant walked over to Marley and placed his arm around her, then faced Al. "Your daughter's adorable." He pressed a kiss against Marley's forehead. "I want to get started with Marley as soon as possible so we can have our own brood." Marley glanced at him. *He what?* She struggled to get out of his hold.

Brant drew Marley tighter against him, so she had no way to extricate herself.

With another chuckle, Al headed out the door.

Marley moved, trying to get out of Brant's clutch. "You need the child's seat from the car," she called.

"Got another one in the truck. See you at the wedding."

The door closed and the two of them stood hip to hip. "Let's get one thing straight, Brant. I haven't said yes to your proposal." She pushed away and started for the door. "I have to meet my sisters."

"No." Unexpectedly, he swung Marley into his arms and carried her into the bedroom.

He plopped her in the center of the bed, then dropped down beside her.

She tried to sit up, but she gave up when she realized it was useless. "What gave you the idea I'd be interested in marrying you, especially after yesterday morning? When I left here, I was livid."

"Oh, I knew you were angry." He stretched out alongside her, caressing her face. "But you slammed the door." He paused. "Twice." Brant reached over for a strip of her hair and curled it around his finger. "It showed me you cared." He brushed her hair away. "And something else." He kissed her gently on the lips. "I saw you avoid Richard's kiss before the bachelor party. I knew then my chances had improved."

Marley studied him. Who could stay angry with him? And he couldn't possibly be serious.

"I plan to do everything I can to prove my good intentions."

"Which won't be now, because I have to get ready for that wedding."

She got up, and he didn't try to stop her.

CHAPTER SEVENTEEN

BRANT FOLLOWED HER to the door and slipped into his sandals. "Have we got enough time for breakfast?"

"Sure, but we need something fast. Let's head to the restaurant we went to the other day unless you have another suggestion." She'd tied her hair back in a voluminous ponytail.

"Nope. Loved their coffee." He rolled the sleeves down on the shirt he'd worn to bed, not having changed after their guitar concert.

Once in the car, Marley asked, "Do you cook?" Weeks seemed to have passed since Richard had made her breakfast.

"Don't cook, but I'll do the dishes if someone else prepares it."

"How do you eat?"

"Usually with a knife and fork, but I'm pretty good with chopsticks."

She swatted his arm. "That's not what I meant."

Brant rubbed his arm where she'd tapped

him. "Mostly takeout. Phoenix has some wonderful restaurants, and I'm good with a grill. What about you?"

"I can cook."

"Why do I feel there's a but?"

"Have you seen my mother's kitchen?"

"No, we snuck out, remember?"

"My grandmother and mother ran a catering business. Mom still does. We nearly had to break her arm to keep her from doing this wedding. She wears herself out and everyone else." Marley paused and glanced Brant's way. "From the time I was old enough to hold a knife, I've been helping with the cooking. My sisters still do. College opened more opportunities than an education for me. It got me out of the kitchen."

"So I shouldn't put my hopes on a home-cooked meal?"

Marley turned into the restaurant parking lot and stopped the car. "I don't know. If you continue to behave, I might surprise you with one of my specialties."

"I love surprises." His expression sobered and he stared out the window. Turning back to her, he said, "I've seen your house, bits of it anyway. It's huge. And it sits on what looks like several acres."

"The house is my grandfather's. Come on— let's get that coffee."

"Is it a sore subject?" Brant asked when they were seated in the restaurant.

Marley shook her head and continued to sip her coffee.

"I met your grandfather. He's about the same age as mine." Brant ate a little of the breakfast he'd ordered, while Marley scooped out her yogurt. "My family's lived with my father's parents all my life, in a house half that size. My sisters shared a room no bigger than Lindy's, and it didn't come with its own bathroom. The four of us had to share one, which can get sticky with three sisters." He sat back, holding a plastic fork and regarded her.

Marley had an image of him dealing with sisters. She finished her yogurt and put the container aside. "Before my grandfather made additions, we all lived on the second floor. Until I was born, my parents lived in what eventually became Lindy's room. Poppy and my nana shared another room and, eventually, I got the third bedroom with the open area for my playroom."

Brant began pouring syrup over his pancakes. "I'll bet you were terribly spoiled."

"I was." She took a sip of coffee. "Five years

later, when my mother got pregnant again, Poppy built one of the additions for him and Nana so our family took over the entire floor. By the time there were six of us girls, Poppy built another addition for my parents."

"Your Poppy's a pretty good handyman and definitely not poor."

"True." She looked up gratefully, as one of the cashiers came over to refill her cup. "Things began to fall apart when I was about twelve. The fighting was nonstop, not just between my parents but also between my father and Poppy. They've obviously arrived at some understanding because my dad's now staying with him."

"All that fighting had to be devastating for you and your sisters."

"You can't imagine how much I wanted to get away." She looked up at Brant while she gripped her cup. "When my grandmother got sick, my mother took over the catering business. There were no extras and Poppy had a mountain of bills for Nana's medical expenses."

"That's when you started dancing?"

Marley nodded. "Because I spent so much time at the parties and weddings my mother catered, I often danced with her customers.

People began asking me to teach them so they could dance at their weddings. One thing led to another, and it helped me pay expenses."

"You're an amazing woman, and I love that you're into dancing. It's one of my personal passions," Brant said, reaching across the table to take her hand. He held it for a moment before releasing it and reaching for his phone. "I want to clear something up." He flicked his finger over the phone's surface and handed it to her. "Are these the ladies you saw sneaking out of my condo early in the morning?"

Marley sucked in her breath, but didn't say anything. "They may do it again sometime. They're my sisters—not my dates. They often drive into town to shop or see a show. The ranch is too far to travel back to late at night, so they use my guest room."

He put the phone on the table, removed the cup from her hand and held both her hands in his. "I am committed to you, Marley. Only you, from this day forward. I will never be like your father."

Marley compressed her lips and nodded, too emotional to express her gratitude.

Brant's phone began to vibrate, inching slowly across the table. He grasped it with one hand, still holding on to Marley with the other.

"It's Carla, my manager," he said, glancing at the phone.

Oh, so that's who Carla is. The name had plagued her since he'd first called her it.

"Pick me up when you're heading to the church." They both rose, and he drew her to him. "I can walk back to the motel from here." After a brief kiss, he sat down again and answered his phone.

Burning with curiosity, Marley retreated to her car. She wanted to know why his manager had called, and why Brant hadn't shared the information with her. Another play, maybe another movie. How would any of that affect them and his proposal of marriage?

"WE'RE DOING IT MY WAY!" Lindy paced the beauty salon, her blond hair in rollers. "This is my wedding. I want it to be different, and for a few hours you can all put up with it." She plopped down and yanked a dryer over her head.

Marley sat in one of the chairs in front of the mirror, watching the beautician, Tristan, pull curls to the back of her head. Each section received a hairpin and a squirt of hairspray. Marley placed a hand over her nose to avoid the fumes. When would this nightmare end?

"You are going to be absolutely lovely." The huge mass of curls was pinned in place, with no possibility of moving, thanks to the can of hairspray that had turned her hair into a solid cone.

Marley glanced at Chloe, who sat to her left, holding her hand over her nose, as well. Marley waved Tristan away when she reached for another can. "That's enough spray." Chloe obviously couldn't tolerate the smell, and she looked as though she might be sick.

"This is the final one, a specialty for the maid of honor." With that announcement, Tristan squirted silver sparkles onto the immovable hair.

Marley raised a hand. "Stop!" The sparkles fell on her hand and arm as well as her hair. She turned to Lindy, who had her nose in a magazine. "Lindy!" Her sister ignored her. Marley glanced at Chloe, who reached in her purse and extracted a package of crackers. She'd been eating them since they'd arrived.

Marley got out of the seat and walked over to Lindy while Tristan continued to follow her, squirting more sparkles into her hair. Stopping in front of her sister, Marley raised both hands to deflect the spray. "Tristan, stop that or you'll be minus a tip." The spraying stopped.

Since Lindy still ignored her, Marley tugged the magazine from her hands. "You've got to stop this nonsense. There's no reason all of us should be miserable just so you can have your own way." Marley had avoided the fake nails Lindy had insisted she needed. At least her sister had relented enough that they all had red nails instead of black.

Marley viewed her other sisters, who were covered in colorful plastic shawls. Each one looked ready to boil. Jen, Franny and Morgan directed dagger eyes at Lindy. How could Marley keep the situation from escalating into a catfight?

Chloe got up from her chair, removed her shawl and walked over to Marley. "You're not going to give us this much trouble, are you, when you get married?"

Visions of Vegas popped into her mind, and Marley slowly shook her head. The stiff hairdo felt weird, and she stopped the motion. "Absolutely no chance. No one will have to suffer through my wedding."

Her sisters heard her and a spontaneous "Yay!" arose from each one.

MARLEY STOOD OUTSIDE the motel door and debated whether she should warn Brant. What kind of reaction could she expect? No way did she want to go public, let alone stand before a church audience, looking this way.

When he opened the door after her knock, it took him a while to focus. When he did, he stepped back and nearly tripped over the chair. "What the...?"

She walked in and closed the door. "What is this?" he asked as he began circling her. Marley stood patiently in the black strapless cocktail dress that ended at her knees. Knees covered in black mesh stockings.

"Black? Aren't you supposed to be in frilly frou-frous in a rainbow of color?"

"Lindy wanted a black-and-white wedding. She and Denny are in white, and, against Lindy's objections, Mom is wearing the same pink dress she wore to the last wedding. She only wears black to funerals." When Brant continued to stare, she added, "And don't you dare say anything about my hair."

Brant glanced up, then gripped his thumb knuckle between his teeth, looking ready to laugh. But he appeared to gain control, possibly something he'd learned in acting school. "Can I touch it?" He made a tentative motion toward her hair, then pulled back. "It looks...

solid, like petrified pink cotton candy," he said, then pressed his lips together.

"Oh, go ahead and laugh." He turned away, his shoulders shaking. "The beautician used a whole can of hairspray to keep it pinned in place. Chloe and I could have died from asthma attacks." Marley started to chuckle. "Then she added silver dust so my hair would sparkle. It'll take me a week to get all this gunk out of my hair. If only I could have brought my own hairdresser from Phoenix."

Brant spun around, grabbed her shoulders and held her at arm's length, still shaking with laughter. "This has got to be the craziest wedding I've ever attended."

"We nearly came to blows over the black lipstick and black nail polish, but I won." Marley dabbed at her eyes, which had begun to tear. She wasn't sure whether her eye makeup was waterproof, and she didn't want it running down her cheeks. "No way was I going to walk down the aisle looking like a zombie." She sucked in her breath. "A clown is bad enough."

Now they were both completely gone, until Brant said, "I'd better get into my penguin suit." He was still laughing when he emerged from the bathroom in his pants and boots. "Can you help me with this?" he said as he slipped into his white shirt. "It has regular buttons."

Marley assisted, then handed him a small gift. "From Denny. Cuff links, for the tuxedo." Brant opened the box and stared, then brought the box closer for a better view. "*D* and *L?* Am I seeing this correctly?" He handed it back to Marley. Sure enough, each link had only one initial.

"Their initials," she said as she fitted them into his cuffs.

"Is it some kind of tradition?"

Marley shrugged. "I've never heard of it."

"I sure hope he didn't spend a lot for something I can only wear once." He started to chuckle again and was still chuckling when she helped him with the bowtie and cummerbund. "And you thought my family getting married in Vegas was weird."

As Marley turned to get Brant's jacket, she felt a gush of air on her back. "What did you do?" Annoyed, she wheeled and said, "Stop fooling around, Brant. Zip me up."

"What?"

"My zipper. Zip it. We've got no time to waste."

He threw his hands in the air, palms up. "I didn't touch you. Honest."

Marley reached around, searching for the zipper and found only a gaping hole.

"No!" She ran for the bathroom and slammed the door.

A few moments later, Brant knocked. "You all right?" He tried the door. She'd locked it.

"The zipper's broken."

"Maybe I can help." After she unlocked the door, he started to walk in but gripped the doorjamb instead.

Marley held the dress up in a vain attempt to provide cover for herself. "Stop ogling me. Lindy picked out the underwear."

"I like it." His face lit with humor that Marley didn't appreciate.

"You're drooling, Brant. This is a catastrophe. I can't wear this."

"Maybe we can sew it or pin it or something." They worked on the dress for several minutes, but nothing could repair the zipper. The hook at the top was the only thing that kept the dress from falling down. "We better get to the church. You can wear my jacket." Fortunately, it was long enough to cover the entire open area.

"I'm driving," he said when they reached the car. "You've got a lot on your plate right now, and you need to concentrate on what can be done to solve this." He started laughing again. "I'm sorry." He looked at her, unable to stop grinning. "Could this day possibly get any worse?"

AT THE CHURCH they found all the bridesmaids clustered around Chloe, who was in tears. "For the hundredth time, Lindy—I'm sorry. I didn't know I was pregnant when I got the dress." She spotted Brant and backed against the wall. "He can't come in here. My zipper broke."

"So did mine," Marley said. "They may all be defective. We'll have to change into other dresses."

"I don't believe this!" Lindy said. "You just don't like my choice of colors. Admit it—you don't want me to have anything different."

Lindy took in a deep breath and aimed her bombardment at Marley. "You figure this out, because I'm having my black-and-white wedding. No one is going home to get her bridesmaid's dress from another time." She whirled and headed for the cloakroom, slamming the door behind her. Marley had noticed the faintest pink on her train. So the cleaner had been unable to remove the stain entirely.

Marley went to grip her head in total frustration but stopped when she felt the stiff hairdo.

She turned to Brant. "You find the groomsmen and bring them here, but don't let Denny come. He can't see the bride. Also, ask the minister to come see us."

"You have a plan?"

"Two. Plan A we get the minister to delay the ceremony. If he can't, we use plan B."

"Which is?"

"Once the groomsmen are here, we'll borrow their jackets. That way we'll all look the same and won't have to worry about further zipper breakage." She hesitated. "Forget the groomsmen—just bring their jackets. And you better bring Denny's, too."

Brant gave her a thumbs-up and made for the small room by the altar, where the groom and groomsmen waited with the minister.

When Aunt Effie joined Marley, they clasped hands. "Brant said there's some problem? What's going on?" Marley explained and lifted the back of Brant's jacket to display the broken zipper. "I suppose we can sew you into it, but that will take time."

Brant had returned with the minister and an armload of jackets. Richard was right behind him with another armload. "There's a name on the slip of paper in the breast pocket in each so we'll know which belongs to who," Brant said and dropped the jackets on a chair.

Richard followed suit. "The bride having another temper tantrum?" he asked. "I could hear her screaming all the way down by the front of the church."

Marley bit her lip to avoid making any comment. The church, full of guests, must have heard Lindy, as well.

"I'll explain," Brant said, grasping Richard's shoulder and directing him toward the altar.

Facing the clergyman, Marley began, "Pastor Williams, we've got some wardrobe malfunctions." His brow furrowed, so she continued, "Several zippers broke, and we need to delay the ceremony." She glanced at Aunt Effie, who mouthed, "One hour."

"Can't," the minister said, backing away from Marley. "I have another wedding here in an hour, and then I have to attend a ceremony at another church. It's now or never. Get your act together and go with the jacket solution."

Marley rubbed her temples. "Plan B," she mumbled and looked at the pile of jackets on the chair. She picked up the only white one and regarded her sisters, who had gathered around her. "Each of you take a jacket. They're black like your dresses and will protect your backs. Roll up the sleeves like this." She demonstrated by tucking the end of Brant's sleeve underneath.

"Don't look for your husband's. Just find one that fits." The women ignored her and checked for their husbands' names on the slips of paper. Thanks to Al's height, Chloe's jacket reached her knees, totally covering her dress. "I'll get Lindy ready. Where's Dad?"

"Marley," a small voice said. She turned to see her cousin, Cheryl, the only one in the party who wasn't paired with a husband. "Do I take Richard's jacket? He didn't leave it."

Marley closed her eyes and tapped her forehead.

"I'll get it," Aunt Effie said. She disappeared into the church and returned almost immediately with the jacket. "Brant got it for us." She handed it to Cheryl. "Better check it for blood."

"What?"

"Just kidding." She turned to Marley. "Your mother's already seated, and your father was outside having a cigarette. If you don't need me anymore, I'll get him and go back to my seat."

Marley nodded and started for Lindy. She stopped and said to her sisters, who were quietly fixing their jackets, "Thanks. You've been wonderful. I really appreciate your help."

"Group hug," someone shouted. The five of them—Jen, Franny, Chloe, Marley and Morgan—piled together for hugs and giggles.

Marley knocked on the door. "Lindy, it's Marley." When Lindy opened the door, she made no effort to hide her displeasure. A storm raged across her face.

"I am not wearing that jacket," she said when Marley offered it to her. "If you all want to look like idiots, go ahead. Ruin my wedding, but you're not going to make me appear like some—some—some…" She caught her lip with her teeth and made a Herculean attempt not to cry.

"This will cover the stain on the back of your dress," Marley said, still holding the jacket out to Lindy.

"Where?" The bride circled herself, straining futilely to locate the discoloration. "Where is it?"

"On the train, which will detach once you're out of the church. Wear this. We'll all match and years from now, we'll all have a big laugh over it." The other bridesmaids had entered the tiny room, dressed alike in the jackets.

"Everyone's laughing now," Lindy said in a bleak voice.

"No, we're not," Chloe said. "And the men won't laugh, either. Brant said no one will even crack a smile. The Roman Warriors will make sure of it."

Every one of her sisters nodded approvingly.

CHAPTER EIGHTEEN

NO ONE LAUGHED. No one made eye contact. No one gave any prepared vows. And the people in the pews looked overjoyed as the bride and groom kissed in the shortest ceremony they had ever witnessed. Marley returned the cluster of calla lilies to the bride. Lindy and Dennis left the altar, and, to everyone's delight, but especially Marley's, began their walk down the aisle as a married couple, to applause and well wishes.

Now that the monumental undertaking had been achieved, Marley could relax. With a triumphant smile, she took Brant's hand and started to follow the newlyweds.

Richard walked right behind them with Cheryl on his arm. "Was I that big of a threat you had to hire an actor to play your fiancé?" Richard asked.

Marley and Brant both stopped and turned. "This whole engagement thing is an act.

Just like the drunk scene. Denny told me all about it."

Marley felt the tension build in Brant's hand, possibly because her own grip refused to let the blood flow. She grabbed his other arm to keep him as well as herself from doing anything unforgivable at the altar. "Ignore him," she whispered. But he didn't. Brant shook his arms free and whirled to confront Richard, creating a bottleneck at the gate of the wooden fence enclosing the altar.

"You want to take this outside?" Brant said in a quiet voice.

"Why? So you can sing and dance around me?"

"Whatever it takes."

"Stop this right now," Marley ordered, holding out her arms to keep the two men separated. "Don't you dare spoil this wedding."

"There a problem, sis?" All six feet and five inches of Al came between the men. He faced Richard. "We've got five Roman Warriors here who say this wedding carries on as planned." After a short pause, he added, "Got that?" He winked at Marley, and would have high-fived Brant if she hadn't grabbed Brant's hand and pulled him down the aisle.

Marley could barely contain her fury. She

closed her eyes and let the flow of people carry her to the reception line. Standing by the bride, she greeted friends, relatives and strangers with the same fixed smile, the same lines repeating in her head until everyone had left the church: *They know. Everyone knows the engagement is fake.*

"Calling Marley," Brant said, waving a hand in front of her face. "I see you in there."

Forcing herself to focus, Marley drew in a deep breath and looked around. They were the only two left in the church vestibule.

"How did Richard find out the engagement is fake?" Her voice was raspy.

"Probably nothing more than a hopeful assumption on his part. You tell me to ignore any of his attitudes that upset me. How about you ignoring remarks from him that upset you."

"I can't," she said through a tight jaw, gazing at the floor.

"Welcome to my world."

She looked back at Brant and gripped his arm. "Who told Richard you're an actor?"

"You ever watch TV or go to the movies?" Brant asked and removed her hand from his arm, entwining his fingers with hers. "I told you I've done pictures and commercials. Even your nephew recognized my voice. My pro-

fession wasn't anything you could keep secret." When she didn't respond, he continued,
"I didn't have to tell anyone. All your sisters
knew. They mentioned it when I danced with
them last night. So did your grandfather."

Unable to deal with this latest calamity, she
pulled her hand free, went back into the church
and sat in an empty pew. "And not one had a
problem with it," Brant said as he sat down beside her. "You planning to talk to me or should
I go and beat the crap out of your old boyfriend?"

Marley had begun pounding his chest, until
he encircled her in an embrace and held her
tight. "Did you know I've been inducted into
the Roman Warriors, that distinct club for
all the husbands of your sisters?" While he
brushed her face with his fingers, he continued, "We meet monthly, dance around huge
bonfires in the nude and wrestle alligators. Or
was it crocodiles? Which ones are carnivo-
rous?"

"Oh, Brant, stop talking. There are no alligators or crocodiles in Pennsylvania. I feel
like such an idiot," she said, edging away from
him. "This whole engagement has been a farce
from the beginning." She looked up in an attempt to read his face. "And, no, I rarely watch

TV, certainly not the commercials. The only actors I'm familiar with or liked died decades ago."

Marley yanked off her engagement ring. "This gets returned along with the other one." Prepared that Brant might object, she said, "It has nothing to do with money. I don't want something that will remind me of this engagement. I'd never have even considered it if Dede hadn't egged me on. I don't even like diamonds. They're too...too impersonal and cold."

Brant reached into his pants pocket and pulled out the box containing the expensive ring. "So I can never give you this?"

Marley stood and Brant did, as well. They moved out into the aisle. "No." She restrained his arms to keep him from pulling her back into an embrace. "Thank you for being my friend—"

"Is that all I've been?"

Marley closed her eyes and bit down hard on her lower lip. She was not going to cry, nor would she cling to him for support. "I've got to face my family, Brant. Make amends for being so foolish."

"Let me—"

"No. Please."

"Is this some kind of kiss-off because—"

"Brant, I—"

He placed his hand over her mouth. "It's my turn. You've had your say. Now I have mine." He drew in a deep breath. "I love you, Marley Roman. I have since the first day I saw you."

"Stop telling me that. Love at first sight never happens."

He pushed her back into the pew and sat down next to her.

"It does. It certainly did for me." He leaned closer and lowered his voice. "I'd been away for months, doing a picture down in Australia. My taxi pulled up behind yours at my condo, and I saw this gorgeous redhead get out of the cab in front of mine. You headed for the door obviously annoyed with the cabbie. I could hear you sputtering under your breath. Not so he could hear. I burst out laughing and tried to catch up with you. By the time I got inside with all my luggage, you were gone. I had no idea you had moved into the condo next to mine."

He shook his head to indicate she shouldn't interrupt. "Days later, when I finally met you in the hallway, I couldn't believe my luck. I decided right then and there, I wanted to get to know you. That you avoided me and turned me down when I did ask you out intrigued me even more."

Marley tried not to laugh and gazed in the other direction. Brant caressed her chin and forced her to look at him.

"I liked your spunk. And I just knew, in here." He tapped his chest. "I knew you were the one for me."

"You realize how insane that sounds?"

He closed his eyes. "Marley, let me finish." He waited a moment then began again. "My great-grandfather came from England and settled in Arizona. On his way crossing the country he met his wife, a Mexican beauty he knew for one day before he proposed. They were married for nearly seventy years. My grandfather knew his bride three days, and my father took all of two weeks. Instantaneous recognition of true love is in our genes. I knew one day I'd find—"

"Didn't you find her when you were in college?"

Brant stopped and stared straight ahead. "Janise had leukemia when I met her. I loved her and wanted to make a life with her. Even though she went through several remissions, I understood our chances weren't good." He looked back at Marley. "I don't give up on people I care about." He gripped her hands. "I never thought I'd find anyone again until I met you. I love everything about you, even your cotton-candy hairdo."

"Brant, I—"

"Did I say I was through?" He paused and waited a moment before continuing. "I acknowledge we're different. You may need a while before you feel the same about me, and I won't rush you. But each minute I'm with you, I see so many things we have in common. We have to give us a chance."

"Here they are," Al said as he entered the church. Brant and Marley turned with blank expressions to find out who had intruded. "The bride's waiting for pictures, and Aunt Effie has some special strong thread to sew you into your dress." He reached past Brant and grabbed her hand. "You two can go back to kissing after the pictures are taken."

As they got up to follow Al, Brant whispered near her ear, "As much as I admire your spunk, I'm not letting you face this alone."

"Al, give us a minute, please," Marley said; then she faced Brant as Al continued out the door. "I'm okay with this. Honest. I'll tell everyone the truth. The engagement was fake because—"

"Listen, Marley. It was fake until I asked you to marry me."

"But I haven't said yes to your proposal, and I'm not about to create even more problems that I'll have to answer to later. Right now we're friends, Brant, and that's all."

Brant's forehead puckered in a frown. He held up his hand, reached in his pants pocket and lifted out his vibrating cell phone. He glanced at it before placing the phone by his ear. "Hi, Carla." When Marley tried to get past him, he hooked her arm. "Right. Send me a text message. I want to show it to my girlfriend." He paused. "Yeah, right, I said girlfriend. She hasn't said yes yet." He snapped off his phone. "That was my manager."

"You told her about me?"

"We have no secrets. She's set up the recording studio for the book I have to read. The publisher wants the book on tape when the mystery hits the bookstores. I'll have to leave sometime after the wedding reception to get started."

"Maybe you should go now. Get a head start."

"No. You're not getting rid of me. I'm your backup."

Marley considered this. She'd always handled everything herself. Having backup gave her mixed feelings she couldn't quite describe.

The church door opened, and Al came back in, more than a little annoyed. "Hey, you two. We want to get this over with before any more zippers pop."

"Another minute, Al, please." Marley clasped Brant's arm. "If you stay, you don't do anything stupid."

"Like?"

"Like asking me to marry you in front of everyone."

"Listen, girlfriend, I'm not into public humiliation. I'm only going to protect you from any lynching or egg throwing or whatever your family does when someone refuses to get married."

"I'm not refus—"

"Please, Marley. Now!" Al said, then led her out.

"HOLD STILL," AUNT EFFIE told Marley. "I had no problem sewing Chloe's dress, but she didn't wiggle all over the place. I'm not doing any precautionary work on the other girls, but I'll stand by in case another dress splits."

Marley held on to the counter in the small

cloakroom to steady herself. "Did you know Brant was an actor when you met him?"

"Of course. I thought I recognized him when you showed me his picture on your phone. I had the hots for him when he was on a program I watch, one of those police things." She pushed her blue-gray hair away from her forehead. "Still do. And he's even better looking and nicer in person. Plus he can dance. Made me feel I was in my fifties again."

"I never even guessed he was successful," Marley said. "In fact, I thought he was barely making a living. You should see the clothes he wears, the rags. Most of the time he looks like someone living on the street."

"Obviously, clothes don't make the man." Effie snipped the thread and checked out her work. "There. That should hold. You'll have to be cut out of it."

Marley thanked her aunt and headed toward the group assembled for photos. *Backup,* she thought. Someone standing beside her, backing her, protecting her. A warm glow began to spread through her. She liked the idea. She liked that it came from Brant.

All the men now wore their jackets, including Dennis. Lindy looked beautiful in her white satin gown trimmed in lace, and the train, positioned on the side, was spot-free, at least from the front.

Some woman Marley had never seen before organized everyone. "You here, and you here," she said, making the mistake of putting Brant and Richard next to each other. However, the Roman Warriors intervened, preventing any problems, and they all stood stiffly at attention. Marley couldn't muster a smile, nor could she take her eyes off the two men, who glared at each other through the entire process.

When they were finally through, Marley walked over to speak with Richard privately, only to have Brant quickly appear at her side. She held up her hands against his chest and said, "Give me a moment, please."

Brant nodded and backed away.

"Richard, you said a few things in the church that were true and some that weren't." She paused. "You were right about the engagement. It's a lie."

Richard socked the air with his fist and mumbled, "I knew it."

Marley heard movement behind her and fanned her hands, motioning Brant to stay away. "But it had nothing to do with you. I did it for me, so all my relatives would leave me alone and not bug me about my turn. I had no idea you were Denny's brother or that you'd be here." She pivoted to motion Brant over to join her, only to find him right beside her. "This business between the two of you," she said, pointing a finger at Brant and Richard, "has to stop."

"So, you're not engaged?" Richard eyed Brant, jutting out his chin. "You can back off now. Marley and I have a lot of catching up to do."

"I don't think so."

"Stop. Stop this now." Marley put her hands up to grip her hair and put them down again after touching the hairspray. "I can't stand this fighting."

Brant stretched out his hand toward Richard. "We better stop before she destroys that hairdo." He looked as though he was choking back amusement.

Richard hesitated a moment before complying.

"See, Marley," Brant said. "We're all 'friends.'" He placed quotations marks in the air after releasing Richard's grip. She stared at Brant, mystified by the strange feeling of loss that clutched her heart. Their engagement really was over, the fake one at least.

The picture taking, including some videos,

now complete, the bride and groom piled into a limo and headed for the reception. Marley managed to get there, as well, going along with the flow, enjoying none of it. Brant remained quiet, texting on his phone during the ride.

At the reception, the bride sat at the head table next to the groom; the rest of the wedding party sat on either side of them. For some reason, Lindy insisted Brant sit next to her, which put Marley next to Dennis at the long table. When Richard took a seat beside her, she didn't bother to look his way.

"Despite all the problems, they made it," Richard said in an effort to draw her into conversation. "So you and…Brant, is it?…are what?"

"We're friends. I thought he made that clear."

"I guess you'd have to be, pulling off a fake engagement and getting everyone to believe it was true. But it's over now, right?"

Marley glanced Richard's way and saw hope. Having had no further opportunity to talk with Brant, she had no idea exactly where they stood. Was it over? She knew then with all her heart she wanted Brant, but she had no idea how to go about having him. What could she tell Richard? Instead of answering, she focused on the food in front of her.

The salad was limp, the chicken overcooked and the dessert a sticky-sweet concoction she didn't like. Marley left most of it on her plate. She'd hear later from her mother about the horrible food, and how her mother could have done better and should have been allowed to.

Richard invited her to dance. Marley shook her head. The thought of dancing made her feel sick. Maybe it was that dessert.

Her cousin Cheryl leaned over past Richard and asked something about a Tupperware order. What order? Her sisters asked her opinion on several matters, and Marley couldn't come up with a comment. She felt as though a plug had been pulled, allowing all the life to drain out of her. And then Brant got up to toast the bride.

To her dismay, Richard drew closer. "Just because he's an actor, he thinks he can…" Richard continued to mumble about Brant's ineptitude as the best man throughout Brant's speech, so she heard none of it. She turned to tell Richard to be quiet, and her lips nearly brushed his cheek. When had he gotten *that* close?

Heat burned her face, and she muttered an

apology. She saw Brant lift his glass in a toast, his eyes on her. Embarrassed, she stood and went out a side door into the garden, only to have Richard follow right behind her. When he put an arm around her, she moved out of his grasp.

Richard sighed and said, "Guess the playing field isn't level, after all."

"It never was. I'm sorry, Richard. You're a nice guy—"

"Sure. But Brant's nicer." He leaned against the brick wall, crossing his arms over his chest. "You know," he said, "actors are more prone to casual sex than your average Joe." He pushed away from the wall. "Seems you fell for someone like your father after all."

"Marley." She pivoted to find Brant walking toward her. "Your mother is about to make an announcement. She asked me to get you."

"Oh, no. She's going to tell everyone she and my dad are getting married again." Marley clutched her stomach. "I'm going to be sick." She deposited her undigested meal on the dirt next to the gravel path. To add to her humiliation, both men stayed on either side of her, each holding a shoulder.

"She hates her father," Richard said.

"I got that," Brant replied. "Can't say I blame her."

Marley backed away from them both and ran to the ladies' room. After rinsing her mouth and patting her face with cold water, she went into one of the stalls, locked the door and sat on the toilet, her feet against a wall. She was still sitting there when a woman entered, calling her name. Marley hugged her knees. The woman left. Marley focused on the fingers of her left hand and pretended to touch her guitar strings, making various chords. She gave up when it provided little relief.

A short time later she heard Brant's voice. "Someone saw you walk in, Marley, and there's no other way out."

She didn't answer. She heard stall doors being pushed in until his lizard boots stopped in front of her door. "Did I say something deplorable during the toast? You ran out—"

"I didn't even hear it. Richard kept talking right by my ear, and I started to feel sick."

"Are you coming out of there? I'm feeling silly talking to this door."

Marley dropped her feet to the floor and opened the door.

"If you want, I'll cancel my flight. The job can wait till tomorrow."

"Don't do that. I've already ruined enough things." She walked past him to the sink and leaned on the marble top. "I don't want that on my conscience, too." She caught her reflection in the mirror and shuddered.

"Al's driving me to the airport." Brant approached her and didn't stop when she waved him off through the mirror. "I'll leave the tux and rings at the motel."

She looked up at him. "What should we do about the guitars?"

"Keep them. Give them to your family. The guitars don't have cases, so you can't take them on the plane."

She stared at him, confused. "Don't they have to go back? You borrowed them, right?"

"No." He came up behind her and wrapped his arms around her while continuing to talk to her mirror image. "I bought them outright. Twelve hundred dollars."

Her eyes bulged, and she faced him. "You spent…?" Her mouth opened but she couldn't form any words. Finally, she said, "They aren't worth that."

"They're worth every penny. They gave me the opportunity to play with you." He sighed and brushed a kiss against her ear. "The best night of my life." He pulled her closer. "I won't kiss you," he said. "I lost my meal, too, and my mouth tastes raw."

"No," she gasped. A shudder ripped through her. "Not food poisoning on top of everything else?" She buried her face in the ruffles on his shirt.

"That certainly would make this the wedding from hell," Brant said, chuckling. "But I doubt it. We're both just a little on edge. And I've never been able to hold anything down when someone barfs right next to me." He pulled her closer. "Got some on Richard's shoe, too, which completely made my day."

Marley started to cry and laugh at the same time. "It's not fun...funny. It's horrible."

They held each other for several minutes until Al stormed into the ladies' room. "Will you two cut it out? I've got to get him to the airport."

CHAPTER NINETEEN

ONCE THE RECEPTION was over, Marley could have gone back to her parents' home to continue with the party, but she chose not to. Brant wouldn't be there. And Richard probably would. Instead, she drove to her motel.

Inside her room, she found Brant's tux hung neatly in the open closet. Both engagement rings sat on the pillow, wrapped in a sheet of paper.

"I agree about the rings," the note read. "You deserve better than diamonds. We never exchanged numbers. Here's my cell." A string of numbers followed. "Call me so I'll have yours. Don't know how often I'll be able to talk once I'm involved with the project. Wish I had the chance to pull that thread on your zipper. I'll do it in my dreams. All my love, Brant." Marley sat on the chair, a lump of depression, as she read and reread the note.

She had to get out of her dress. Effie had sewn it way too tight, and it was beginning

to cut off her circulation. She couldn't reach
the back. Every attempt to pull the formfitting
garment around so she could reach the zipper
ended in frustration. Marley fell on the bed exhausted and lay on her stomach as she tried to
focus on a solution to her problem.

She missed Brant. Ached for him. How
could he mean this much to her in such a short
time? She took the note he'd left and typed in
his number on her phone. The call went directly to voice mail. Maybe he was already
on the plane and had turned off his cell. She
didn't leave a message. What could she say?
*I miss you. I love you. Come back and get me
out of this dress.*

Marley pounded the bedspread in agony.
She wanted out of this stupid dress so she
could shower, cool down and get all the gunk
from her hair.

Someone knocked on the door.

Marley did a push-up on the bedspread,
waited, still supporting herself with her arms
and looked at the doorway that separated the
two rooms. Who could that be? She maneuvered to the side of the bed and placed her bare
feet on the rug. The pounding continued as she
headed for the door.

"Marley, you in there?"

"Richard? What are you doing here?" she said as she opened the door.

Richard had changed into a blue golf shirt and a pair of tan pants. "Now that Brant took off, I'm back to being the best man."

"Best man? Why?" Marley shook her head. "The wedding's over."

"Right, but not the final cleanup. I came for the tux. Have to return it tomorrow. Everyone else has changed into casual clothes, and they're planning a barbecue at your parents' place."

Marley stepped aside so he could come into the room. "Really? Tomorrow's Sunday. I thought—"

"With so many outfits to collect, I figured I'd get a jump on it. Why wait till the last minute?" He glanced at the open closet and went toward it. "How's the dress situation working? You need any help?" he asked as he took the hangers off the rod.

Marley considered for a moment before saying, "No, I'm fine."

He held the tux over one arm and walked over to her. "You sure? I hear your sister had a hard time getting hers off. Your aunt did such a good job sewing her in she had to be cut out of the dress." Richard dropped the tux on the bed and reached into his pocket. "I brought some scissors."

He took out a pair of tiny nail-clipping shears. "Let's get you out of that dress and into something more comfortable. Your sisters changed already, and they asked me to bring you back to the party."

Marley hesitated. She really wanted a shower before going anywhere, and she *hadn't* been able to get out of the dress herself. "Okay," she said, turning so that her back was to Richard. "Just cut the thread in a few places so I can take the dress off."

She felt the metal touch her skin in several different spots, each time increasing her sense of freedom. "That's enough," she said, moving from Richard's reach and grasping the back of her dress. "I'll handle it from here."

And then Marley turned—to find Brant standing in the doorway.

"I left my cell in the tux." Brant, wearing the same clothes he'd arrived in three days ago, walked over to the bed and removed the phone from his jacket pocket. He held it up and showed everyone, including Al, who stood by the door.

"Come on. You got it," Al said. "Let's go."

Brant placed the phone in his pocket and

walked purposely over to Marley. "Call me so I can have your number." Wrapping his arm around her shoulders, he pulled her against him so that they both faced Richard. With one hand, Marley continued to hold on to the back of her dress, but she wrapped the other around Brant's waist.

"This is my woman, and I want you out of here." Leaning closer to Marley, he added, in a softer voice, "Okay if I say 'woman' instead of girlfriend? It sounds so much more Roman Warrior." Brant looked back at Richard. "Have I made myself clear, or do I have to sing and dance around you in the parking lot?"

Ignoring him, Richard said, "You coming with me to the barbecue?"

Marley was thankful Brant didn't answer for her. At least he wasn't taking his "woman" thing beyond what she could tolerate. "No," she said. "If I decide to go, I'll go alone."

"Al," Brant said, "would you get him out of here so I can say goodbye properly?"

"Okay, but make it snappy." Al guided Richard by the elbow, and they did an awkward two-step through the doorway. Over his shoulder, Al said, "You can do all your talking on the phone."

"I don't want to talk." Brant drew her into

his arms. "I want to kiss her," he said, "so she'll never be able to forget me." And he did.

When they separated, she gazed up at him, still breathless from the kiss. "I miss you already," she whispered.

He smiled down at her. "Call me." As he walked over to the door, Brant blew her a kiss and mouthed, "I love you."

He was out the door and rushing to catch Al's truck when Marley said, "I love you, too."

IT TOOK MARLEY MORE than two hours to get herself back to what she considered normal. Thanks to the cut thread, the dress had come off with ease and now lay in a heap on the bathroom floor. But her hair required several washings to remove all the gunk the hairdresser had sprayed over it. Finally, dressed in yellow pants and a black T-shirt, Marley was ready to face her family.

She lifted the two guitars with annoyance. How could Brant spend so much? Although both instruments had good tone, the rosette around the sound hole on one had begun to deteriorate, and the wood by the bridge on the other had started to warp.

Marley couldn't remember a time when she wasn't conscious of costs; she'd never spent on a whim. *It's his money,* she reminded herself. *Still, how could he throw it away like that?*

Well, she'd leave the guitars with her grandfather after she played for him. Might as well have as much enjoyment out of them as possible.

If Richard had come to the party, he'd already left, because, thankfully, Marley didn't see him anywhere as she walked around to the back of the house.

"You brought guitars," Poppy said joyously when he greeted her. Suddenly the expense didn't seem that great. He found a folding chair without arms and pulled several other chairs around for the audience that gathered. She handed Poppy the guitar with the nylon strings and began tuning the one with steel. "I'll play as long as Arthur doesn't cripple my hands." He began tuning the guitar.

They played several tunes until requests were tossed at her. "Hey, Marley, how about that Mexican song, you know, the one you and Brant played." Someone else said, "Yeah, the wedding song."

"La Bamba," she noted under her breath. The song was fast and difficult and sounded so much better with a band backing her. *And, of course, Brant singing.* She sighed and hesitantly started the song. Finishing with a flourish, Marley smiled at her family, who clapped, several offering a standing ovation.

She remembered her discussion with Brant. When would they be together again so they could continue to share their passion for music?

"I'm hungry," Marley said as she got up, took the other guitar from Poppy and placed both against the wall. "Let's eat and we can play again later."

"Don't think I can join you." Poppy kneaded his gnarled hands. "Sure hope you don't get this. It sucks an awful lot of joy out of life." He put an arm around her shoulders and directed her to the picnic table.

Her mother had prepared a spread for everyone to enjoy. Her exceptional pork ribs in a flavorful sauce, along with several salads, baked beans and other specialties overflowed on one table. The grandchildren devoured hot dogs and hamburgers on another table.

Marley made a plate for herself and joined her sisters under a string of lanterns in the backyard, where the smell of roasted corn on the cob permeated the air. She enjoyed the food and the company, finally able to relax without tension from the wedding or her dealings with Richard.

Poppy sat down next to her. "I really liked last night's concert with you and your young man." He nodded several times. "He sure has several talents. He's an actor, not a rancher?" He looked around. "I don't see him here. Where'd he take off to?"

"He has work in New York recording a book." Marley sighed. "It might be a while before I see him again."

Poppy chucked her chin. "Don't you worry that pretty little head. He's a keeper." He got up and went back into the house, taking both guitars with him.

People mingled, and Chloe patted an empty folding chair beside her and invited Marley to join her.

"Feeling better?" Marley asked. For the first time she realized that one day she could be pregnant, too. The possibility made her smile broaden with expectation.

"Yes. I finally feel human."

"Did Al get Brant safely to the airport?"

Chloe nodded. "I'm afraid all your secrets are out. Brant asked a million questions about you, and Al—"

"Did I hear my name mentioned?" Al edged an empty chair closer to them and joined the circle. "How long have you two known each other?" he asked Marley. "Brant was clueless."

"What did you tell him?"

"That you and I were lovers and—"

Marley whacked him in the arm and nearly upset his plate of food. Al chortled. "I told him how you and I dated in high school. But," Al said, leaning closer to Chloe, "your sister had a thing for me, so I dropped the redheaded beauty for this blonde bombshell and married her." He gave Chloe a quick kiss then picked up his roasted corn.

Marley glanced up as her mother approached, followed closely by her father. "You missed my little speech," Nora said, reaching back to take Red's hand. "We're getting married."

"I couldn't stay because I was sick. Lost that entire meal."

"Good. Then when you have your wedding, you'll let me do the catering." Nora smiled, obviously forgiving Marley for being absent during the announcement. It dawned on Marley that her mother, for that matter all her relatives, had no clue that she was no longer engaged. Just as well, since Marley had decided to tell Brant, yes, she would marry him, the next time he mentioned marriage. "Maybe we could make it a double," Nora said.

Marley grabbed her stomach, feeling the roasted corn and spicy spareribs begin to rise. She sat back in her chair and forced herself to swallow the bile. "No, Mom, Brant and I have other plans. We intend to elope—to Las Vegas."

"Vegas! That sounds like fun," Red said, putting an arm around Nora's shoulder and pulling her close. "Maybe we should do that, darling. What do you think?"

Marley stood quickly, upsetting the chair, and headed for some privacy behind the garage, where she lost her second meal of the day.

THE MONDAY AFTER Marley arrived in Phoenix, she returned to her job—following a quick visit to her hairdresser. Her hair now brushed her shoulders in a state of relaxed curl, the tightness and frizziness she had endured in Pennsylvania gone. Dressed in a cool summer dress of pale green, she met Dede for supper.

"Tell me, tell me, tell me," Dede said as Marley joined her in the Arizona Center. Dede wore her black hair in a French braid intertwined with red ribbons that matched her red dress. "And don't you dare leave anything out." She inspected Marley's hand. "Where's your ring?"

"I returned it during lunch." Marley held up her hand to silence Dede and motioned to the waiter. "I'd like a virgin Mary, please."

"Since when are you off the sauce?" Dede glanced at the wine in her glass before taking a sip.

"The last week was an eye-opener. I will never risk getting even a bit tipsy. It's moderation from now on."

"So the store took back your fake ring?"

"No, I still have that tucked in the back of my jewelry box. I returned the five-thousand-dollar one Brant put on his credit card."

Dede reached across the table and grasped Marley's hands. "He bought you a five-thousand-dollar ring?" After Marley explained about the mix-up, Dede said, "Brant wanted you to keep the *five-thousand-dollar ring,* and you refused! Are you insane?"

"Oh, Dede, there's so much more. I'm absolutely crazy about him and—"

"This is the same guy you wanted nothing, I repeat nothing, to do with when we made up that engagement. What was it, ten days ago?"

Marley explained briefly, hitting only the

highlights. "Because he's an actor, I couldn't take him seriously at first. But…" Marley smiled and caught her upper lip between her teeth. "He's wonderful. He wants to marry me. And I plan to marry him."

"Whoa." Dede held up a hand before reaching for her black cloth purse. She removed an iPad and turned it on. "That's right. He said he was an actor. What's his full name?"

Marley's brow furrowed. "Don't do that. Brant told me not to look him up on the internet."

"What's he hiding? Come on. Full name. Brant…?"

With a deep sigh, Marley said, "Brant Westfield." She sat back, looking at the virgin Mary she had ordered and considered ordering some vodka to add to it.

"Mes Dios!" Dede shouted and positioned the iPad so that Marley could see. "Half a million hits. Did you know he's been acting on some pretty popular TV shows? Dramas and late night talk shows?"

Marley covered the iPad with her napkin. "Don't say another word, Dede. No more." She used a shooing motion to indicate she wanted the iPad put away.

Marley and Dede placed their order before

Marley continued, "I haven't told you everything that happened with Richard Brewster." After she explained about Richard and recounted the events at the wedding, Dede appeared intrigued.

"So this gorgeous guy you turned down is available? How about introducing us?"

Marley laughed. "Sure. Next time I see him, I'll mention you want to meet him." After a long pause, Marley added, "My father was there."

"Right. How did that go?"

Marley sighed. "My parents are getting married again."

Dede seemed unsure how to respond. Finally, she said, "How are you handling it? I know you've had issues with him."

"Not well." Their food arrived and Marley dived into her Cobb salad. "I just don't want my mother hurt again."

By the time they left the restaurant, the evening had turned cool. Lightning flashed in the distance, and they hoped to get home before the summer monsoon drenched them both. Boarding the light-rail, Dede said, "You and Mr. Wonderful keeping in touch?"

"As much as possible. He has to concentrate on the book he's recording."

"I want more details, girlfriend. Call me tomorrow."

Marley was running through raindrops when her cell phone rang. She ducked under the awning at her condo building to take the call. "Let me phone you back," she said to Brant. "It's lightning here." Minutes later she called him from her condo.

"Hi, how's your work going?"

"I finished reading the book, excellent by the way, and hope to start recording once I go over what needs to be done with the producer tomorrow. And the author, my friend from college, is in town. We plan to get together." He paused. "You got home safely?"

"Yes. Al drove me to the airport. I understand you had quite a talk with him when he took you there."

"Oh, yes. One of your many beaus." Brant paused. "I have a question for you."

"What?"

"You're the oldest, right? And Chloe is next? What's the age difference between you two?"

"Five years."

"Hmm. I've been doing the math. If you and he were seventeen and eighteen in high school—"

Marley burst out laughing. "Chloe was thirteen and Al was eighteen. She had crushes on every guy I ever dated."

"Al said she chased after him. Please erase these images that have plagued me since he told me that—Al with this girl barely into puberty."

"Nothing happened between them at that time, although my sister was persistent. He joined the army, probably to get away from her. Chloe started writing to him. She was seventeen when they finally began dating, and they were married the moment she turned eighteen. Is that better?"

"Yes. Thank you. Now the other subject that's haunted me. Any more run-ins with Richard?"

"No. Didn't see him again. But, Dede, you remember her?"

"Of course. The woman who got the ball rolling."

"She wants to meet him."

Brant burst out laughing. "Fine, as long he's nowhere near you."

"I had supper with her tonight and…"

"And?"

"She went on the internet and looked you up." Marley heard a deep sigh. "I wouldn't let her tell me what was there. I'd rather you tell me next time—"

"Marley, speak to my sisters. I'll contact Elaina. She comes to Phoenix on a regular basis, and she can tell you anything you want to know. A lot of what's out there is horse manure, and she can fill you in on what's real and what's not." They spoke a little longer before Brant said, "I better go. It's really late here and I'm exhausted. I love you, woman. Dream of me tonight."

CHAPTER TWENTY

PHONE CALLS BETWEEN Marley and Brant were irregular. She could tell he was stressed, and, not wanting to add to it, she kept her own tensions under wrap. And there were many, all of them involving her mother and her parents' forthcoming marriage.

"We've decided on doing it quickly and settled on the second Saturday in August," Nora said when she called. "I want all my girls in the wedding, with you as my maid of honor. Everyone can pick their favorite dress from past weddings." Her mother actually sounded giddy when she added, "Of course, I won't wear white. But I thought maybe cream. What do you think?"

When had Marley become her mother's best friend? Nora asked for advice on who to invite, what menu to plan and how to word the invitation. "We don't want gifts, but an RSVP would be nice, don't you think? Your father contacted Pastor Williams, so the church service is arranged."

Marley spent the days in a funk. When her phone rang, she hesitated to answer it, attempting to avoid calls from her family. But what if Brant called? Why couldn't she make her family understand her parents' wedding was not something she wanted to participate in? She didn't want to know the details or be part of it, yet when she tried to distance herself, her mother said, "But, Marley. You're so good at this. And I really need some help." Each time Marley received one of the calls, she felt sick. Not to the point of losing her lunch, but her unease rankled her nerves. She spent hours strumming her guitar just to calm herself.

Marley took care of what she could long distance, giving advice and using the internet and her phone. Ever the planner, the handler of all family dilemmas, she longed for someone else to take on the responsibilities. At least this would be the last time she'd have to make wedding arrangements for anyone in her family. Her own wedding…

Marley didn't pursue the thought. Nothing in Brant's phone calls or brief text messages indicated he still wanted to marry her. And even those calls had dried up during the past week. She longed to hear his voice, but instead had to settle for short text messages.

ONE EVENING, THE A STRING on Marley's guitar broke. She was restringing it when the door-bell rang. Not the intercom bell in the lobby, but the bell in her hallway. Who could that be after ten o'clock? she wondered. Although she had become friendly with several people in the building, they rarely visited so late at night. Marley checked the peephole. All she saw was black hair.

"Who is it?" she asked.

A woman tossed long black hair away from her face. "Elaina. Brant's sister."

When Marley opened the door, Elaina said, "Sorry it's so late, but I just got out from the theater, and I'll be leaving early tomorrow. Brant asked me—"

"Come in," Marley said, stepping aside so Elaina could enter her living room.

Elaina walked in, circled the room slowly and faced Marley with a grin that resembled Brant's. "I love it!" she said. She threw open her arms and wrapped them around Marley.

"What?" Marley said, when she could step away from the embrace. "What do you love?" Marley looked around at the furniture she'd purchased after hours of plundering used furniture stores. Most of it had served several apartments during her twelve years in Phoenix until she could afford to buy the condo. The fine art on the walls were framed children's drawings done by her nieces and nephews. The room had a comfortable rural quality that she enjoyed, right down to the knitting basket by the rocking chair. Some might consider her interior decorating eclectic, especially where she mixed Native American baskets with heirloom quilts, but Marley considered the place home.

Elaina grabbed her hand and pulled Marley toward the hall. "Come with me. You've got to see Brant's place." Marley followed her into the hall and waited while Elaina unlocked Brant's door. After opening it, Elaina stood aside and gestured toward the huge room. It had to be three times the size of Marley's living room. Nothing decorated the walls. Nor were there any curtains or blinds on the windows. A guitar and a banjo stood next to a grand piano, and an assortment of black instrument cases sat on the floor. Except for the piano bench, several folding chairs and a card table, the white-walled room lacked furniture and any kind of personal touch.

"On to his bedroom," Elaina said, waving a hand toward another room. Besides a single bed, neatly made, the room had two walls lined with bookcases Marley had seen at IKEA, something she'd considered investing in herself. Although Brant's had a decent supply of books, most of the shelves contained CDs and DVDs. Nowhere did Marley see any electronic gizmos that might make any of these items workable.

With a flourish, Elaina pushed open a set of double doors. There in a walk-in closet, nearly the size of Marley's bedroom, sat a desk, computer and file cabinets. The wall on the right formed the backdrop for a lot of electronic equipment; the center wall behind the desk was covered by a huge TV screen; and a very small area on the left wall had a built-in dresser as well as a door to a bathroom. A selection of clothes and garment bags filled the only spot that still remained a closet. At least Brant did have some clothes besides the Goodwill collection she'd seen him in.

"There are two other bedrooms, with furniture my sisters and I provided so we'd have a place to sleep when we visit. Don't get me wrong. We love him, and he's generous to a fault, but not one of us can get him to make this place a home."

Marley recalled his remark about five mothers but didn't comment. "How long has Brant lived here?"

"Over two years. And you moved in less than four months ago. I know because my family was considering buying it before you did. And look what you've done in that time. It's wonderful. Look what Brant's done with this place." Elaine gestured at the living room. "Nothing."

What should she say? Marley remembered Brant's concern about his father's request to return to the ranch. Had that somehow influenced Brant to limit what he did in the condo?

"Would you like some tea, a drink maybe? At my place," Marley said.

"Iced tea would be lovely." Elaina started for the door. "Brant said I should answer any questions you might have." She stopped. "And I will. Welcome to the family, Marley. We're all delighted he found you."

They talked for nearly an hour at the booth-style table Marley had in her kitchen. "It's unbelievable how much misinformation gets put on the internet," Elaina said after sipping her tea. "Once it's out there, that's it, unless the person who created the information changes it." She put her glass on the table. "I checked it today, and you're already listed as Brant's latest girlfriend, along with pictures of him and you at the wedding. There's even a segment on YouTube of the two of you dancing."

Marley's jaw dropped. "How is that possible? *I* haven't even seen the pictures of the wedding."

"Someone figured they could make a buck." Elaina placed her hand on Marley's. "And if you see anything at the grocery store—you know, at the checkout line where they have the magazines—ignore it." Elaina's face lit up. "Calla lilies, really? Aren't they for funerals?"

MARLEY DIDN'T CALL Brant, knowing he would only have time to speak on his own schedule. She did text him at least once a day. She'd contacted him after Elaina had showed her his condo, but he didn't reply. One night when he called, she couldn't contain her curiosity. "So who are you today? The Englishman or the Texan?"

In his British accent, Brant said, "Thanks for asking, my darling. I've been Baron Rochester, and I think my tongue is about to fall off." The last part of the remark lost all sign of an accent. "Sometimes, it's really hard remembering what voice to use for which character."

"I'd love to hear them all."

"Really? After all the times you told me to stop talking with different voices."

"Back then, I considered the different accents annoyances coming from an overconfident actor with an overinflated ego. Now I know they have a purpose."

"And the actor?"

"The actor is charming." *And sweet and lovable. And I so miss him.*

"Elaina mentioned she'd shown you my condo. As my biggest critic, I'm sure she listed all my shortcomings. It didn't seem to scare you off, though." He paused. "She liked you, by the way. Thought you'd be a good influence."

"I liked her, too."

"Did she leave the key?"

"No."

"I'm going to contact the manager and have him give you one. There are copies of the novels I've recorded, two of them by this author, and you can listen to them."

"Where would I find these novels? Your 'man cave' has shelves full of so much stuff."

Brant chuckled. "Believe it or not, everything is organized. When you walk into the bedroom, go to the shelves on the left. I keep books on tape on the second shelf from the top, one, two, three cases in. Use a step stool. They might be too high for you."

"What do I look for?"

"They're organized by author's last name. Look for Stanzer, Sam Stanzer. There are others I've recorded, but these are my best, and Sam's an excellent writer."

"How many of those DVDs are of you?"

"A few. But I don't want to give you too much stimulation. Wait till I get back."

"When will that be?"

"When I stop tripping over my tongue." He paused. "Did Elaina mention anything to you about my father?"

"No."

"He's turning seventy soon. I'm pretty sure the family's planning something. Whenever we've spoken, he's mentioned how we need to talk. It's weighing on me. I don't know what to do." He sighed. "I miss you so. I'd really like to hold you, talk to you about all this."

"Finish this assignment so we can have time together. I miss you, too."

"OKAY, YOU GUYS. Settle down." Marley had three fellow guitarists in her condo who were interested in starting their own band, The

Three Ks. The two youngest, Kevin and Kenneth, still attended high school, while Karl had started his freshman year at the local community college where he played in the guitar ensemble. They'd met when Marley had been carrying her guitar into the elevator the day she'd moved into her condo. That day they'd learned that not only could she play guitar but she could also teach it, too.

The boys took over her condo on Friday nights whenever she was available. Karl played the keyboard, as well, but preferred to work with his electric guitar. They were practicing several songs Karl had composed when the doorbell rang.

Marley wondered all the way to the door who it could be. It was after eleven. Were they so loud that someone had complained? She opened the door and stepped back in surprise.

"Brant? What are you doing here?" He wore the familiar black pants and another Western shirt with the sleeves rolled up to his elbows. He looked scruffy, with a beard that had to be several days old.

"Long story. May I come in?"

"Of course." She pulled him inside and backed into the three young men standing in the hallway.

Brant stood stock-still. "Who...?"

Marley laughed as she shooed the boys back into her living room. "Enter and meet an up-and-coming band." She introduced each of the boys. "And this is Brant Westfield, my fiancé."

Brant's lips formed a small, questioning, "Oh?" but he didn't contradict her. Was he put off by her announcement? She'd never actually said she'd marry him, and they hadn't discussed marriage since he'd left Pennsylvania.

As he shook hands, he glanced around the room. It took her a moment to realize he'd never seen her place. When he settled on one end of the couch, the young men each took their chairs in the semicircle and began strumming their instruments.

Brant sat up and pointed. "Don't I know you? The Whalen boys on the fourth floor, right?" Ken and Karl nodded. "Had no idea you played." He turned to Kevin. "And you are?"

"Their cousin."

Kenneth, the youngest, a junior in high school, gave Marley a shy smile and said, "I didn't know you were engaged."

Brant moved forward and leaned on his thighs. "It's an interesting story, one that I intend to clarify first chance I get."

Kenneth's expression went blank, and Marley rushed to the rescue. "Ken, you've really improved since the last rehearsal. Have you done anything differently?"

"Yeah. Practiced the chords like you said, same ones every day over and over."

Marley shot him an answering smile. "Now your fingers have that memory embedded in them."

"About time," his brother commented.

Ignoring the remark, Marley said, "Why don't we play the 'Diamond' song we were practicing. One, two, three, four." And they all began to strum.

Brant sat back and sent her a smile that lacked its usual intensity. He looked so tired, drained, to put it mildly. What to do? The group usually stayed until midnight, and she didn't want to cut back on their time, especially when they had really started to mesh. This was by far the best practice session since they had started. She wouldn't have to do anything, because the next time she glanced at Brant, he had thrown his head back against the couch and was snoring softly.

When they finished, Karl started to snicker. "Never thought my music could put anyone to sleep." He played an extra loud riff on the electric guitar. Brant didn't move.

Marley stood and put her guitar back in its case. "He just flew in from New York, so he's dealing with jet lag."

All the fellows took the hint and began packing their instruments. "What are you going to do about him?" Kenneth asked.

"They're engaged." Karl added a rough swat to his brother's shoulder to accentuate his point. The three gave her veiled looks, as they exited her condo. Well, there went her reputation.

Once she got the boys out the door, Marley returned to look at Brant. Standing with fists on hips, she wondered what she was going to do with him. She tried moving him, but he only snuggled deeper into the couch cushions. Too tired to deal with Brant, she decided to leave him there till morning, with enough light so he could find the door and go back to his own place.

She quickly got ready for bed, then went back to the living room to check on him. He was sitting on the couch, holding his head in his hands. When she walked over and stood in front of him in her summer nightgown and robe, he looked up.

"We need to have a serious discussion." He pulled her onto the couch. "Tomorrow's my father's birthday party, and I'd like you to come with me to the ranch." He issued the invitation in a monotone that wasn't exactly enticing.

"Is everything all right?" She wondered if his uncharacteristic lackluster was more than jet lag.

Brant got up and drew her to her feet. "I don't know." He pressed his forehead against hers. "The long ride will give us a chance to talk." A quick kiss left her with an irritating itch from his beard. He started for the door, made a sudden turn and glanced around her home. "I like it." And he was gone.

CHAPTER TWENTY-ONE

MARLEY AWOKE AFTER 5:00 a.m. with the sun shining through the window and the telephone ringing. "What now, Mom?" she mumbled as she rolled over and picked up her phone. Marley used to remind Nora about the time difference between Pennsylvania and Arizona, but her mother refused to pay attention, saying, "I never know if I should add or subtract. You're the math whiz, Marley, not me." Marley had finally given up.

"I didn't wake you, did I?" Her mother asked the same question every time she called. Without waiting for an answer, Nora continued, "We have less than a week. Have you made your reservations? Al can pick you up at the airport." And then the long sigh. At least it no longer contained tears. "Won't you reconsider? We have such beautiful gowns."

"Mom, please. I won't be in the wedding, I have my plane ticket, and I'm arriving Friday night close to eight."

"No! You can't come so late on Friday. You'll miss the bride's dinner. The wedding's Saturday. We need—"

"Everything is arranged. I have no more vacation time left, so I can't get there any earlier." Which wasn't true because she'd saved a week for her own wedding and honeymoon. Just in case. "Relax and enjoy your special time. I'll be there with bells on."

Once her mother hung up, Marley rose. Brant hadn't mentioned when they'd be leaving, but she wanted to be prepared. She showered and dressed in green pants and a yellow blouse and added a green headband to keep her relaxed curls away from her face. She examined herself in the full-length mirror. Was she too casual? Should she wear a dress? High heels?

Had she imagined Brant's presence? For a moment the whole evening seemed more like a dream than reality. Should she make breakfast? Call him? About to start making coffee, she was startled when her doorbell rang. It wasn't even six-thirty.

Brant had shaved—*thank goodness*—and looked more like his clean-cut self, with hair still damp from his shower. He wore jeans and a Western shirt in solid red. So there obviously wasn't any need for her to wear something dressier. His smile, the one he usually had for her, was nowhere to be seen. Her heart sank. How could she get that smile back?

"Ready?"

She nodded. "I was going to make coffee." Marley held open the door, inviting him to come in. He stood aloof, and she felt slighted. Could their time apart somehow have created problems between them?

"We'll have breakfast at the ranch. You might want to bring a sweater. It can get chilly in the higher elevation." He held a black felt cowboy hat in one hand and an overnight bag in the other.

"Should I bring a card, a gift, something for your father's birthday?"

Brant managed a halfhearted smile, not up to his usual standard. "No. You're the birthday present."

Marley raised an eyebrow. *Exactly what is that supposed to mean?*

Armed with her green sweater and a purse, Marley rejoined Brant and they walked in silence to the elevator. On the ride down, she leaned against the cool metal side and remembered the first time they'd ridden in it together. Brant had hovered over her then, trying to make a connection. Now, after they'd connected on many levels, he stood by the door with no interest in her at all, watching the light flick from one floor number to the next.

So much had happened between them since that first elevator ride. She focused on him, totally confused. What had turned him into this quiet, moody person she didn't recognize?

Once in his truck, Brant said, "It'll take more than an hour to get there. You need something to eat? We can stop for some fast food."

She appreciated his offer even though it was more a social nicety than a personal concern. "No. I'm fine." She sat in the middle of the truck, shoulder to shoulder with Brant, yet she felt as though he were miles away. When they reached I-17 heading north, he entwined their fingers, the first real attempt at intimacy this morning. They had passed the exit to Route 303 and turned onto Carefree Highway, heading west, when he squeezed her hand.

"Are we really engaged?" He gave her another smile that didn't quite make it to his eyes. "You've decided to marry me?"

Marley pulled her hand free and placed it on her lap. "I don't know."

"You…don't know?"

She looked at him, trying to read his expression. "Are you acting?"

"What?"

"Are you playing another character? Because you haven't been the person I know since you arrived back."

Brant made a quick turn off the road into the entrance to a park. For several minutes, he sat there, gripping the steering wheel with white knuckles, staring through the windshield. Marley sat quiet and watchful, as well as a little fearful, struggling to figure out what could possibly be wrong with him. "I'm not acting." He faced her. "This mixed-up mess, you see, is really me. I've been trying to figure out the right words…"

He gazed at her. "Come here," he said. He pulled her into an embrace and held her, not saying anything more.

She heard what sounded like deep breathing, then several attempts to clear his throat. When he finally eased back, she saw tears in his eyes. She felt a flutter of panic. What was the matter with him? He quickly wiped them away and gazed out the window again. "I'm very happy you want to marry me. It's just…" He sucked in his cheeks before continuing. "You may not want to after I tell you—"

Marley grasped his chin, forcing him to look at her. "What is it?" *Is he sick? Dying?*

"I'm going to tell my father I'll take over the ranch."

That's it? All this angst. She had no idea how to respond. Finally she asked, "And that affects us how?"

His brow furrowed. "We'll have to give up all our plans."

"What plans? Outside of getting married in Vegas, we never made any." A different fear gripped her. *We aren't getting married?*

He averted his eyes once more. "Okay, *my* plans. I expected to continue in my career." He swatted the steering wheel and drew a deep breath before regarding her again. "Sam Stanzer, the author of the book I've been recording." He closed his eyes momentarily. "He's been offered a movie contract for his first book. He wants me to play the main character. Said he'd modeled him after me."

"That's wonderful, Brant." Would this mean they'd postpone the wedding? Was that why he was so upset?

"I can't do it."

Marley sat back and stared at him. "Why?"

"It's about time I took on some responsibility. I've been the baby in the family long enough. I need to give my sisters some relief and do what my father expects of me."

"But you said Elaina handles everything brilliantly, really fits in at the ranch and you thought she deserved to continue. What changed your mind?"

"You."

"Me?" Marley felt appalled. How could she be responsible for this? She fought to understand Brant's logic.

"You and your family. Elaina's the oldest and gets all the responsibility, and the youngest, like me and Lindy, take advantage. I can't expect my sister to shoulder all the duties anymore. It's time for me to carry the weight."

Marley gasped. "You're basing this all on me and my family?" She peered out the side window. "I'm sorry I complain so much. It's how I release pressure and has nothing to do with how I would change anything. I like being the oldest, the responsible one." At least in most instances. She'd like someone else to relieve her of all the tensions with her mother's wedding.

Marley turned back to him. "And I don't care where I live." She paused and removed her seat belt. "But it won't be with a man who gives up on his dreams. Because if that's what's going to happen, we aren't engaged."

She wished she could hand him his ring, something to indicate the engagement was over. Marley edged over to the door and folded her arms across her chest.

Brant went back to gripping the steering wheel.

"What you're considering, turning your life upside down, can't possibly be what your father wants from you. Please take me back to my condo. I don't want to spoil this celebration for your father." Sighing, she added, "I already can't stand him."

Brant started the truck, and Marley put on the seat belt by the passenger side door. "Don't lay your father issues on him. He's a wonderful man. I wouldn't even consider this except that I admire him to the fullest."

Brant didn't turn the truck around.

"Where are you going? I said to take me home."

"You owe me, Marley. We had a fake engagement for your family; now we can have a fake one for mine."

"I'm not an actor. I can't carry it off."

Brant pulled to the side of the road again and faced her. "Right up until I exited the highway, we were engaged and planning to marry. That was five minutes ago. Unless that was a total lie, you should at least be able to keep up the pretense for a day and show some affection toward me that's not totally fake."

He closed his eyes and leaned his head against the steering wheel. "You didn't want to be considered an old maid. Well, I'm the male equivalent. My parents have been overjoyed that I finally found someone." He looked at her then. "Please. Stay engaged to me until the party's over."

Marley undid her seat belt and moved next to him. "I didn't stop loving you, Brant," she said, caressing his face. "It's just…" She wasn't about to pound her reasons into the ground. She sighed. "The engagement's on until we leave."

He drew her to him in an awkward embrace. "I love you so much," he whispered against her cheek. "Thank you."

Once they started again, Brant appeared to concentrate on the driving. Marley felt numb. Would living at the ranch be so bad? She couldn't picture the place. She could give up city life if Brant really wanted to live there. And part of her admired his desire to help his father. *Muddle. That's what my life has be-come. A complete muddle.*

"You talk about me giving up on my dreams, what about you?" Brant asked.

"What dreams?"

"Music."

"I never—"

"Your grandfather told me at the bride's dinner you always loved music, and he's the one who pushed you into math."

Frustrated, Marley blew a stream of air through her teeth. "I've told that man a dozen times he didn't do that. I had already made up my mind to major in math, and just asked his advice because I knew it would make him feel good to be asked. I love music. But I knew I could never make a decent living playing the guitar."

"Yes, you could. You're good."

"Stop." She held up her hand. "It's not what I wanted. My goal has always been to combine my love for math and music with my love of teaching. I always wanted to be a teacher."

"Then why aren't you doing that instead of… What do you do? Punch numbers into a computer? You're a creative person. Doing book-keeping all day has to drive you up the wall."

"Teachers don't get paid well, so I use my

talents where I'm paid. Teaching I do for my own enjoyment whenever I can."

"And when is that?"

"Were you totally out of it when you showed up at my place last night?"

He glanced her way. "What are you talking about?"

"I've been working with those boys for months, teaching them all aspects of music so they can start their own band. And for the last two semesters, I've taught math in the evening at a community college. Once I have more experience and have taken additional higher math courses, I can apply for full-time employment there." She turned to him then, her chin jutting out. "Which I'll consider only if it pays enough."

"Never knew you were such a mercenary."

"Well, I am." *And I'd never throw money away the way you do.* She turned back in the seat and faced front. Brant kept quiet for quite some time. Finally, he said, "Would you consider becoming my accountant? I really need a competent person to handle my money."

Marley smiled. "If we were ever to marry, I'd handle the money and put you on a very tight budget."

His eyes opened wide. "Well, that's certainly the best reason so far to end our engagement." He started to laugh, then he smiled at her, his "I want to make love to you" smile in full blaze. He was finally back to the person she loved. Maybe this day with his father would work out, after all.

Marley relaxed and leaned against his arm, enjoying their companionship. Yes, she very much wanted to marry this man. And if he intended to settle down at the ranch, she'd adjust, just so she could spend her life with him.

CHAPTER TWENTY-TWO

BRANT LOOKED AT the fieldstone house they were approaching and felt the usual sense of home. This had been his residence during his youth and whenever he wasn't away at college, traveling or working. It had a warmth and ambiance not present in his condo. But Marley's... The few glimpses he'd had of her place gave him that same homey feeling.

Would she be able to live here? Her roots back in Pennsylvania weren't urban. She should be able to adjust. She had to. If he had anything to say about it, this engagement was leading to marriage, and the sooner the better.

Brant pulled off the main road onto a gravel drive surrounded on each side by metal fencing painted white. Trees lined lush green fields bordered with irrigation ditches, and a good dozen horses stood grazing nearby. Several houses and barns sat under tall eucalyptus and cottonwood trees at the end of the road. The main house had bunting and balloons draped around the porch.

After Brant stopped the truck and got out, he walked around to open Marley's door and help her down. "Remember what I said when we arrived that first time at your parents' home?"

"Yes. You said 'break a leg' and implied I was an unfeeling mannequin."

"Because you wouldn't kiss me even though we were engaged." He pulled her into his arms and whispered, "Let's give my family a more convincing performance."

He loved the way Marley melted against him. When his lips touched hers, he expressed all his love and yearning. Long after the kiss, Brant continued to hold her close. "Break a leg," he said, then stepped away.

Elaina ran down the steps, black hair flowing, arms extended. "Welcome. Welcome." His oldest sister. His first love.

Ignoring Brant, she said to Marley, "I'm so glad you could be here. Everyone's dying to meet you."

Delighted by her warm welcome to Marley, Brant picked up Elaina and twirled her. "Aren't you glad to see me?"

"Of course I am, you big lug. Put me down." Once on the ground, Elaina hugged him, then took Marley's hand and led her toward the porch. "Francesca has made the most sumptuous breakfast."

Marley faced Brant and mouthed, "Francesca?"

He mouthed back, "The cook." Francesca was third generation at the ranch. Many of the people who had worked for his grandfather had raised their families there. Brant had grown up with them and considered them kin.

The large room they entered contained a long table, at which sat about twenty people of both sexes, their ages ranging from two to seventy. Several people rose and yelled greetings. Brant's eyes immediately went to the tall man with a full head of white hair and the white mustache who had started toward them.

"Dad, I'd like you to meet my fiancée, Marley Roman."

FOR A MOMENT she thought Mark Twain had risen from the grave. His father took her hand between his and beamed at her. Instantly, Marley recognized where Brant had inherited his smile. "Delighted. And you must call me Dad, no formal Mr. Westfield or Robert." He turned to a woman and placed his arm around her. "This is my wife, Julian, and we're both thrilled that you could be here with us." He kissed her cheek. "She prefers Mom, and we both couldn't be happier Brant found a lovely bride who shares his interests."

Julian, whose hair was as white as his and coiffed in an attractive style, took Marley's hand in a light touch. "We are truly happy. Welcome."

After more introductions, Marley and Brant took seats next to his father, opposite Elaina and her husband. Mounds of huevos with chorizo, enchiladas, chilies, fruits and other Mexican delicacies festooned the table. With the food, and the mix of Spanish and Native American artifacts, the room's flavor was definitely Southwest.

One of the younger boys, who was sitting next to Brant, said, "Your lady is very pretty," in Spanish.

Immediately Mr. Westfield corrected, "Stick to English, Bobby. It's impolite to talk in front of a guest in a language she won't understand."

Flipping to Spanish, Marley said, "Thank you for the compliment, Bobby."

The boy sat back abashed, red creeping into his cheeks.

Brant started to chuckle and gave the boy an affectionate knuckle tap on his chin. "You have to watch out for Marley. She's forever surprising me, as well."

"So how is that book coming?" Mr. Westfield asked Brant. "I'm really looking forward to listening to it."

"Nearly done, and the author has another one in the works."

"And of course you'll be doing that one, also." His father beamed at him, then turned his attention to Marley. "Have you had a chance to hear my son read? He does it beautifully."

"Yes, I listened to the first two books of the author's, and I'm looking forward to the next one." She spoke directly to Brant now. "I can tell which character is speaking by the tones, the cadence and the accents. And I particularly like the accents."

Brant leaned over and kissed her. "I knew it would only take time." She tasted the spicy salsa he'd added to his food and licked her lips.

Marley was sure her cheeks had to be a blazing pink. She wasn't used to him kissing her in front of his family, although it never bothered her when he did it in front of hers. But back then they'd been acting. Glancing around the table, she saw all the love reflected there and realized she had no reason to feel embarrassed. Living with Brant's people wouldn't be a hardship.

After the meal the group retired to one corner of the room while several people from the kitchen cleared the table. Mr. Westfield sat in an extra-large recliner and motioned to Brant to have a seat on the piano bench in front of a grand piano similar to the one Marley had seen in Brant's condo.

"I want you to play for me, and I don't want to hear any birthday songs."

Mr. Westfield scowled at several people to emphasize his point. Julian came over and sat beside him on the lounge. "Now, now, dear. No one plans to force happiness on you."

Brant lifted the keyboard lid and turned, bracing himself with a stiff arm on the bench. "I'd like Marley to join me. She plays the acoustic guitar." Elaina was already walking toward Marley with a guitar, and another family member brought over an armless chair.

"Brant has talked about nothing but how much he's enjoyed making music with you."

Marley took the guitar and checked the tuning. When she was through, she looked at Brant. "What should we play?" She'd never heard him play the piano, so she looked forward to seeing how well they could mesh the two instruments.

"Let's try 'Some Things Don't Come Easy.'"

She smiled and nodded, remembering how he'd first sang it to her. While they played and sang, he watched her, his fingers skimming the keys effortlessly. Yes, her insides were tingling and she was definitely having one of those musical afterglows.

After their presentations, which received thunderous applause, Brant asked Marley if she'd like a tour of the ranch. They headed outside to where the horses were grazing and observed them. "What do you think?"

"About what? Your family, the ranch, the horses?"

"About how I can convince you to marry me and live here."

"I like your family, Brant." Marley leaned on the fence. When one of the horses approached, she backed up and the horse shied away. Brant enclosed her in his arms. "You afraid of horses?"

"I've never been this close."

"Blackie won't hurt you." Still holding Marley, he scratched the horse's forehead. "He's mine. Getting a little long in the tooth, now, right, boy?" The horse nuzzled Brant's hand.

"Oh, you think I brought a treat?" Brant chuckled and pulled out an apple from his pocket along with a pocketknife. He cut the apple in two.

"Where'd you get that?" Marley asked.

"I stole it off the table. Here." He handed one half to her. "Offer it to him, but look out for his teeth."

Hesitantly she held out the apple. When he came for it, showing those enormous teeth, Marley pulled her hand away.

"Don't tease." Brant grasped her hand and positioned it so Blackie could get the apple. "Haven't you ever been to a farm or petting zoo?"

"Yes, when I was little. A goat chased me all over trying to get my bottle." Marley petted Blackie where Brant had scratched him. The animal felt like soft velvet. "I wanted the bottle. Had no intention of giving it to that goat."

"You must have been very young." Brant offered the horse the other half of the apple.

"About Michelle's age, I think."

Brant placed his arm around her and guided her from the fence as several more horses started toward them. "I didn't bring enough treats for the whole herd, so let's not tease them with false hope. We'll go to another place." An arm wrapped around her shoulders, Brant led her to the other side of a white barn. He captured her face, a hand on either side, and with the utmost care, began to kiss her.

Marley was entranced. It had been so long since he'd kissed her like this, outside of her dreams, that is. When he slipped his arms around her back and pulled her close, she forgot any of her concerns. The grounds were beautiful, the people friendly and Brant was the love of her life. How could she not marry him? She'd accept anything he decided as long as they'd be together.

"The ranch is a great place to raise children," he whispered against her lips, then kissed her nose. Had he expected a comment from her? If he had, he didn't press it. "I can teach you anything you need to know about horses—how to ride them, groom them, clean their stalls."

Marley laughed. "Right. Nothing I'd like better than shoveling horse manure." She stood holding his hands, gazing into eyes that promised so much happiness. "Are the duties here so intense that you can't pursue what you love doing?"

"Working the ranch is a full-time job. And I enjoy those aspects I'm already familiar with.

However, if I continued to record books or act, I'd have to devote weeks, months of my time to those activities. Someone would need to take over duties here, and it would all fall on my sisters again."

"Couldn't you do it here? You know, make your own recording place?" When he didn't respond verbally, just shot her a questioning look, Marley quickly added, "I'm sorry. I really don't have the slightest idea what you do. What it involves."

"Creating a recording studio in the middle of nowhere would take most of my time. I wouldn't be able to concentrate on doing what's necessary here."

She regarded him, tortured by what he planned to give up. "But would you be happy?"

"You make me happy. I could handle anything if our wedding is on again."

Marley avoided answering him. She stared down at the dirt path as they headed back to the house. "When will you be talking to your father?"

"After lunch."

"Do you need backup?"

Brant stopped, forcing her to stop, as well. "What are you suggesting?"

"When I was going to talk to my family,

you offered to cover my back. I'm making the same offer."

Brant glanced up at the treetops before turning his attention back to her. "Thank you, but no. I'm afraid you might do something crazy, like twist Dad's arm behind his back and drop him to the ground until he agreed to let me off the hook."

"I wouldn't get that physical." She smiled. "But you're probably right. I wouldn't let him push you into anything you don't want to do."

"I appreciate you watching my back. I really do. It's just..." His expression had turned serious. "Handling the ranch is something I have to try. I owe it to my family." He paused and they both stopped walking. "I'm flying back to New York to meet with Carla and go over my plans, whatever they may be."

"Has she been your manager for long?"

"Since college. A long and very satisfactory association. Expect she'll really lay into me if I stop." He sighed. "I've finished recording the book, and I still have that commitment at the Civic Center."

They began walking again. "When do you leave?"

"Right after my talk with Dad. I'm taking a private plane from Prescott."

Marley stopped, gasped and covered her mouth. "How will I get home?"

"You can drive my truck. It's an automatic and not too much bigger than a car. You can use it until I get back, if you want." They continued on to the house. "If you'd rather not, I can have Jose drive you. He makes regular trips to Phoenix for supplies, so it's no problem."

"I'll drive, but you better give me good directions so I can get back to Phoenix."

"I will, but right now I'd like to show you more of the house. My room, where I grew up and stay whenever I come to the ranch."

Elaina greeted them in the vestibule. "Dad's playing some game on the TV with the grandkids. Lunch will be ready in about an hour."

"Can I help?"

Elaina chuckled. "No. The kitchen staff handles everything for the house and ranch hands. But thank you. Brant told me you're pretty nifty in the kitchen."

Brant pressed his hand against her back. "I'm showing her my room." He aimed her toward the staircase.

"Did you tell your sister everything about me?" she asked as they climbed the stairs.

"Of course. Didn't you tell your family everything about me?"

"No way." Marley chuckled. "I made almost everything up." She stopped in front of an open doorway.

"This is it, where I spent most of my youth, except for summers when I went to Connecticut."

The room, definitely done to suit traditional masculine tastes, had knotty pine walls and brown plaid drapes, with a matching bedspread on the double bed. Photographs of horses adorned the walls. Several photos were of Brant as a young boy, riding a horse and wearing full cowboy gear, including holstered six-shooters. Brant stopped in front of a large framed photo. "That's me and Blackie."

"Who were you pretending to be in that getup?"

"The Sundance Kid."

"Are the guns real?"

"No. Cap guns. I wasn't allowed to touch the real thing until my father took me hunting."

"I thought you said you didn't hunt."

"I don't kill. I learned how to shoot and became good specifically so I could avoid hitting the deer or antelope. Dad gave up on me and began taking Elaina. If there's any venison in the freezer, it's because of her skill."

He led Marley to the desk with a laptop computer and turned it on. "It's about time I educated you."

"About what? Horses?"

"No. About me and what I do. Or did, I should say."

While they watched the screen slowly take on color and icons, she asked, "What will I do if you give up everything to move here? I've always worked, first with my mother's catering business, then—"

"You can manage me and my money. There won't be as much, but I'll have residuals on what I've already done plus my investments. And I'll definitely need someone to control my spending."

"You're offering me a job?"

"Yes. On top of being my wife, and the mother of my children, which will probably take up a great deal of your time." He gave her another one of those smiles of his that always softened her heart. "If you need to keep busy, be my accountant and charge anything you want for the service."

Marley shook her head, as though she hoped to fling out the images that had come into her mind. "Is that how you hire people? You don't know any of my credentials. I could rob you. I—"

He placed his hand loosely over her mouth. "You got your master's at ASU at night and have worked at three different places since you moved to Phoenix, including those teaching jobs you mentioned. Good recommendations all the way around, by the way."

"You looked me up, but you didn't want me to check you out?" Miffed, she started to walk away, but he held her arm so she couldn't. She attempted to break free, but Brant drew her against him and rubbed his cheek against hers.

"My love, you are a godsend. I find the one woman in the world who actually listens to me and isn't consumed by curiosity."

"Oh, I'm curious, all right," she said, pulling out of his grasp. "It's just I've been so worried about what I might find. To hear you and Elaina—"

"Hold that thought. Let's go over everything now." He sat in the only chair in the room and patted his lap, motioning her to join him.

"I know how to use a computer, Brant."

"Yes, but this way I can have a little control." He grinned. "Like placing my hands over your eyes or tickling you to distraction anytime something comes up I'd rather not have to explain."

"Well, you're not going to have that kind of control. You promised me you'd tell me everything, and that's what you're going to do." Marley reached for the laptop and carried it over to the bed. "This could end up being a long session. We might as well both be comfortable." She lay on her stomach and placed the computer by the pillow. As Brant lay down next to her, she said, "And this way, if I don't hear a believable explanation, I can knock you off the bed."

When Marley typed Brant's name into the browser's subject line, "England" came up. "What's this?"

"I spent a year in England when I got the scholarship—" Brant flipped onto his back. "Oh, that's right. You don't want to know about that."

Marley sat up and looked down at him. "Brant Westfield. You had a scholarship to Oxford? For real? It wasn't something you were making up to impress my family?"

"For real." He remained on his back, his eyes closed. "After Janise died, I pretty much lost myself in classes and the theater. It helped me get through that time. Paid off unexpectedly in excellent grades and recommendations."

"What else should I know about you?"

He opened one eye. "You weren't too interested before."

"In what?"

"My scar."

She sat back on her legs. "Tell me about it."

He grabbed her hand and placed it near his waist. Propping himself on one elbow, he said, "When I was eleven, I went horseback riding with my sisters."

"On Blackie?"

"Yes, on Blackie. I had been having some pain in my side, but I really wanted to go riding, so I ignored it. My appendix burst, and I had to be air lifted by helicopter to the Children's Hospital in Phoenix. I almost died. My whole family was in a panic. Another reason I don't believe in wasting the moment. You never know when your time is up." He pulled her back on the bed and lay next to her with his arm wrapped around her.

They surfed the internet, entering Brant's name in all the search engines, checking out the movies, TV shows and any other information they could find. Marley was fascinated, but for the most part, Brant merely supported his head and watched her. He brushed at her hair and curled a section around his finger.

"Your hair's lost most of its curl. I like it curly. What will our children have? Straight, curly, black, red or possibly blond, if they get any of your sisters' genes." He tucked the curl behind her ear, and she swatted his hand. "I'm looking forward to creating our brood."

He propped his chin on his hands. "Once I've talked to my father, we can live here. Move into the guesthouse on the property. When we have children, we can move into a larger place to raise our family." He sighed.

Marley glanced at him before entering his name in Google. As she continued to scroll through information on the internet, he said, "You planning to have that cotton candy hairdo for your mother's wedding?" He created another pipe curl and brought it up to his nose, but she refused to let him distract her. "As much as I liked it, I still prefer your hair down, wrapped around your shoulders."

"Brant, stop that." She drew her hair over to the other side. For the most part, he ignored the information she pulled up, but on occasion, he'd check out the screen when she asked a question. "So this last picture. What did you do in it?"

"I rode a horse. I may have mentioned before, I—"

"I know. You own a horse ranch."

"Smart aleck." Brant reached over and turned off the computer. "That's enough for now. We better go join everyone for lunch." He got up and carried the laptop over to the desk.

Marley kneeled on the bed. "Do you do anything else in that movie besides ride a horse? Like talk? Kiss the girl?"

"I don't do much speaking in this picture, but I have a lot of riding."

He hadn't answered her last question, the one that interested her the most. "So, do you get the girl?"

"No." He came over and helped her off the bed. "Might as well deal with this now," he said, kissing her nose. "I have on occasion gotten to kiss a girl, but I'm more what people call a character actor, not the star of the show. I'm fortunate to have plenty of work, but I'm not the one who draws the crowds to the theater. So I don't get to kiss the girl very often."

"Has that been your goal? To be the star?"

"My goal is to be a star in my own life, marry the beautiful woman in my arms and make love with my wife every chance I get."

"You haven't explained the kissing part. Did you—"

"Does it matter? I won't be doing it anymore."

"Show me. How do you kiss the ladies in the movies? I want to see if it's different from the way you kiss me."

Brant gave her a quick smack on the lips.

"Oh, no you don't. Show me."

With a reluctant nod, he took her in his arms and supplied a satisfactory sample. *Okay. But nothing great.* "That's how I kiss onstage. This," he said, placing his hands on either side of her face, "is how I kiss my fiancée." His demonstration turned all her bones liquid, and she melted in his arms. "Notice any difference?"

She nodded.

His voice deepened. "And this is how I kiss my wife." He kissed her again with the same intensity.

Elaina knocked on the door. "Time for lunch," she said with a knowing smile, then disappeared down the hall.

"You hungry?" Brant asked, still holding Marley tightly to him.

Barely able to form any words, Marley said, "Starved."

After lunch, and extended hugs with the family, Brant walked Marley to his truck. He took her in his arms again and skimmed butterfly kisses across her cheek.

"You've got plenty to deal with, including that drama with your parents." He paused, looking deep into her eyes. "I've handed you a lot to think about, as well." Brant pressed his forehead against hers. "Next time we meet, you give me a definite answer."

CHAPTER TWENTY-THREE

MARLEY MADE IT safely home, all the while curious about Brant's meeting with his father. She sent a text message, but she didn't expect an answer since Brant would be traveling. *Hmmm. A private plane. How much had that cost him?* Brant might have plenty of money now, but his funds would dry up once he no longer worked as an actor. Especially if he kept spending frivolously at such a rate.

Maybe she was too conscious of money and how it should be spent. She judiciously dealt with her employer's costs and payments every day on a large scale. Her own money she managed equally carefully, budgeting it to the penny.

There would be no way for her to earn anything on the ranch. Acknowledging once again that she had always worked and provided for herself, she couldn't picture a lifestyle where she didn't. She could help on the ranch. However, cleaning out horse stalls held no appeal.

Any other work would require an extensive commute. So many questions, and she had minimal information until Brant answered her text.

His reply finally came.

Glad you made it safely. Meeting with the author, going over his next book. Busy, busy. Lots to tell you, love Brant.

Marley looked at the words, which lacked any kind of answers, and felt totally frustrated.

She sent another message to him, stating she'd be flying back to Pennsylvania that Friday before her parents' Saturday wedding. Although she'd complained about the wedding, possibly way too much, she'd never had a chance to discuss it with him. Would he be able to attend? He'd finished the book. What did he have to discuss with his manager?

Marley had no idea, and he hadn't mentioned it in his last text. She took out her guitar for therapy and checked to see if any other strings needed replacement. If only Brant could be at the wedding with her to hold her hand and provide backup. Something she knew she'd most definitely need.

HOW DO PEOPLE disentangle themselves from their family? Marley posed this question to herself when her mother called a few days before she had to leave. Her nerves could barely handle the calls any longer. "Look what you've started. Now Chloe won't be in the wedding. You have to take her place."

"Why won't she?"

"She's started to show and can't fit in any of the dresses."

Impossible! Chloe couldn't have gained that much weight since Marley last saw her. And when had she decided to tell everyone about the pregnancy?

"Mom, listen, please," she said. "I'm trying my best not to be rude, but I do have a life here, and I can't deal with every problem you have. Please, accept that I won't be in your wedding."

"You're not coming?"

When her mother's voice cracked, Marley made her hand into a tight fist and hit her thigh over and over. She wasn't going to give in. This time around she was saying no and sticking to her resolve. "I didn't say that. I'll be there to see you and Dad marry again, but I won't be in the wedding."

Desperate once she'd hung up for someone

to talk to, Marley called Dede and arranged to meet her for lunch at a local Subway near their offices.

"I need your help. My mother keeps asking me to be in the wedding, and, although I've told her no, she gets my sisters to nag me. I don't want to participate, but I'm afraid they'll wear me down. I can't get them to listen to me."

"Of course they won't accept a no. You've given in and done everything they've asked in the past. They won't let this matter go."

"Well, they have to. No way will I stand up there at the altar and be party to this…I don't even know what to call it. He's only going to walk out on her again." Marley placed her elbows on the table and rested her face in her hands.

"How can I help?"

Marley reached over and grabbed Dede's hand. "Come with me."

"Yeah, right." Dede pulled away and picked up her sandwich. "I have no desire to be a third wheel to you and Brant."

"He can't make it. He's having trouble dealing with his manager." That's what she'd learned in his last text.

"What kind of trouble?"

"I wish I could say. He won't answer my voice mail and only texts me minimal information. He won't tell me what went on with his father. I'm so frustrated. I understand he's busy but..." Her voice faded. Finally, Marley asked, "Please. I need a friend."

"I don't know." Dede looked down as she pushed her napkin around. "I haven't met any of your family. You'll be off with them and—"

"I'll introduce you to Richard."

Dede glanced up, her black eyes dancing. "Your Richard?"

Leaning forward, Marley said, "*Your* Richard. I'm giving him to you."

"How can you even say he'll be there? He's not part of your immediate family."

"I can because Lindy told me." Although Dede continued to appear hesitant, Marley knew she'd won her friend over. The prospect of bringing her best friend and Richard together made Dede glow. But Marley was happy for herself, too. Because she needed all the support she could muster.

"GREAT TO HAVE YOU HERE," Al said when he met them at the Pittsburgh airport in the early evening on Friday. He had Michelle in hand, who immediately grabbed her aunt's legs.

Marley picked the little girl up and spun her in circles while she hugged her. Back on the ground, Michelle clung to Marley's hand while Al gave his sister-in-law a kiss on the cheek.

Turning to Dede, Marley said, "This handsome devil is Al, Michelle's father and Chloe's husband." As Al reached for Dede's hand, Marley continued, "And this is my best friend, Dede, who knows every intimate detail of my life." She put her free arm around Dede's shoulders. "She's sworn to protect me from anyone who wants to force me into a bridesmaid's dress."

Al made a face. "Sorry about that. Chloe said she was sick of weddings and decided to play her pregnancy card."

"Mom believes it's all my fault."

"It is. You think any of your sisters would have bowed out if you hadn't insisted on watching from a pew?"

Marley gasped. "The rest of them quit, too?"

"No, just Chloe. And I expect you to stand together with her as an unbreakable unit."

Once they reached his truck, Al threw their luggage into the truck bed and helped Michelle into the child's seat, located behind the driver. "Sit here," Michelle begged and Marley took a seat next to her.

Dede sat in the front. After Al got behind the wheel, he asked, "Has Marley ever told you anything about me?"

"Of course. She even told me you dated each other."

"We were lovers," he said, grinning from ear to ear. He gave Marley a wink in the rearview mirror.

Marley reached out and smacked his shoulder. "Why do you tell everyone that? It's totally untrue."

Al laughed outright. "It gets her going so much that I can't help myself." He continued to laugh as they headed toward her parents' home. At least the weather had improved. No more rain.

Starting another topic, Al glanced in the rearview mirror again. "I take it you're not too thrilled about this wedding."

"True. I don't figure my father's changed, and I hate to think what this will do to Mom when he leaves her for someone else."

"And your sisters aren't too happy with you. They didn't want to do this wedding without you. The only reason Chloe got out unscathed is that they sympathize with her condition. They've all been there."

"The subject is closed, Al, so don't waste your breath trying to convince me otherwise."

"It's just...Your sisters. They want a father, and they're ready to put up with Red." Al stopped talking and concentrated on his driving. But within moments, he glanced in the rearview mirror again. "People can change, can't they? I know your mother has. Why else would she take him back? She wants this, and she's willing to make it work. She's forgiven him. Why can't you?"

"Like I said, I don't think he's changed."

When Al spoke again, his voice was low and harsh. "If he hasn't, the Warriors will take him behind the garage and take care of him."

"Sounds like a plan," Marley said with a grim smile.

After a short pause, Al spoke to Dede. "I hear you're about to meet the great Richard Brewster."

Her expression brightened. "That I am."

"He's one lucky man. First Marley and now you."

Dede started to laugh. "Marley's told me about you and the Roman Warriors."

"Nothing bad, I hope."

"No, just that you're all full of meaningless flattery. I love it."

As they got close to her hometown, Al turned into the parking lot of the motel Marley had stayed in, drove up to one of the rooms and stopped. Hadn't Marley told him they planned to stay at her family's home? "We're not staying here, Al. I'm—"

Marley stared at the tall man leaning against the open motel door and gasped. As he starting walking toward Al's truck she noticed that he wore the same black boots, black pants and Western shirt with pearl snaps he'd had on the last time she'd seen him. She definitely had to talk to him about changing his wardrobe. "Brant!" she said when she recovered her voice. She released the seat belt, opened the door and was in his arms before her feet hit the ground.

"Miss me?" he said as he swung her around.

Marley pressed her cheek against his and wrapped her arms around him as tightly as she could. "Yes, yes, yes," she said. She kissed him before slowly sliding down until her feet touched the ground.

"Me. Me," Michelle shouted.

They both turned to see the little girl

stretching toward them, her fingers doing a wild beckoning dance.

Brant released Marley and reached in to Michelle. She grasped his hand and refused to let it go.

"Can she come out for a minute?" Brant asked, undoing her seat belt before getting an answer. "Hi there, Michelle." He lifted her out of the truck. "My goodness, you've grown at least ten feet since the last time I saw you."

She gave him an I-adore-you smile, and he grinned. He put his other arm around Marley and said, "My two favorite girls." He noticed Dede in the truck and nodded in her direction. "I see you made it. Welcome."

Al emerged from the truck and came over to them. "She's here to meet Richard, who's attending the wedding. Marley set it up with Lindy. We're not going to have any trouble, are we?"

With a shake of his head, Brant leaned over to Marley and pecked her on the cheek. "Nope. I've got what I came for, and I'm sure the Warriors will take care of any flak."

"You can count on that." Al reached for Michelle. "Okay, honey. We have to go."

Michelle put a stranglehold around Brant's

neck and faced away from her father. "No. No. I want Unky Brat."

Choking, Brant began to cough. "Let her stay awhile," he managed in a hoarse voice. "We'll call you later."

"There is no later. I've got a dozen chores that need doing before the wedding. Nora's insisting on having the reception at her place, and tables, chairs, everything still have to be set up."

"Isn't there a bride's dinner, dancing?" Brant glanced at Marley, a worried frown crossing his face.

"Nope. You missed it. Marley's flight arrived too late." Al checked his watch. "They should be through by now." He reached for Michelle again. She still refused to leave.

"Either I get her now, or she's staying the night with you two."

Brant turned to Marley. "What do you say?" He moved closer and whispered in her ear. "We can do like the last time. I have a similar suite." When Marley nodded, he said to Al, "We've got Michelle tonight. I don't have a car, so can you pick us up tomorrow?"

What plans would they have beyond tonight? Marley had so many questions.

"Chloe and I'll be here for breakfast. Eight o'clock."

"What about me?" Dede asked, opening the door and preparing to exit.

"You're with me. Richard awaits. He's supposed to help the Warriors with tomorrow's setup. If you play your cards right, you can get him out of it, and he'll be eternally grateful." Al closed her door.

"My things," Marley said as Al took off in his truck. He'd stowed her suitcase in the truck bed and hadn't bothered to leave it for her.

"You won't need anything." Brant looked down at Michelle. "What do you say we use my shirts for pajamas for you and Aunt Marley? Would that work?"

Michelle totally agreed, nodding and smiling as they walked into the motel room. Brant picked up Michelle, and bounced her in his arms to her glee. "You know, love," he said in his British accent. "I'm going to remember this and make your life completely miserable when you start dating." He turned to Marley and used his normal voice. "Usually these crushes only last a short time. She should be over me by now."

Marley started to chuckle. "Oh, and you know this because?"

He strolled through the bedroom doorway over to the one bed, a king-size, and dropped Michelle on it, where she began to jump up and down.

"My nieces had this same infatuation, so I'm well aware Michelle's affections for me will soon disappear, and I'll just be old Unky Brat." He placed an arm around Marley's shoulders. "And as much as I enjoy being adored, I wish she'd gotten over it before I showed up. I had all my hopes on you adoring me." He kissed her forehead and directed her to a chair. Once she was seated, he dropped to one knee and took her hand, only to have Michelle slide off the bed and come over to him.

Brant blew a puff of air through his teeth, turned to Michelle and said, "You want to help me?" She nodded. "Okay, get down on your knees." She did. Brant started to laugh. "Maybe we should take a picture of this. I doubt if anyone would believe it." Although Marley considered recording it for posterity, she knew this moment would never fade from her memory.

"Marley Roman," he said, removing a ring from his pinky. She looked down at the ornate band of gold and silver encrusted with bits of colorful gemstones. "It's not a diamond. Not even an engagement ring—" Michelle made a grab for it, and he pulled it out of her reach "—but a wedding ring that serves both purposes." He placed it on her ring finger. "It says I love you with all my heart, and I want you to be my wife. Please say you'll marry me."

Marley grasped his hand and brought it to her lips. "Oh, Brant, I love you. Yes, I'll marry you." She slid off the chair and knelt next to him, throwing her arms around him. The unexpected exuberance sent them both sprawling. Michelle joined the mix, giggling joyfully. They remained on the floor in an embrace, laughing, too weak to pick themselves up.

"It's beautiful," she said, holding her hand above them so that the light caught the colors in the ring. "Exactly what I wanted."

"David Wildhorse, a jeweler friend, made it from everything in Arizona. The gold is from my family's ranch. After you returned the diamond ring to Gus at the pawn shop, I called there and got your size. And," he said, propping himself up so that he could reach into his pocket, "I have one just like it for me." He showed her a larger version of her ring. He cupped it in his hand, then closed his fingers over it when Michelle tried to get that one, as well.

"Then you must wear yours, too." Marley took it and placed it on his finger.

Brant stood and pulled her to her feet. "I've made reservations. A flight for two to Las Vegas." He paused. "If that's okay."

"When?"

"Tomorrow, after your parents' wedding."

Marley clasped her hands around his neck. "I can't wait."

Brant removed her hands, held them against his chest and watched her with somber eyes. "You didn't even ask."

"Ask what?"

"About where we'll live...about anything."

"I don't care, Brant. I just want to be with you. On the ranch, in Phoenix, wherever."

Brant picked her up off her feet and placed her on the bed. The moment he lay down next to her, Michelle began whacking his back. "If that young lady doesn't give us a moment of peace, I'm going to lock her in the bathroom." He flipped around and shouted, "Boo!"

Michelle backed away, fell on her rear and burst into tears. Immediately, Brant got off the bed and lifted her into his arms. "I'm sorry, sweetheart."

She glared at him and pouted. He looked back at Marley, containing his laughter. "It's over. No more infatuation." When Michelle squirmed to get away from him, he put her on the bed. Immediately she crawled over to her aunt for comfort.

Brant dropped onto the chair. "Isn't it her bedtime? I've got so much to tell you."

Michelle directed all her affections at her aunt, entangling herself in Marley's hair. The moment Marley freed herself, Michelle found something else to cling to. "Why don't you go to the other room? I'll call you when I'm available."

With a sigh, Brant stood. "Goodbye, Michelle." She turned and gave him the evil eye. Chuckling, Brant went to the door, paused there a moment, blew a kiss and was gone.

Once Michelle fell asleep, three stories and several drinks of water later, Marley went to the bedroom door. Brant arrived in seconds. Before he pulled her into his arms, he glanced at the sleeping child. "Will you get any rest with her flipping around?"

"A little. But then I'm sure I'll make up for it on my honeymoon."

"Not on *our* honeymoon." He shut the bedroom door and directed Marley to the sofa, where he sat next to her, his arm around her shoulders.

"Oh, that voice." Marley withdrew from his embrace for a moment so she could kiss him. "I'm trembling with expectation."

"I'll do my very best to live up to it." The radiant smile he gave her told her how much he loved her. "We have less than twenty-four hours. I'll answer all your questions now. Ask away."

"So what happened with your father?"

"We're not moving to the ranch."

Marley's brow furrowed. "What did your father say when you offered to take it over?"

With a sardonic smile, Brant gazed at the rug before glancing back at her. "He wanted to know where I got such a wacky idea. I did what any intelligent son would do. I blamed you."

"Brant!" Marley punched his shoulder. "Stop playing games. What happened?"

"For the past few months, ever since I did that movie in Australia, Dad's been after me to have a talk, as you know. I thought it would be a follow-up on what we discussed years ago—my taking over the responsibilities at the ranch. It wasn't. He's perfectly satisfied with how Elaina runs things. What he wanted from me was my name. I'm the only Westfield capable of having the name survive." He smiled.

"And I plan to make sure it does, if you'll co-operate."

"You realize there are nine females in our two families and you're the only male. What are our chances?"

"We'll just work at it until we have a son or you get too tired of having babies."

Marley cuddled against him. "You're nuts. So what else did your father say?"

"He wants the trust, which has the four children equally sharing in the property, put in my name. He wants to retire, take my mother on a world cruise, but he needed me to take over responsibility for the trust. We signed the papers with his lawyer before I left."

"Okay. So where do we live?"

"You've seen my place." Brant sighed. "Although I didn't see all of yours, I like the decorating. Something mine totally lacks."

"You have something I don't."

"What?" His expression sobered.

"A grand piano. When we talked about music, and I said I wanted to learn to play the piano, you said you wanted to learn, too. But you already knew how, since you played for your father. Why did you lie to me?"

"I didn't lie. I'm always learning." He brought her hands to his lips. "If you'll recall, when we talked, I was more concerned with discussing the merits of music and how it affects us internally."

"Right."

"I totally stand by everything I said and plan to spend some time demonstrating it this coming week. I'm open to suggestions about the condo."

"A walk-in closet is supposed to hold clothes, not a big-screen TV." Marley pulled her hand free and brushed his hair back, enjoying its texture.

"It's my office and keeps everything in one place. I close my door and don't have to run around putting things away when other people use the condo."

"Do you have any other clothes?" she asked. "Another closetful, maybe?"

"Nope. This is pretty much it. My sisters gave me the shirts for Christmas, and I left my jeans and work shirts back at the ranch. And you've seen all my casual stuff." He grinned. "Do you think I need more?"

"Absolutely."

"Okay, but I hate shopping. I'll let you pick out anything you want me to wear...within reason."

"As long as it's Western-style?"

"Well, I do have that horse ranch."

"Right," she said laughing.

Brant leaned forward and pressed his forehead against hers. "We'll decide where we'll live when we get back from Vegas." He continued to hold her. "There's something else. Have you made plans for this fall?"

"Like what?"

"Teaching? You said you teach math at the community college."

"No. I signed up for advanced math classes at ASU, and I can't do both, teach and..." She paused, wondering why Brant's expression had gone blank. "Why?"

"Production for Sam's book starts this fall. I'm not sure when, but I'd like it if you could be with me."

"The one about that great-looking detective who has to fight off all those women?"

"Sam's doing a rewrite. I'll be playing a hunchback with one eye and a limp." He waited a moment and added, "And a beard and terrible acne." He caught his lower lip between his teeth.

Marley closed her eyes and snuggled against him. "And a potbelly and a bald spot." She looked up into his face. "I wouldn't miss it."

SOMEONE KNOCKED ON the door. Not another interruption. Brant had so much to discuss with Marley. If this was Richard...Brant strode to the door, determined to send the annoying pest on his way. When Brant opened the door, he stepped back, hesitated, then turned toward Marley. Her father? Why was he here?

"Okay if I come in?"

When Marley didn't offer a protest, Brant moved aside, and Red walked slowly past him into the living room. He took the stuffed chair opposite the sofa, and Brant retook his seat next to Marley. Immediately, she pressed against him and held his hand.

"What do you want?" Brant asked.

"I'd like to speak with my daughter."

Marley's grip tightened, and Brant feared he might lose some fingers. "Whatever you have to say to her, you can say to me, too. Since I'm a little bigger than she is, I can throw you out if we don't like it."

Red chuckled. Not exactly the response Brant had expected.

"I'm glad to see you have her best interests at heart." Red pulled in a deep breath, then focused on Marley. "I came to reason with you. I know I don't deserve it, but I hoped you, too, could forgive me. I've tried to correct my mis-

takes. Your mother is giving me that chance.
I want my family back."

Brant winced when she tightened her grip
even more as she said, "The one you walked
away from?"

Red hung his head and rubbed his hands together. "Yes, that one."

Brant managed to unlock her fingers and
free his hand. "I need a drink. Can I get you
something?" He got up and went to the refrigerator, where he'd stocked several bottles of
water. He returned to the couch, handed one
each to Marley and Red. She looked ready to
throw it at him. After retaking his seat, Brant
placed his arm around her shoulders, tense
boards that definitely needed a massage.

You need to forgive him, Brant thought, but
he wasn't about to butt in. The decision had to
come from her. Whatever she chose to do, he'd
stand beside her. He was her backup, after all,
even if it forced him to back up bad choices.

Marley got up, walked over to the tiny
kitchen and placed the untouched water on
the counter. For several moments she stayed
there, her back to the two men; then she turned
and looked at Brant with an expression that
pulled at his heart. He moved over to her, determined to support her through the turmoil.

She clasped his hand again before facing her father. In an emotional voice, she said, "Okay, I forgive you."

Red slowly got to his feet but didn't make an attempt to get close to her. This wasn't exactly a moment that included hugs and kisses. Brant hid a smile and felt his chest expand with love. She'd made the right choice: family over payback.

Red cleared his throat. "Chloe said she'd be in the wedding, if you'd—" He bowed his head again and started for the door. "Sorry. I promised I wouldn't push."

Marley straightened and dropped her arms. "Who did you promise?"

"Your mother. She didn't want me to. I better go." He turned at the door. "Thank you for listening to me." Red reached out to Brant, and they shook hands. "I'll see you tomorrow. And thanks. Thanks for taking care of my girl. The first one is always special."

CHAPTER TWENTY-FOUR

SEVERAL MOMENTS AFTER the door closed, Marley let out a frustrated scream.

"You'll wake up Michelle." Brant kept his distance, something she appreciated. Right now she needed her space.

"Why did he have to say that? 'The first one is always special.'" She began pacing, knocking her fist into her palm. She glanced Brant's way and saw no telltale expression that might explain what he was thinking. The actor.

When he took a seat on the sofa, she decided to join him. "So what should I do?"

He placed an arm on the back of the sofa and stared at her. "That is by far the most loaded question I've ever heard. And I won't risk my life to answer it."

Marley shrugged. "If I do the wedding, I'll need to pick out a dress. Mom stores all of them in the spare room."

Brant bounded off the couch and went into

the other room. He pivoted. "How superstitious are you?"

"What are you talking about?"

"Do you believe the groom shouldn't see the bride's dress before the wedding?"

Marley shrugged. "I haven't even thought about a wedding dress."

Brant disappeared, then reappeared with a garment bag. "No need to."

Marley gently pulled the dress out of the bag, marveling at the heavy white lace trimmed in pearls. She looked at Brant, too stunned to speak.

"It was my grandmother's. Elaina thought it would fit you, and you do need something special." He picked up the dress. "Put it on. You can wear it as one of the bridesmaids."

"Brant Westfield, you have no idea...." She took a deep breath. "Only the bride wears white to a wedding, so no, I will not wear this to my mother's wedding. And I won't try it on in front of you. Not before our wedding. It's bad luck."

Marley began repacking the dress. Coming up behind her, Brant grasped her shoulders and whispered, "But you will consider it, right?"

She turned into his embrace. "Absolutely. It's beautiful."

MARLEY AWOKE TO something tickling her eyelashes. She opened one eye.

"You 'wake?" Michelle asked.

"I am now." Marley rose to a seated position and swung her legs over the edge of the bed. She wore the long *PITT* T-shirt Brant had packed in his suitcase, something she'd put on after last night's shower. Michelle still had on yesterday's clothes.

"Come here and give me a good morning hug." Michelle climbed onto her lap. "You know what we're doing today?" Michelle shook her head. "We're going to see Grandma and Grandpa get married. And guess who's going to toss rose petals?"

Michelle pointed to herself. "Me?"

"Yes, you. And then Grandma's going to walk all over them." *Right after I've walked over them.* Yes, Marley had decided to be in the wedding.

A rap on the door brought Michelle to total alertness. She scooted off Marley's lap and ran to the door. "You don't come in, Unky Brat."

Silence.

Marley quickly got to her feet and approached the door. "Who's there? We're not dressed."

"It's me. Al. I came for Michelle."

"Daddy!" Michelle screamed and began jumping in place.

The door opened and there stood Al. He picked up his daughter and walked into the room, dragging Marley's luggage. "Unless you're planning to wear that shirt, you better get dressed."

"Thanks. I'll change into what I'd planned to wear to the wedding." Marley grabbed the luggage and walked over to the bed.

Lindy peeked in behind Al. She was wearing a frilly yellow bridesmaid's dress and carrying another, a chiffon full-length one in green, one Marley had worn at another sister's wedding. She couldn't remember which one. Lindy pushed past Al, followed by Chloe.

"Lindy insisted on bringing the dress," Chloe said once she got past her husband. She had on a dressy maternity outfit in pink, with plenty of extra room that she might need eventually, but certainly not today. "I tried to tell her you wouldn't wear one of the old dresses, but she wouldn't listen." Chloe looked hopeful. "You do have something better, don't you?"

Marley reached for the green dress. "I think this should go well with my bone sandals." She turned to Chloe. "I'm sorry. I know I promised Al I'd support you but—"

"Out. Everybody out," Al said, pushing everyone but his wife and Marley from the room. He turned to Chloe. "I brought several choices. I figured Marley might change her mind." He started for the door. "I'll be right back."

"IT'S A WEDDING DRESS," Lindy squealed when they joined her at IHOP for breakfast. "Your wedding dress? Brant showed us while you were getting dressed."

The group consisted of Chloe and Lindy, their husbands and little Michelle. They had gathered before heading to the eleven o'clock wedding. Michelle hadn't changed into her flower-girl dress, yet, since she could spill syrup on it. However, everyone else had on their wedding attire. Brant wore a black tux in a Western style with his boots, something he intended to wear at their wedding.

Marley extended her hand to show off the ring. "Brant gave me this. We're getting married in Vegas, leaving right after Mom's wedding."

"Vegas? But we want to be in your wedding." Lindy's eyes brimmed with tears, and she brushed them away. "We want to go to your wedding. How can you do this to us?"

"You had your wedding the way you wanted. I'm entitled to have mine the way I want."

"But all the times we played with Ken and Barbie. We planned to be in each other's weddings." Lindy looked to her sister for support. "Right, Chloe?"

"I can relate," Brant said, joining in the conversation before Chloe had a chance to speak. "I have three sisters and got dragged into playing with them and their dolls as I grew up. They let me be Ken while they all pretended to be Barbie, and everyone had a big wedding with Ken."

"See," Lindy said, leaning across the table. "Even Brant wants a big wedding."

"I never said that." He reached for Marley's hand. "I want whatever my bride wants. It can be here or in Vegas. It's up to her." Brant kissed Marley near her ear and whispered, "But the honeymoon won't be delayed." He sat back. "What do you want, Marley?"

"I want..." She looked around at her family and her future husband. "I want to be Mrs. Brant Westfield by tomorrow morning in Las Vegas. Just pretend today's wedding is mine, as well. This is the last family wedding I plan to attend until Michelle gets married." She picked up the menu. "Should we start with coffee? I didn't get much sleep last night, and I can really use a pick-me-up."

"Oh, not much sleep." Dennis chortled.

Marley waved offhandedly at her niece. "I slept with this little girl, who used me as a punching bag all night long."

"And I," Brant said, sighing and placing an arm around Marley, "slept by myself, hugging my pillow and wishing it were Marley. And it's the last time I plan to do that."

"Get used to it," Al said. "Unless you don't want kids, because once the little ones come, having them in bed with you is your life."

Brant moved his head so that his lips brushed the side of Marley's forehead. "Can we adjust?"

She snuggled closer. "We'll have to."

"It's TIME TO GET READY," Chloe said when they had finished eating. "I'll dress Michelle." She took the skipping little girl to the ladies' room, carrying an outfit suitable for tossing rose petals. When Michelle emerged in layers of pink, she went right up to Dennis, took his hand and tugged.

"Oh, what have we got here? Don't you look pretty." He bent over, adjusting his height to

Michelle's, when Lindy grabbed his arm and pulled him away.

Michelle looked crushed.

"Your sister..." Brant didn't bother to finish. Instead, he went over to Michelle and picked her up. "Okay if I take this beautiful princess out to the truck?"

Marley expected Michelle to protest, considering how she'd acted earlier, but the little girl contained her tears and held on to Brant. However, the look she sent in Dennis and Lindy's direction showed that they were now both toast. Oblivious to the hurt feelings they had created, the two took off in their car, leaving everyone else to crowd into the truck.

"It's still so early," Chloe said once they were on their way. "Have you packed everything at the motel, Marley?"

"No. And we have to be out of there before the wedding."

Once Al stopped at the motel, Brant said, "Why don't you three go watch TV. I need to talk to Marley."

"Yeah, right. I'm monitoring you, buddy." Al glanced at his watch.

Brant placed a hand on Marley's back and aimed her toward the room she had shared with Michelle. "Are you all packed?" she asked.

"It can wait. You want to check out that gown. See if it fits?"

For a moment, Marley hesitated. "Right. That's a wonderful idea. I'd really like to show Chloe." She faced him. "But you can't look."

"I'll get your sister."

Before he was out the door, Marley slipped into the bathroom with the dress. It weighed several pounds, an old-fashioned style that really appealed to her, with grosgrain ribbons following the pattern of lace along a bodice encrusted with pearls. The lace from her waist to the floor had swirls of pearls scattered throughout. Lovely, exactly what she would have chosen.

The little buttons at the wrists were difficult to do up, but the back was worse, making it impossible for her to get into the dress by herself. When the outer door closed in the other room, Marley called out, "Chloe, could you help me? I can't get the back buttoned."

She stood leaning over the sink, in front of the mirror, when the bathroom door opened. And Brant walked in...wearing a black tie wrapped around his eyes.

Marley gasped and turned to him.

"I can't see. Honest." He took several steps toward her, holding his hands out, giving a believable performance of a blind man searching for her. Another acting routine, for sure. Definitely. How else could he place his arms around her and clasp the buttons on her back?

She grabbed hold of his arms and pushed them away, all the while attempting not to laugh at his antics. "Get Chloe."

"No. I can do this." He slipped out of her hold, turned her around and began buttoning the back of the dress. When that was done, he started on the openings from her wrist to her elbows, and easily flipped over the tiny pieces of fabric covering the pearl buttons.

"You can see, Brant."

He didn't bother to deny it. "Are you really superstitious?"

"No."

"Good, because I'm not, either, and I want to get a good look." Brant pulled off his blindfold and sucked in his breath. "My bride. So beautiful." Stepping away, he held her hand and turned her around. When he was through, Brant wrapped his arms around her, kissed her neck and gazed at her in the mirror. "Why can't you wear this to your mother's wedding?"

Marley moved out of his embrace, only to have him capture her again. "That's way beyond superstition. Competing with the bride on her day is totally rude."

He sighed. "You're right. Completely unfair." Moving over to the door, Brant gave her his special smile. "I'll get Chloe."

THEY ARRIVED AT the church with fifteen minutes to spare. Marley saw Dede waiting outside with Richard and went over to greet them, holding on to Brant's hand so he couldn't sneak away. The two women hugged, while Brant and Richard looked uneasy and didn't say anything to each other.

"So you're in the wedding?" Dede asked. She clasped Marley's arm and drew her away from the men. "Meet me Monday after work. I've lots to tell you."

"Can't." She showed Dede the ring. "We're getting married this weekend."

Dede squealed and pulled Marley into an embrace. She whispered something endearing in Spanish and then turned back to the men. Richard looked perplexed as Dede took his arm and led him into the church, but Brant had a contented expression. At least he kept his thoughts to himself and didn't gloat.

Marley entered the room where the bridesmaids waited. Her mother wasn't with them, so Marley assumed she was behind the closed door in the cloakroom. Memories of Lindy's wedding flashed, and Marley forced herself to concentrate on the now.

"Is she here?" Nora called from the cloakroom. "I want Marley."

Marley walked over to the door and knocked lightly. It was opened immediately by Aunt Effie, who yanked her into the room.

Nora wore a suit in cream, with a full-length narrow skirt and Chanel-style jacket. The attire was chic, without the frivolity of previous weddings. "You look lovely, Mom."

Nora smiled at Marley. "Thank you."

Marley went to her mother and hugged her. Yes, she had made the right decision. She'd never have to look back with regret for missing this precious time with her family.

AS MENDELSSOHN'S WEDDING March began, everyone stood. Michelle walked toward the altar on the white cotton carpet that had been placed in the aisle. She tossed rose petals here and there. Some actually landed where they were supposed to. The moment she saw Aunt Effie, Michelle dropped the basket of petals, ran over to her and demanded to be picked up.

The rest of Marley's sisters followed, each

wearing a different gown. Lindy was the last one before the maid of honor.

And then it was Marley's turn. She walked down the aisle, concentrating on the cowboy standing next to her father. When she reached the altar, Brant stepped down to help her up the two steps.

Brant whispered by Marley's ear, "I've seen this movie before. It's called *27 Dresses*."

Marley elbowed him in the ribs and tried her best to keep from laughing just as her mother came down the aisle with Poppy.

Marley focused on Brant while Pastor Williams went through the service. It wasn't until the recessional started that she turned to look at her parents, married again, walking to the front of the church.

BRANT GAVE THE garment bag containing the wedding dress to the flight attendant to hang for him, while Marley continued toward the back of the plane. "Where are you going?" Brant caught up with her and led her to their seats in first class.

Marley's jaw tightened, but she didn't say anything. Instead, she took a comfortable leather chair next to the window. Once seated, Brant leaned over her and reached for her seat belt. "I can afford it." He kissed her on the cheek before sitting back and buckling her safely into her seat.

With a sigh and a nod, Marley reluctantly forced herself to relax in the luxurious seat way beyond anything she'd ever experienced.

"Will there be any more surprises?" she asked.

"Like?"

"I don't know. This is the first time I've ever been a bride."

"And last."

"And I don't know what to expect. I've handled most of the planning or been involved in the past five...no, six weddings in my family, and I haven't arranged anything for my own. Have you planned everything?"

Brant shook his head. "Elaina and my other sisters set it up, because everything's new to me, as well. I'm hoping to avoid any publicity, so it'll be pretty low-key. We're staying at a discreet hotel that will provide absolute privacy."

"With a heart-shaped bed and a Jacuzzi tub?"

Brant laughed. "If that's what you want, I'll arrange it."

"Don't you dare. I was only kidding."

Marley shook her head and looked away. The plane had started down the runway, and she felt a little panicky. Flying into the unknown this way with a man she'd known for such a short time.

"I wish we could have brought the guitars," Marley said. They had played them at her mother's wedding reception.

"I myself think we'll have enough to do without them, but if you feel a guitar is necessary, I'll buy one for you."

She turned to him ready to object, only to encounter his smile, the one that gave her goose bumps and heart palpitations at the same time. "I'll manage without." She leaned against his shoulder, their hands joined and she lost her fear of the unfamiliar.

She wanted this man with his "I want to make love to you" smile. And she had every intention of finding out what that smile promised.

* * * * *

LARGER-PRINT BOOKS!

GET 2 FREE
LARGER-PRINT NOVELS
PLUS 2 FREE
MYSTERY GIFTS

Love Inspired

Larger-print novels are now available...

LILPDIR13R

Reader Service.com

Manage your account online!

- Review your order history
- Manage your payments
- Update your address

---

*We've designed
the Harlequin® Reader Service
website just for you.*

Enjoy all the features!

- Reader excerpts from any series
- Respond to mailings and special monthly offers
- Discover new series available to you
- Browse the Bonus Bucks catalog
- Share your feedback

Visit us at:
ReaderService.com